BLUE HOURS

BLUE HOURS

A Novel

DAPHNE KALOTAY

TriQuarterly Books/Northwestern University Press
Evanston, Illinois

TriQuarterly Books
Northwestern University Press
www.nupress.northwestern.edu

Printed in the United States of America

10 9 8 7 6 5 4 3 2 1

Library of Congress Cataloging-in-Publication Data

Names: Kalotay, Daphne, author.
Title: Blue hours : a novel / Daphne Kalotay.
Description: Evanston, Illinois : TriQuarterly Books/Northwestern University
    Press, 2019.
Identifiers: LCCN 2019006332 | ISBN 9780810140561 (trade paper : alk.
    paper) | ISBN 9780810140578 (e-book)
Subjects: LCSH: Female friendship—Fiction. | New York (N.Y.)—Fiction. |
    Non-governmental organizations—Afghanistan—Employees—Fiction.
Classification: LCC PS3611.A455 B58 2019 | DDC 813.6—dc23
LC record available at https://lccn.loc.gov/2019006332

For Xavier Collard

And turning towards each other in the dusk.

—J. L. Carr

Contents

Part I

THE ISLAND

no man's land

We were college graduates, blasé about it, diplomas rolled into tubes. It was 1991; a diploma couldn't save you from having to stand behind a shop counter or sit answering a telephone at the front of some office. Saddam Hussein was back again, Yugoslavia was at war, the U.S. economy was sadly napping. With two school friends, I'd come to Manhattan straight from graduation, knowing only that I wanted to write. You could do that then, move to the city without a job or a plan, just some unreasonable dream, and survive.

We took what work we could find. I spent the days folding sweaters at a clothing store, and Adrienne, who was going to be an actress, waited tables at a place on Mercer. The other girl took a job as a receptionist at a dental office. We had managed to find a three-bedroom walk-up on a nondescript stretch of Lafayette that wasn't quite SoHo and wasn't quite Chinatown. Little Italy, too, was a block away. Exposed brick walls, two crumbling bathrooms, and an apparent mild gas leak. If there was money laundering going on, that was not our business. Our windows looked out over a cement traffic island that turned the street suddenly, uselessly, one-way, so that few cars ever passed. Vagrants spent long hours there in looping conversation.

He looks at me says I'm a let you go now. I'm a let you go now. Just like that.

Or maybe gone into shoe repair with my uncle.

I mean, come on, it was just two times!

Tied a yellow ribbon, sure, just don't ask what else she did.

Ancient grievances lobbed back and forth. The men never begged, or at least not from me. They probably knew I had little to offer, with my crumpled paper bags from the corner deli.

The stupid hunger of college girls who never learned to cook. Macaroni from a box with its little packet of orange powder, or brittle bricks of curly noodles plunged into broth. When my shift at the clothing store ended, I'd walk home along Broadway empty-bellied, light-headed, swooning at the pungent gusts from food carts. Too-sweet gray smoke of candied almonds, or toasty pretzels covered in big square flecks of salt. Once I found myself in a cheap accessories shop paying for a necklace whose red glass beads looked like cherry candy. Only when I'd left with necklace in hand did I understand that I wanted not to wear it but to eat it.

In my memory of that time I'm always famished, from fear of running out of money and from never having learned how to prepare a piece of meat. My mother had died when I was ten, and even after my father remarried we continued to just stick things in the microwave. The most I knew to do was sauté something: grayish mushrooms with a chopped onion, or a gloppy sauce of tomato paste, garlic, and water. My housemates were no better. When we grew ridiculously hungry, we went to Adrienne's restaurant, a cheap poly-Asian place where big bowls of sticky white rice disguised how little there was of the beef we had gone there for specially. For lunch, at the deli near the store where I worked, I always ordered the liverwurst sandwich—to stave off anemia, and also because liverwurst was the cheapest item on the board.

These days, of course, no upstarts can make a go of it in that city without someone to subsidize them. But back then there was still a chance. And so we lived by the peculiar American wisdom that has it better to tough things out in a questionable rental unit and charge one's life away on a credit card than to room at home or ask family for help.

Also, my father had officially cut me off. He was on to his third marriage by then and complained about the alimony.

Not that I expected his help. For four years on a walled campus of historic buildings near the Hudson, I had obscured the humble facts of my upbringing. The little house in Brighton, Massachusetts, with its stubby, crumbling driveway; the crappy public school; the Oldsmobile with the door rusted shut. What did it matter? Hadn't all great Americans worked their way up the economic ladder? Now we were the ones with the menial jobs, the desperate Friday paychecks. The nightly visions of mice, of stolid cockroaches . . . the too-quick flutter of something down the tea towels.

I told myself it was just a stage. Temporary, the postdated checks, the fearful sorting of mail, envelopes with stern messages in red ink. Every once in a while, a moment of dumb luck: a twenty-dollar bill found on the sidewalk, or a trial-size sample of something handed out on a street corner. There was no shame in this. We were in a recession! Other friends worked in a bakery, a photocopying place—a chiropractor's office! My demotion from cum laude French major to retail clerk wasn't an insult, just something to get through. We weren't minions; we were "assistants." I wasn't broke; I was *trouée au coude*.

This was before Giuliani blustered in and swept everything up, before frat boys from the trading floor moved into what had been rent-controlled apartments. The city was everyone's and everyone had to deal with the grit. When you blew your nose at the end of the day, black crud came out. If a pipeline burst or some minor urban disaster took place, a long while passed before it was fixed. Forty-Second Street was still triple-Xs and peep shows, and Tompkins Square Park had just been closed. Squeegee men accosting cars with slimy mops . . . Panhandlers, loud, on the subway cars . . . Some unfortunate soul waiting for you to slip your token into the turnstile, so that she could try to suck it back up from the slot with her mouth.

Which is why a person could live there on a scrap of a job and still have as good a shot at a future as anyone. This, I suppose, is what I meant today, a full twenty years later, when I told Roy there was nothing left. That city doesn't exist anymore. Just as the girl I was no longer exists.

It's only an hour or so ago that he called. Found me through my agent. Two decades since we last spoke, but his voice ruffled me just the same. A Rhode Island telephone number, as if he never left home. He told me Kyra's missing.

That's how he put it: "She's gone missing. It's been three days."

My heart did something it hadn't done in a long time, a sort of hiccup but sharp. I said, "You mean she's run away?" Can a fortysomething-year-old run away? Well, why not, if you're Kyra. Midlife crisis, probably. I had mine two years ago and nearly ended up divorced.

But I must have already sensed it was something else. Roy said no one seemed to know what had happened. "Her posting mate says she went to meet a friend."

Posting mate. So, she's still with that NGO. Red Cross, Doctors Without Borders . . . Years ago I allowed myself to look her up online, before quickly shoving her back into the locked trunk of memory. I asked Roy which ruined country she had touched down on now.

To my surprise, he seemed to think I should know. Apparently she sends out regular email broadcasts to friends. Now he was gathering any information he could get.

"I can't help you." I didn't mean to sound cold. It's just that I haven't spoken to Kyra in twenty years.

"If you'll kindly let me finish." Roy said it slowly. "I'm calling because I've received a package from her with your name on it."

"But—I don't believe it."

I heard him sigh, loudly. He explained that she had sent the package via diplomatic pouch, with a note instructing him to please make sure to get it to me. "So it seems to me she must have known she could be landing in some sort of trouble."

Give it to *me*? *My* name on it? I asked how he even knew she was missing.

"AidNow called this morning. I'm her emergency contact. Don't ask me why they waited three days. These nonprofits don't know how to do anything."

So, Roy hasn't changed.

"And now this package arrived. Look, what's your address? My secretary will have it couriered."

Kyra, in some sort of trouble. Gone off somewhere and disappeared. Roy was still speaking, asking me to be sure to please let him know when the package arrived. "And you'll tell me if there's anything in it about where she might have gone, right?"

Just when you think you've made it through the rough part—ushered your child past so many daily perils, reconciled with your beleaguered husband—the past returns to make demands. Just when you've begun to believe in the possibility of a peaceful life.

Roy must have misunderstood my silence. He said, "Don't tell me you still haven't forgiven her."

That confused me. For one thing, it's not true. I love Kyra. And I'm the one to blame, not her. It made me wonder what she had told him.

He said, "It's the past—can't you let go of all that?"

There's nothing left to let go of. That world is gone. Even the old apartment no longer exists. In its place is a twelve-story building of darkened glass—luxury condominiums, with a doorman and an exercise room. I've seen it advertised in the magazine section of the *Times*.

"Mim, I need your help. We're all she has. And those AidNow people are incompetent."

We.

I gave him my address, though few people in the universe are allowed to know it. Let him send that package on its way to me. Kyra, missing. I keep replaying the conversation, trying to understand. I keep hearing Roy saying, *I need your help.*

Last we spoke, twenty years ago, it was me saying that, to him.

emergency

Impossible, now, not to think of Carl. His big duffel bag slumped in the corner, his cigarette butts in the jam jar on the window sill. Really it would be months before I met him or Kyra. I had just arrived in New York and was consumed with trying to become some new version of myself.

My face was rounder then, and I wore my hair in a bob, the tips curling in at my cheeks; I wanted to look like Anna Karina in *Vivre sa vie* and trimmed the bangs myself. I was convinced that if I could just perfect my look, I could erase the parts of my life I wanted to leave behind. My eyebrows were thick and dark, and I began shaping them with tweezers, because Adrienne, who had already been cast in a number of plays and knew about this sort of thing, told me to. To dress up I had either a short red woolen kilt or a stretchy black dress patterned with tiny orange polka dots, which I wore with black round-toed pumps of putative suede. Even with my discount at work, I was afraid to spend the little money I had. Nor did I peruse the thrift shops like Adrienne, who was always wearing some lace or satin or velvet thing that carried the scent of past decades. For that you need patience and vision.

Adrienne—jaunty, cool, in her Salvation Army finds. Her father was black, her mother half-white, half-Japanese, giving her enviable cheekbones and that rare combination of brown skin with light eyes. Long, thick, curly hair she could do all kinds of things with. Through her left nostril she wore a small silver hoop, and she had a wool cap she liked, with a little brim at the front, like a train conductor. But without the hoop or the cap, when she smoothed out her curls with a hair iron, she could transform into anyone.

By late summer she had been cast in a recurring television role, as a nameless ER nurse on one of the afternoon soaps. I still remember the surprise of seeing her on the screen that first time, wearing a white lab coat and carrying a clipboard. She spoke her line ("Does the patient have any kin?") very sternly and, without really listening for an answer, jotted something down. Then, in a burst of improvisation, she put the stethoscope in her ears and walked away.

We had a fourth roommate by then, a last-minute attempt to help with the rent, a guy working his way through medical school. He would record the soap opera daily, for the simple pleasure of pointing out everything Adrienne's nurse did that was medically unsafe. Thirty-second takes in which she would blurt out some vaguely authoritative line ("I need to check his vitals!") and then, to show she meant business, roughly plump the pillow behind someone recovering from brain surgery, or give a small shove to a gurney or to an extra in a wheelchair.

Then, just before Christmas, my ex-stepsister, Janet, called from a real hospital, in Boston, and I had to get on a bus and go home.

She had been in an accident and needed a lot of surgery on her face. On the phone all she said was, "I fell."

She was four years older than me, petite and pretty, with pale blue eyes. Her mother had been my father's assistant and married him soon after my mother died. The cliché of it bothered Janet as much as the notion of a stepmother had bothered me. But for the three years we lived in the same household, Janet had been a savvy older sister to me, with her boyfriends and shoplifted bras and little swigs of my father's Jim Beam. Three piercings in each of her earlobes. Cigarettes hidden in an eyeglass case. Her hair was permed, her eyes rimmed with black liner. (Wet n Wild was the brand, the cheapest of drugstore makeup, but as a girl I thought it a statement of her nature.) In those years of my sadness and anger at losing my mother, Janet was the one who showed me how to weave my hair into a French braid, how to wield an eyelash curler, and later on, how to insert a tampon, how to light a joint. Before she had finished high school our parents split up—a big angry finish—and Janet and her mother moved back to an apartment over by Fenway. My father and I stayed in the Brighton house, and then began his Don Juan period. But Janet remained kind toward me.

Now her nose and cheekbone were broken, her forehead fractured. There was a white cast-like thing across the bridge of her nose. She was lying on the sofa in her apartment on Summit Avenue, not far from the B-line. On the other side of the hill lay the town of Brookline, with its well-appointed houses, underground power lines, and no overnight street parking (to keep the riffraff out). But on Janet's side—my side, the Allston-Brighton side—the telephone lines hung heavy with melting ice, and cars slumbered under husks of faintly blackened snow.

"It's amazing, Mim, the doctors used this new method so they wouldn't have to cut up my face. Since a lot of the damage was under the skin. They cut around the outer edges, see?"—Janet brushed her bangs from her hairline with a pale hand—"and then they just lifted the skin, like a flap on a suitcase. So they could reconstruct the bone and cartilage and everything underneath."

I felt ill and didn't want to picture it. I told her I still didn't understand what exactly had happened.

"I told you. I fell down the stairs."

Something made me wonder if that was all. Had she blacked out? She liked to drink. "Who called the ambulance?"

"Tim was with me. My boyfriend. Luckily."

Ah, right. She always had a boyfriend. "Where is he now?"

A small motion of the hand, these things happen, he'll be back. Her chatter stopped me from asking more—though it strikes me now that I must not have wanted to know.

The fact was, we had been growing apart. It started when I left for college, long conversations on the telephone becoming shorter, my replies elliptical. How could I explain to her the strangeness of life on a walled campus, that sheltered world of creaky dormitories guarded by loving matrons, of friends who had attended prep schools, of evening meals at *la table française?* The last time Janet and I had really been together was the summer I interned at the *Atlantic.* We had barely spoken since my move to New York. I suppose she was angry with me. She had wanted me to come back to Boston.

Only now do I see the strange truth of it: that it's because of Janet—because of her accident—that so many of the things that were about to happen happened.

At the time I was aware only of the awkwardness of the visit, and leaving Boston again as if I were fleeing. In my backpack were a lot of colored tights, Janet's Christmas gift to me. Impractical colors like orange and red and metallic silver, not to mention a lacy pair that I'm still not certain she realized had a big round purposeful hole where the crotch should be.

I mention this because it mattered to how I felt that day—to how I felt about my life—to be heading back to New York at year's end with a backpack full of hopeless stockings.

Janet had bought me a train ticket so that I wouldn't have to take the bus again. This was back when the Amtrak ran on diesel north of New Haven. Everyone would get off and pace the long platform and smoke cigarettes and watch the electric engine slide away, the old heavy diesel one dragged back on again. But it was so cold that day, only a few of us lined up to exit the train. Ahead of me was a girl about my age, with a perfect oval face and long, sleek hair as dark as mine. She had already taken out a cigarette and was sniffing the tip, impatient. For some reason I thought I knew her.

We stepped out into the frigid cold. *Frileux* was the word the boarding house manager in Paris—where I'd won a semester's study-abroad scholarship—had used when I asked to turn up the heat. *Vous êtes frileuse.* The dark-haired girl was already lighting her cigarette. I wondered if in fact I did know her. She was tall and slim, her back very straight, her coat a long fitted one of a neo-military style. She looked lapidary, imperial, as she walked farther down the platform, shoulders back, coattail flaring behind her. I took out my own cigarette, but I wasn't a real smoker and my matches kept snuffing out.

A man swept in with a lighter. He looked to be in his late twenties, and asked if I was heading home. I nodded. I had decided to no longer think of Boston as my home.

He told me he worked in Boston but was spending New Year's in the city. Friends of his always had a big bash. To his question of what I did for work, I mentioned the Benetton job, shrugging so he would know I didn't care. "I'm going to be a writer," I explained. "I'm writing a book." I was young enough that I could say such a thing and not expect someone to smile sympathetically.

The man asked what sort of book. Stories, I told him, and as proof unzipped my backpack to search, among the scrunched stockings, for the notebook where I was writing my newest story, about a girl who spent her days folding sweaters in a clothing shop. . . .

The man nodded at my pages. "Ever tried to publish?"

"Not these. They aren't good enough." I wasn't being modest; it was the truth. At my *Atlantic* internship I had seen firsthand

13

the onslaught of hopeful letters, the stories no one would pursue beyond the first paragraph, the manuscripts already frayed at the edges from being sent round to so many places. I was determined never to land in the pile of to-be-returned ones, or pinned up on some corkboard for people to laugh at.

My fingertips were already numb, and I saw that the girl was stamping out her cigarette—a decisive twist of her sharp-toed boot. I remember thinking the man must not have seen her, to have chosen to talk to me instead.

He was introducing himself, and I shook his hand. "I'm Mim."

"Not much of a name, hmm?"

"Oh—Miriam. Woodruff." It was the first time I understood that these things mattered if I wanted to be thought of as someone.

The man slipped a calling card out of his wallet, scrawled something on the back, and handed it to me. "Come to my friends' party."

I thanked him and tossed down my cigarette, giving a twist of my shoe the way the girl had. But it kept burning, and I had to stamp it again before reboarding the train.

a new year

The party was in the East Village, one of those walk-ups where you had to shout from the sidewalk until someone tossed down a sock with the door key stuffed inside. I wore a black cap-sleeved angora sweater and a microscopic black velvet skirt I'd bought with my store discount, with the red tights from Janet, the Minnie Mouse pumps, and the cherry-candy necklace.

My roommates came with me, although in the welter of bodies we soon became separated. The room throbbed with voices and cigarette smoke, and I looked around for the man from the train. Someone said, "Hey, we're collecting New Year's resolutions."

All I could come up with was that I was going to have to do something with the colored tights. I proffered this to my new friends, two young men in button-down shirts. One had his cuffs rolled up casually yet perfectly, while the other looked rumpled, his shirt frayed at the collar, his nubby tweed jacket decidedly second- or third-hand.

At that age I was still fickle and judgmental. I would meet a man and think him utterly fantastic for about twelve minutes, and then he would mention, for instance, that he didn't like beets, and I would think, "I can't be with him." So I quickly sized up these two and decided I preferred the rumpled one, for being not quite so perfect. As for my resolution to wear the colored tights, the neat one wished me success.

"Success," said the rumpled one. "Achievement. Victory. Accomplishment." His resolution, he said, was to practice his vocabulary. He was a writer, working on a novel.

Well, so much for him, I told myself. But I shook his hand. "Miriam. Woodruff."

The neat one gripped my hand firmly. "I'm Jack." He was quite strapping, actually, with a Mediterranean complexion and thick dark hair. On his wrist he wore a substantial, gleaming watch, like some kind of navigational equipment. His eyes had a slight puffiness at the lower lids, which I decided countered his neatness.

It turned out he didn't know the hosts either. He was getting a PhD at Columbia, in comparative literature: Italian and French. When I told him about my semester abroad, he said, "You should come to some of our lectures. Practice your French."

"Practice," said his friend. "Rehearsal. Training. Repetition—"

"*Endless* repetition," Jack said, arching an eyebrow. The more he spoke, the more I detected an accent. Not recognizably French or Italian, but certain words were slightly off. Newark came out as "New Ark."

The big fancy watch began to make sense. This was the accent of the worldly rich, the sort who learn English at a Swiss boarding school, or in a baccalaureate program in Tokyo. People who could afford a nice stint at an American university and then go sailing around Sardinia for the summer. There had been a handful of students like that at my college, ones with continental airs and not the slightest worry about money. An instinctual dislike filtered through me.

It was a familiar feeling, and about more than just money. As much as I wanted, badly, to be like my college friends—to navigate the world without the deep-down fear that kept me eating liver-wurst daily—a broader, lurking envy had defined me ever since my mother died. Envy of *them*: the people with mothers, the random lucky majority. Sometimes I even felt they owed me something, some small piece of their good fortune.

A girl with an astonishingly large beaky nose had come round, along with a woman wearing a white feather boa. Birds, I remember thinking. The one with the nose said she worked as a secretary but was writing a novel. "I've got thirty-six pages."

"A novelist—so's my comrade here!" Jack said cheerfully, and perhaps maliciously; his friend in the shabby tweed jacket looked visibly affronted at this girl having staked a claim to his vocation.

The feather boa said, "See that guy over there?" She pointed to a skinny young man who was showing a magazine to a cluster of guests. "His sister has a story in this week's *New Yorker*."

We all gazed at him in a moment of silent respect.

"Which writers do you like?" the beaky girl asked, and before anyone could answer took from her purse a thick, beat-up paperback, *The Portable Faulkner*, its ruffled pages fanning like an accordion. "He's my all-time favorite. A poet, really." She opened randomly to a page teeming with little slash marks and the shorthand of metrical scansion penciled above each phrase.

"You scanned . . . the entire book?" I didn't mean to sound aghast.

"That's how you learn."

"Learn. Study. Master. Be taught . . . Acquire knowledge, become skilled . . ."

"I want my prose to do what Faulkner's does." She pointed at a line, and the rumpled novelist bent to have a look. But Jack was squinting at me.

"What about you? What is it you do?"

I couldn't bear to admit that I too considered myself a writer-in-training—that in my coat pocket I carried a little notepad and pencil at all times, that I made lists of words like "wraith" and "propinquity," and rose early each morning to work on a story about a shopgirl. Instead I explained that I was a subaltern at the Benetton down on Broadway, and that I had only just graduated from college in May and was still looking for more appropriate work.

Jack said, "I suppose all that matters is that you learn something from it."

That irked me. I was about to say, "What matters is that I'm trying to pay my bills" but heard myself say instead, "You're not from here."

To my surprise, this small attack worked. Jack seemed uncomfortable as he explained that his father was Corsican, his mother French, that when he was fifteen they had briefly decamped to New York, but he had gone to university in Paris before deciding on the PhD. "I suppose my goal in life is to keep learning and never stop."

"Stop," I said. "Quit, end. Halt—"

The feather boa nudged us. "Do you think that guy tried to slit his wrists?" She nodded toward a young man wearing some sort of wristbands.

"How awful!" We looked at him and his bandaged wrists, and I remember thinking how strange it must be to walk around with visible proof of emotional pain, for all to see. And then a flutter of confusion as I thought of Janet, her face, the doctors lifting the skin up like a mask.

What strikes me now is that I didn't think of all the wounded people who walk this earth with no visible scars at all.

Jack said, "But would he be out at a party if he just tried to kill himself?"

"I wouldn't know," the woman said. "I don't believe in suicide." She took a swig from her beer and realized it was empty. "Time for a refill." Jack's friend, perhaps to escape the *Portable Faulkner*, followed her.

"If you ever want to come to one of the lectures," Jack said in a rush, as if I too were about to run off. From his wallet he slid out a business card. This was before those machines became so common that anyone could print one up; only people with real jobs, like the man from the train—whom I now glimpsed across the room— were endowed with a neat stack of calling cards. At least, that was what I thought. This one was thick, letterpressed, in black ink:

JACQUES "JACK" CATALANO

HOMME

(MAN)

Below that, just a telephone number, with the 212 area code.

I admired his aplomb. He had never had to work, so why not advertise his good fortune?

"Let's see?" The bird girl shoved poor Faulkner back into her purse, and Jack handed her a card.

"Oh, hey," he said to me as the girl admired the card. "If you write down your number"—he was taking out yet another card— "I'll let you know if there are any good lectures coming up." From his shirt pocket he plucked a slim silver pen, the sort given as prizes to bright students.

I felt flattered and wrote my name and number on the back. The other card I tucked into the pocket of my miniskirt. Then I glimpsed the man from the train and went to chat with him before finding my housemates again.

Plastic cups filled and abandoned. Conversations half heard, shouting into the faces of strangers. Art gallery intern, clothing designer, cabaret singer . . . By day these same people would be spell-checking at some bridal magazine, or switchboard-operating at a radio station, or taking dictation for an eminent professor. But off-hours we were band managers, screenwriters, television hosts . . . The room teemed with aspiration. All the while the skinny young man went about clutching his *New Yorker*.

And then my med school roommate said, "Carl!"

A guy in jeans and a T-shirt turned to us. "Whoa, small world." He was broad-shouldered, with short-short hair like the boys in the sports bars back home. He laughed but his laugh was more like a soft, low cough.

He and our med school housemate had grown up together somewhere in Ohio. Carl said he had just gotten into town, was staying with a college friend until he could find a room to rent. It was the friend who had brought him to the party. "He's here somewhere." His eyes darted round the room, and somehow it seemed less that he was searching for someone than keeping sentry.

He had fair skin, light-brown eyes, and a lovely pink mouth. But with his faux-leather sneakers, and the T-shirt with the name of a sports store, and the flat-top haircut shaved close at the sides, all I saw was that he looked like the boys I had grown up with, who had been my friends once, and with whom I no longer kept in touch.

He hadn't looked for work yet, he was saying, but hoped to make some money doing carpentry.

"Right, I remember you built that treehouse."

"I built a whole loft for friends at State."

His muscles were tight under his T-shirt. But when he took a swig from his beer, his hand trembled. It gave him the shabby look of an addict, or a person who pays for things in coins. He could be a recovering alcoholic, hopped up on coffee and cigarettes.

It made me uncomfortable. Not just the trembling hands. The cheap clothes and keepsake necklace and paramilitary haircut, they were reminders—that like him I wasn't truly of this set, of this crowd. Everyone else, they were all on the brink of something, even the girl with the thirty-six pages. They all had plans, were going somewhere. And badly as I wanted to believe I too had a future, Carl reminded me how hard it was to trade up in life. That I was merely attending the party, not truly a part of it. Not on the same track, not the same speed. Like the train from Boston: diesel versus electric.

I turned away and searched for Jack. Across the room, the young man whose sister had been published in the *New Yorker* was trying to eat a plateful of crackers without letting go of his magazine. I thought despondently of my story about the girl in the clothing store. And then I saw, next to him, reaching for a paper plate, the girl from the train.

She was picking out a few squares of cheese, carefully, as if they had been rationed. There was a calm look to her, very still. Her hair, long and dark and shiny, was swept casually to one side.

I went to her. "We were on the train together."

She looked up without surprise, just the slightest angling of her head.

"The train from Boston," I told her.

She flicked her hair over her shoulder and took a good hard look at me. Something almost Asian about her eyes. She said, "I thought I was going to freeze to death."

She was tall like me but her face was more oval, no makeup. Dark eyebrows that arced softly, her eyelashes very fine. She wore a pale blouse with many tiny pearl buttons up the front, the sleeves culminating in wide floppy cuffs of delicate lace—a shirt for someone who need not labor with her hands. The lacy cuffs draped her wrists as she picked sedately at the waxy squares of cheese.

"I was coming from Rhode Island," she told me. "My mother lives there." At her clavicle a tiny diamond dangled on a chain so fine it was like the glint of raindrops. Even I could tell the diamond was real. But her jeans had a hole in the knee, and her shoes were pointy black leather boots. She asked if I'd gone to Boston for Christmas.

21

I told her about Janet, about her accident. It was the first I had told anyone how awkward the visit had been. "She wouldn't look me in the eye. And I still don't understand how she fell."

That same flat gaze. "Did you ask her?"

"Yes! Well, I mean, kind of."

She just barely raised an eyebrow. "Maybe you should try again."

I felt chided, and somehow rattled. A loud bleat came from one of those cardboard-and-paper noisemakers, and I asked if we had missed midnight.

She flopped back a lacy cuff to peer at her watch. "Ten minutes."

I was still thinking about what she had said, wondering why I hadn't pressed Janet more about what happened. But all I said was, "New Year's is so awful."

A slow nod. The nearly invisible necklace shimmered. "I've never understood why everyone else doesn't think that. Here another year's ending, and the world's still a mess."

They were handing out the noisemakers, and the awful honking increased. Despondent, I said, "You're right. It's already half a year I've been living here, and what have I done?"

"What *have* you done?" She laughed.

I told her about the Benetton job, and then, probably because I'd had too much to drink, that what I really wanted was to be a writer.

She gestured with her chin. "That guy's sister has a story in the *New Yorker*." At the other side of the room, the skinny young man was conversing with the girl with the nose. "Well, so, I mean, what are you writing?"

I mentioned the story about the shopgirl, though by now it was seeming really dismal. The loud quacks and bleats around us sounded mocking. "I know writing isn't a practical profession, and maybe it doesn't seem worthwhile. But it's my calling."

"You call that impractical, guess what I do for a living."

22

She was a dancer, had switched from ballet to modern, named a company I had heard of. "I was a poli-sci major and thought I'd go into the Foreign Service. But when I came back from my study-abroad year, this visiting choreographer at our school told me I should audition for the company. I found out I got the spot the same day I found out I'd been awarded a scholarship to Oxford."

She didn't seem troubled at having given up Oxford. She said her job had health coverage, if not a great salary. She was lucky to have a salary at all. "Hey, what's your name?"

My mind was soggy with drink, and it would have taken too much energy to say all three syllables. I didn't even bother with my last name.

Hers was Kyra. She leaned back against the wall as if too tired to continue the conversation. Cigarette smoke hung in the air, punctured by the quacking noises. It was nearly midnight, and everyone pushed forward—but there was no television on which to watch the ball drop, and the movement stopped. Someone handed me a bottle of champagne, and I began filling people's glasses.

The chant of voices counting down, mincing time. "Ten. Nine. Eight . . ."

Kyra must have gone to find whomever she had come with. I searched for handsome Jack.

"Five. Four. Three . . ."

A room full of bodies and hopes. Who knew that in just a few years most of us would no longer be able to afford our rented rooms? That we would leave our part-time gigs, and novels and guitars, and go back to school, or become paralegals, or settle into some temp job we couldn't afford to leave. No more half-time paychecks, or internships at some magazine that wouldn't exist come the millennium. We didn't know that the dollar would surge, rents rise, that we would move out to neighborhoods that didn't yet have names. *NoLIta. NoMad.* Or Philly or Providence or Lincoln, Nebraska.

How could we know that? Everyone, it seemed, was on the brink of something magnificent.

And then it was midnight and people were toasting and kissing. I kissed the suicidal guy and the bird girl and the guy whose sister was in the *New Yorker*. I couldn't find my roommates or the man from the train, but across the room my gaze found Jack. He was handing something to the feather boa. She glanced at the little card, smiling, laughing, and wrote something on it, then handed it back to him.

I recall only two more things from that night. The first, when the med school guy had gone off with Carl to some other party, and my two other roommates and I were making our drunken way home, was Adrienne saying, suddenly and apropos of nothing, "It's carpal tunnel syndrome. They're some sort of muscular support. The guy didn't slash his wrists or anything. He just types a lot. He's writing a novel."

The second thing was that when we were almost home the other girl said, "Oh, hey, guess what? That hot French guy asked me for my number!"

a bed

Our med school roommate suggested Carl move in with us—to help him out, and to shave some more off our rent.

Adrienne and I each had a bedroom, but the other girl had been sleeping on a futon in the living room; Carl built her a loft bed in my room, so that he could have the futon.

Carl, with the buzz-cut hair, the tremor in his fingers. When he measured the bedroom walls, the measuring tape made a tiny metallic rippling sound. Winter-pale midwestern skin, forearms flecked with house paint. He had found work on a contractor's crew and spent his days atop ladders in uptown apartments, dipping rollers into creamy trays of "Dijon" and "Cypress" and "Lavender Dream." He used the sample paint chips as scrap paper, one of the little things I later noticed about him.

I remember testing out the loft bed. It was sturdy and didn't budge, and sunlight from the window shone over it like a warm blanket. Though I couldn't see down to where the men outside sat on their crates, I could hear a familiar loud cackling laugh and someone's hacking cough. *I mean, come on, it was just two times!*

I had begun to recognize these neighbors of ours. The one with stringy hair and the endless repertoire of obscenities. The one who never stood still. *Left me waitin' by the gate!* The one with some sort of tick. *What I'm trying to say is, see, what you don't understand, what I'm saying, what I mean to say . . .* The one with the long white braid and a voice so cigarette-hollowed he might have been a frog. And the coughing one who toughed it out even on the coldest of nights. The others went somewhere else when the weather became harsh, and turned up again in the morning as if reporting for work.

I climbed back down from the loft bed and went to pay Carl. We had pooled some money together, but when I handed him the check, he said it was too much. "I get the wood wholesale. Here." Crumpled bills from a pocket, counting them with a shaky hand.

I was embarrassed and shoved the bills into my skirt pocket. But there was already something there. A business card. "HOMME" letterpressed in black ink.

It still bothered me that he was a cad. I tossed the card at the wastebasket but it landed mere inches from my feet. Facedown. Something written on the back, lopsided script.

"Kyra" and a telephone number.

Experience has taught me that our intentions (despite the assurances of so many self-help books) often don't matter. Some things—like the slowly widening crack that for a time threatened to engulf my marriage—cannot be avoided. But to admit that simple truth, back when I was in my twenties, didn't suit my notion of myself or my future.

And so I was taken aback when, at work the next day, as I folded my millionth sweater, someone called, "*Coucou!*"

I shouldn't have been surprised to see Jack there. The place was filled with exactly the sort of thing he wore, corduroy pants in autumn colors, finely knit pullovers of Merino wool. "Ah, good, you're here!" Jack kissed my cheeks and asked what time I got off work.

It was that simple question that made me start to like him. Not that I didn't still wonder which unfortunate girl had ended up with my telephone number in *her* pocket. But I liked that he wasn't afraid to ask a direct question that might be construed as the preface to a date.

We went to a Rodin exhibition uptown: drawings, mostly nudes, many depicting intimate acts. Jack chatted lightly, easily, even as he planted himself appreciatively in front of some naked woman flaring her vagina at us. He was the son of diplomats, with a baccalaureate from the American school and a degree from the Sorbonne. He had hoped to go to art school but wasn't talented enough. He said this without a trace of hurt or regret; perhaps he felt he had been saved from a more painful existence. When I asked if he ever painted for fun, he gave the French "tsk" of contradiction, as if such an enterprise were pointless.

With my notebook concealed in my pocket, I briefly considered offering some comment on art's integral value. But something stopped me. Instead, I spoke of my semester in Paris, trying to make myself sound worldly. Really much of what I knew of French culture came from Éric Rohmer films and dinners at *la table française*.

I liked the light touch of Jack's palm on my arm as we moved from one nude to the next. Still, the thought that wafted through me was that it must have been Kyra he wanted to be with. Kyra, but he hadn't been able to find her number.

Afterward, at the gift shop, I deliberated a long time over the postcards while Jack thumbed through the exhibit book. Though the cards didn't cost much, I felt I could allow myself just one, and kept examining the various bodies and couplings as if choosing which lovers to spend my life with.

And then Jack was there beside me, saying, "Here, which would you like?"

Flustered, I grabbed a watercolor of reclining lovers embracing. Warm sandy hues. Jack added it to his little pile and went to pay, and I noted how easily he passed his money to the cashier, and how the gleaming wristwatch made his skin look nearly tan against the platinum.

It was late afternoon by then. The dusky sky glowed blue. Lights glimmered in shop windows, and garlanded trees twinkled with holiday bulbs. A last streak of daylight was barely visible below the deepening blue.

"This is my favorite time," Jack said. "When the sun is setting and the streetlights are just turning on. *L'heure bleue.* The time just between the darkness and the light."

I had heard the expression before and liked that it attempted to express something that couldn't quite be captured.

"One thing about to end," Jack said, "and another about to begin."

At home, I laid the postcard atop my dresser. Two naked bodies, very faint, more like water stains, their warm flesh orange-toned, hair a faded brown, legs partially obscured by a blur of gray blanket. One edge had bent a little, but I straightened it out. The card lay against the base of the lamp, next to the others: the one from the man on the train, and the one I hadn't told Jack I still had. His.

Within his first week with us, Carl had fixed the gas leak, the grouting in the bathrooms, and the fluorescent light over the kitchen sink. He was always moving, fiddling, frowning at some tiny metal spring or wire, unable to sit still. He would find broken things on the sidewalk—a cassette player, a toaster oven—and make them work again.

His duffel hulked in the corner behind the futon couch, by the small desk where he kept his other belongings. Paint flecks on his hair, on his jeans, on the bandana hanging from his belt loop. When I came home late after a date with Jack, or not until morning, Carl was often awake, smoking a cigarette by the window, cold air slipping in. Just a "hey" and barely a glance. I never took it personally; he had spent much of the day perched on a ladder, trying not to tip paint buckets, and was probably tired.

One night, very late, as I headed to bed, I heard a knocking sound, very fast, from Carl's corner. The entire frame of the futon was shaking. This was because Carl was shaking—his entire body, shaking beneath the covers. The sound was the wooden frame reverberating against the scratched, nicked floor.

Carl's eyes were closed, his face covered in sweat. In the faint light from the streetlamp, he looked ill. Strangest of all, a sharp odor rose from his bed. Not the musky smell of perspiration. This was fierce and potent, like something toxic.

Carl made a strangled sound. I supposed he was delirious, and hurried over, touched his shoulder. I expected his skin to be burning, but it was cold.

I asked if he was all right. He was looking right at me, eyes wide open. But it was as if he didn't recognize me. He gave a violent kick. And then, just like that, the shaking stopped.

Within seconds the crisis seemed to have passed. Even the toxic smell seemed to subside. Carl's eyes closed, his chest rising in quick, exhausted breaths. I hurried back to the bedroom. But I couldn't get back to sleep. I kept wondering about the toxic smell, and about the look in Carl's eyes. He hadn't even seen me.

This was back when every day across the city scores of young men were dying. I would see them on the street, especially when I cut along Greenwich Avenue past St. Vincent's. Bony, hollow-eyed, with gaunt cheeks and thin hair. There were no medications yet, just a blood test to label you, and even those of us who lived blithely outside that world had at some point panicked that somehow, in some small lapse of precaution, we had risked that baroque death sentence. This is to say that, for a moment, I wondered—but Carl seemed too strong to be ill, his muscles too solid on his bones, his spine too straight. Maybe it was drugs, some kind of addiction: withdrawal symptoms, something like that.

For a long time I lay there, wondering. Listening to horns and car alarms, spasms of offense from the street below.

Bitch. Last time I saw her, she was wearing that striped dress.

I mean, shit, man, c'mon—it was just two times!

But with Carl I had witnessed something private. I didn't tell anyone what had happened that night.

another bed

I remember the gray-blue mornings, frost etching the windows.
The crisp newspapery smell of the city in winter. Vapor plumes rising from coffee carts, and bitter winds funneling down the avenues,
tugging at coats and hats. I felt guilty every time I passed the bleak
cement island with its sorry, dutiful congregation.

In our apartment, my roommates and I greeted each other with
exclamations: "Bianca told Justin she's pregnant!" or "Someone's
sending Brent anonymous letters!" On Adrienne's soap opera there
was a comatose patient—the only living person who knew the code
word to a safe-deposit box that held the key to some mystery—and
the men who had tried to kidnap him were convinced that, in a
brief moment of consciousness, he might have murmured the code
to the attending nurse. As a result, Adrienne's character was now
being stalked by two very handsome men in leather jackets.

In exchange for this hardship, she had been assigned a name:
Nurse Miranda.

We were all pretty caught up in it. Even Carl, greeted with a cry
of "Grayson caught Bobby Sue and Brent together!" would sort
of smile and say, "What about that Bianca chick?"

I was spending more time with Jack. I liked his enthusiasm, whether listening to jazz in the West Village or showing me how to cook a frittata out of whatever might be wilting in the fridge. I liked waking in his apartment up near Morningside Park, in the big bed with the fluffy duvet. In bed Jack was exuberant, trying this and that. In my memory, he reaches over to take my ankles in one hand, gives a little whistle—*allez hop!*—and flips me onto my stomach. Much of his sexual experience had taken place solely in his imagination, a fact he did not try to hide. "I read about this once . . . ," he would say, or "There's something I've always wanted to try . . . ," or "There was a drawing, in a book. . . ." I liked that he never feigned expertise. I had even begun to think of our lovemaking as constitutional, my one consistent form of exercise. I particularly liked that, unlike other pastimes, it did not require money.

Those hours with Jack were lessons in pleasure. Not just tumbling among the bedcovers but the many other shared delights, even our morning ritual of fig jam on warm crusty bread, the espresso carafe shuddering to a boil on the stove. Jack's fridge contained Kona coffee beans, a demi-bottle of Veuve Clicquot, real Pick salami, real Comté. He taught me how to pan-fry a steak, whip up an omelet. I don't think he ever quite knew that I subsisted on liverwurst.

The silver-spouted espresso maker was too small for the electric burner. We had to set it on a wire triangle atop the coil and watch carefully as it began to bubble up. The coffee drew out thick and dark. "*Le marc*," Jack said one morning, of the silty grounds at the bottom of our little ceramic cups. "That's what we call this."

I swirled the dark residue with the tip of my spoon. Jack said, "I've never been able to figure out how you call it in English."

"That's because we don't have a word for it. We just call it coffee grounds."

Jack shook his head at this failing.

I tried to think of other words. Sediment. Dregs.

32

Jack said, "They say one can read one's future in it."

"Ah, like reading tea leaves." I looked down at the mess of grounds at the bottom of my cup. "Do you believe in that?" It seemed too unjust that my future might already be decided. I wanted to believe in self-determination—that to become the person I yearned to be was simply an act of will.

And so I laughed at the coffee grounds. "The natives and their superstitions, how exotic."

Jack furrowed his brow. "But you don't even have a word for it." He reached over roughly, took our depleted cups, and hastily rinsed them under the tap.

His gruffness alarmed me. What had I done?

There was another episode, too, that perplexed me: We were in the little bakery on Thirteenth Street, drinking tea at one of the tiny round tables. Someone cried out from behind us, *"Mais, alors . . . !"*

A tall handsome woman beside an equally handsome man. "Well now, who would have thought . . . and on our first day in town!"

This was all in French, and as Jack introduced me, the couple formed pleasant, if distant, smiles. They were finely dressed, and the man—it took me a moment to note—wore a watch identical to Jack's.

And what, they asked, could Jack possibly be doing in Manhattan?

Jack told them about his PhD program, and they gave the polite bored nods of people with certificates in more sensible fields. He hurried to name some eminent professor, but it was too late, it did not matter. "And you,"—they turned to me—"are you at the university also?"

I felt myself bristle as I told them no. And then I heard myself say, *"Je suis écrivaine."*

Jack looked surprised; I had never spoken in any great detail of my literary efforts. But the husband and wife must have known lots of writers. They smiled blandly and asked what I wrote. Stories, I told them, and they nodded, how nice, our son Alain likes to read stories.

I wanted Jack to stand up for me, for both of us, but the couple was already asking after his family—with an odd breezy sweetness, as if inquiring about someone's small children. In a rush, Jack spoke of his parents' recent travels on behalf of the government. Fast, no room for further questioning. When it seemed the wife might say something more, he said quickly, "I'm very sorry, but Miriam and I must be going."

Untroubled, the couple said they too were just leaving. They buttoned themselves back into their fine coats. "Enjoy your program . . ." As if Jack's PhD were some small entertainment to be completed in an afternoon.

"Who are they?" I asked when they had left. I wondered if they might be famous.

"Neighbors from our apartment building in Paris." Jack rolled his eyes. But he looked somehow diminished.

How much wealthier could they be, I wondered, if they lived in the same building? I decided it must have to do with something else, politics maybe, or old money versus nouveau riche—but I didn't ask Jack, lest I unintentionally insult him.

Even so, another voice in my head said flatly, *Did you ask him?*

Hours later, I still heard it. *Maybe you should try again.*

roommates

So strange, like being in two places at once. Here I am at my big oak desk, the slight crack of my window admitting the sharp, clipped peep of the cardinal, the slow plunking drops of snowmelt, while my ears ring with the clamor of the city, and voices from two decades ago.

I say her name aloud. Rusty, like a word from a cast-off language. I say it once more, but it still doesn't feel right.

What happened was that the other girl went to live with her boyfriend, and we had to scramble to find a new roommate. On my bureau I still had Jack's calling card—the back of it with "Kyra" written in script.

It no longer concerned me that he had swapped numbers with so many women. I knew it was simply his delight in his own declared identity. Even Carl, the first time I brought Jack home, said, when I introduced him, "Yeah, you gave me your card."

I wondered if Kyra had given her actual number. In the living room, I dialed, then stretched the long telephone cord to my room, so that I could sit on my mattress on the floor.

I immediately recognized the voice that answered. She said, "Yeah, I remember you." Slow, saturnine. I thought she might ask how I had come by her number, but she didn't seem to find it strange. I told her about the apartment, asked if she knew anyone who might be willing to sleep on a loft bed in a shared bedroom with a recently repaired gas leak.

It was cheap, I told her. "And I sleep at my boyfriend's a lot, so it's kind of like having a private room."

"I'll do it."

"Oh." I hadn't meant to sound put off. I was just surprised. "I didn't realize you were looking for a place."

"Yeah . . ." Her voice was suddenly farther away, and I heard the distinct sound of her lighting a cigarette, taking a long drag. "It's time to move on."

"Well, I mean, do you want to see the place?"

"Oh. Okay."

I should have worried, I suppose. Instead we arranged for her to come by the next morning.

Carl was just leaving for work when she arrived. He said he remembered her from the New Year's party, and looked hurt that she didn't recall having met him. Probably she simply didn't recognize him. The buzz cut had grown out, into short bangs that made his eyes look darker, his face softer.

I said, "Come see the loft Carl built."

In my room, Kyra climbed the wooden ladder, and I saw that she was not just slender but skinny, all muscle and bone in her jeans and turtleneck. She leaned precariously from the edge of the bed toward the window. "Great view of nothing."

"Well, drunks, actually. But they never bother us."

Now she was lying on the bed, arms and legs fanned out like a snow angel. "How do you know they're drunks?"

"You know, troubled. Addicts. Or mentally ill or whatever." I wanted her to take the apartment, and so I did not state the real reason, which was that they sat there on their crates drinking all day.

Kyra rolled from one side to the other. "It's comfy up here." Then she sat up and began making her way down the ladder. "How's the writing going?"

I was surprised that she remembered, or maybe just that she had thought to ask. I told her I thought I was improving, but that nothing was as good as I wanted it to be.

"Yeah," she said, "sometimes at rehearsal I cry because my body doesn't do what I want it to. And then the next day it all goes well, or even great—but a great day is even worse, in a way, because then the next day you do the same leap but it just doesn't feel as good." She wasn't even looking around the room any more.

I told her that that morning's writing had gone well. "But probably tomorrow I'll read the pages over and wonder what I was thinking."

Her face became suddenly drawn. "I'm cutting into your writing time."

No one had ever said those words to me before. "It's no problem. But I have to leave for work soon. I'm supposed to be there a half hour before opening."

Kyra said her dance rehearsal was over on Eighth Street, and together we headed out into the affront of February. It was so cold, only two of the usual men were there, their breath becoming white puffs. *Tied a yellow ribbon, sure. Sure she did.* Loud cackles at recollected calamity. The other man sipped from his bottle. I wanted to say, "See," but Kyra was looking across the street. "Oh, good," she said, and hurried across to the deli, from which she emerged with two coffees and a package of donuts. She was wearing the fitted military-style coat, making her look, as she handed the food over to the men, like an officer with her regiment.

I supposed she thought me cruel for not offering anything. "Are you going to do that every day once you start living here?"

She just shrugged. She said, "I like your stockings."

37

I was wearing the orange ones from Janet, with the black mini-skirt and an ugly striped sweater my father had sent me for Christmas. (He and his wife had moved to Texas a few years earlier, and I didn't have the money to fly out there.) I explained about the many pairs of tights, and suggested she might make better use of them than me. I asked if she had always known she wanted to be a dancer.

"I wanted to be a ballerina like my mother. It was only in my teens that I started to see the warped side of ballet. I knew that if I switched to modern, I could have a more balanced life, eat what I want, go to college, not just beat my feet up and become obsessed with my body. Oh—"

Kyra stopped. We were near the doorway where a couple regularly slept burrowed into bedding covered with black trash bags and a large handwritten sign: THIS IS NOT GARBAGE.

Kyra said, "Do you think a garbage truck . . . tried to toss them in the dumpster?"

It had occurred to me too. Something had caused them to write that sign. Though I had passed them many times, I'd never allowed myself to wonder who was under those black bags. "How long can they survive like that?" I asked. "It must be below zero today."

"A long time, probably," Kyra said matter-of-factly. "People can subsist on practically nothing." She had lit a cigarette but at the next corner market passed it to me—"Hold this a sec"—and went inside.

She was buying them coffee, and brownies wrapped in cellophane. She placed these provisions quietly beside the slumbering trash bags. Squatting in her shiny pointy-heeled boots, the flaps of her fitted coat draping the sidewalk.

When she had finished, I handed back her cigarette. "You can't do this for every single street person."

"I know." Her boot heels made a hard sound on the concrete.

"Then why this time?" To me there was something less noble about random charity.

"Because people thought they were trash!"

"It's the same for the rest," I told her. "They don't have to be wearing garbage bags for people to think they're trash. Oh, here's where I turn off."

"Okay. I'll call you about getting the key and all that."

Only after I had turned down the street toward Broadway did it occur to me that I still didn't know where she had been living.

more sweaters

Funny how quickly one becomes privy to a roommate's habits. Just as I knew from the music Adrienne was blasting what kind of a day she'd had, and from Carl's shy laugh precisely when he was about to join a conversation, it soon became clear to me that Kyra didn't wash her hair. That was the secret to its shine. Every day she sweated through dance class and rehearsals and performances, then rinsed off without worrying about her hair. When she did wash it, maybe once a week, her hair became thick and not quite so dark.

I can still see her sitting at the table in the living room, sipping her coffee, in her baggy pajamas and layered sweaters. When she was cold she wore multiple sweaters at once, giving her the look of a bag lady or a senile person. Quite different from that first view of her, on the train platform, in her long fitted military-style coat. Yet she looked no less imperial drinking her morning coffee, one leg draped over the other, socks bunched up around her ankles. She had the habits of a rich girl, with her half-smoked cigarettes (they were less healthy closer to the filter, and she needed her lungs to dance), her discarded hair elastics, her never-worn scarves with the tags still on. I don't think the others knew she gave away her loose change, or how often she bought donuts and coffee for our outdoor neighbors. Even her diamond necklace, with its nearly invisible chain, she sometimes left in a little puddle atop the wooden crate in our room. This mistreatment seemed to me particularly egregious; I thought the necklace exquisite and couldn't help coveting it. When Kyra caught me eyeing it one day, I quickly said, "Watch you don't lose that," trying to sound casual, though something in her face told me she had glimpsed how I really felt.

Some nights she didn't come home. Other times she came back very late, smelling of smoke and sweat from some club, with a paper band around her wrist, like a patient just released from an institution. In the morning her voice would be hoarse, as if from too much revelry. Often she woke early, while I was writing, and would come down the ladder to stretch on the floor, legs extended, draping her torso over herself like a shawl, the little diamond swinging like a fleck of stardust. While I typed at my computer, she would slowly knead the knots out of her muscles, and there was the pleasant sense of the two of us working in tandem.

It was soon after she moved in that I completed the shopgirl piece. At the time it seemed to me a major accomplishment. To summarize:

> At the clothing store one day, someone leaves his *own* sweater folded into a stack of men's pullovers. None have been stolen. The next day, it happens again, someone's old sweater there in the pile of brand new ones. The shopgirl tries to recall who stopped in that day, but the same thing occurs yet again.

> The girl keeps the sweaters and begins to look forward to work, scrutinizing the patrons. But she cannot find the culprit.

She now has a collection of sweaters and imagines the man who fits them—someone strong, quiet, thoughtful. But as soon as she fantasizes this way, the pranks stop. She waits and waits, until weeks have passed and she understands her fantasy man is not coming back. So she takes the sweaters and sets them out on a blanket on Sixth Avenue.

A skinny old man in a tracksuit comes by and tries them on, but they're all too big. He sighs and says his entire life he has looked for a comfortable sweater and still hasn't found one. Hearing this, the girl understands that life is endless yearning, for love, food, entertainment, sex, acceptance, recognition, peace, rest—and for a fantasy man she realizes never existed at all. So she passes the sweaters along to the Rastafarian guy selling a bunch of random stuff nearby, and goes home.

For the first time I had completed a story that satisfied me. Believing it worth the cost of ink and paper, I printed it out on my med school roommate's printer—an endeavor of glacial slowness, each page inching out in tiny buzzing fits and starts. When at last the pages were printed, I paper-clipped them together, slid them into a manila envelope, and sat down to compose a cover letter to my contacts at the *Atlantic*.

Something stopped me. From my bookshelf I took up the thick paperback guidebook I had never used before, the one listing all the magazines and literary journals in the country, even ones that were just pamphlets of folded paper stapled together. But I had my sights set on larger fare. I found the page I wanted and addressed my letter to *Harper's*, where I knew no one at all.

Perhaps it was fear of being rejected by my former colleagues. But there was something else, too. I wanted objective, completely impartial, affirmation of my brilliance. I am not ashamed to admit this. I thought I'd written something really terrific and wanted to hear it confirmed by people who felt no obligation to praise me.

The next day I woke earlier than usual, in order to arrive at the post office the moment they unlocked the doors. Though it was another brutally cold morning, already a queue had formed, which meant God was trying to thwart me—but no, I would not give up, my story must be posted now! I felt lucky when the window that opened for me was that of the friendly, efficient clerk rather than the scowling one. I wondered if she could guess that inside the manila envelope was a story awaiting review, if she might say, "Ah, *Harper's*," and regard me with new respect. But she just stamped the thing and told me how much to pay.

As she handed me the receipt, I was seized with worry, that my envelope might somehow slide off the counter before making it into the mail bin, or get caught at the bottom of a mailbag, never to see the light of day. The clerk looked suspicious at my lingering there. But I wanted to know for certain that my story had begun its journey. Only when she had tossed the envelope, indifferently, onto the pile with the rest, was I reassured, and went on my way.

Kyra and I had begun having lunch together at the deli near where I worked. She too was a fan of the exuberant young man who worked the deli counter. Johnny (he said to call him that, though he was from some faraway place and had some other name) was saving up for culinary school, always concocting new twists on standard fare, offering a taste of something on a plastic fork, "You try! You try, it's fresh!" or "Tuna salad is delicious today," his dark eyes twinkling beneath long lashes—and then would look crushed when I ordered my liverwurst.

Kyra always ordered whatever he had on special. She would eat half and tenderly wrap up the rest, to give to whichever forlorn person first appealed to her.

I remember sitting with her in the deli the day that I mailed out my manuscript, telling her I had finished the story.

43

Her face lit up. "That's fantastic!" Then, almost shyly, "Do you need a reader for it?"

It hadn't occurred to me to show it to anyone. "I already sent it out." My heart sank at my folly.

Kyra seemed to notice. "Well, if you ever need another set of eyes . . ." I had never seen her look bashful before. "I mean, I'd love to read your work."

My work. Maybe I wasn't wrong to have sent it out.

Kyra was peering at me. "You don't show your drafts to anyone?" She looked perplexed. "What about Jack?"

When I told her he had never asked to see my writing, she said, "Huh."

"Well, I mean, I've never asked if he wanted to see it."

That same flat gaze. "Well. I guess maybe it's too personal."

I couldn't take her stare anymore and pretended to concentrate on my liverwurst. But I could feel my ears turning red. I had never thought to wonder why Jack wasn't curious about my writing. Now, just by Kyra having said it, she had made it somehow problematic.

I felt I should defend him. Or at least offer some explanation. "You're always working together with other dancers, so you're used to sharing work in progress. Writers work alone. It can be scary to show your writing to someone else."

It's true. That hasn't changed in all these years. But I see now that I was making excuses. Not just for Jack, but for myself. For not caring enough to share with him the things that mattered to me.

queen of diamonds

Already I had begun holding my breath each time I slid the little silver key into the mail slot, though really it was much too soon for a reply from *Harper's*. I would twist the key and open the box to find, stuffed inside, more bills, some from collection agencies.

Meanwhile Carl had contracted whooping cough. It was Adrienne who gave it a name. Since becoming the ER nurse, she handed out diagnoses left and right. She was the one who told me the tiny white splotches on my nails meant I was anemic, and when our med school housemate complained that he was unable to digest ice cream, she explained that he was lactose intolerant. Muscle spasms, sleep apnea . . . She had absorbed the confidence of Nurse Miranda, and it was hard not to take whatever she said as the truth.

I was still dating Jack and for Valentine's Day decided to wear the crotchless tights. They were a beautiful pale lace pattern, of some synthetic material that had a slight sheen to it. As I primped at the mirror in our bedroom, Kyra said, "Here, wear this."

She held out the slippery chain with the tiny diamond.

"Are you sure?" I was embarrassed to think she might have noticed how I coveted it.

But she was already draping it round my neck. "For Valentine's Day." As if it were a gift rather than a favor. I had never worn a real diamond before and could feel Kyra fastening the clasp at my nape, her cool touch a kind of blessing. I felt like a princess, a debutante, as I headed out to meet Jack.

Instead of a fancy ball there was a prix fixe dinner in the West Village, where Jack and I clinked flutes of champagne and I promptly tucked into my steak frites. I remember thinking that I was finally doing what other people did, sharing a Valentine's meal in a restaurant with a lover. Yet it still didn't feel quite real. That I was a girlfriend, part of a couple, seemed flukish, fleeting. Like the bright diamond at my neck—something lent but not owned. I couldn't help feeling I was in disguise, trying for a role in a play for which I might not be cast.

It was at the end of the meal, as Jack was paying our bill, that a picture slipped from his wallet. A small playing card, glossy and firm.

I slid it toward me. Queen of Diamonds. But the theme of the deck was something rural, and instead of the standard queen, this was a country version, her hair thick with dark curls, her skin rosy, eyes a shiny black, crown a wreath of bright flowers.

Jack said, "It's from a pack I found years ago. She looks like my first love."

Little bells of alarm rang in my ears. But I dared ask: Who was she?

"Clementina. We met the summer I was sixteen. In Liguria. She looked just like this. Well, a real-life version of this."

I pictured some buxom Italian girl lounging on a jetty in a bikini, and realized I was jealous. Jealous even of the playing card, that it could inspire such possessiveness, to be carried closely at all times.

"Now she's in Perugia. Getting her degree in literature, becoming a 'Dottoressa.'"

46

I regarded the image, the strong, confident gaze, and immediately felt inferior. Who did I think I was, to be in the running with someone like Clementina? Yet I couldn't stop myself. "What's she like?"

"Beautiful. Angelic. Hard-headed." He thought for a moment and added, without a trace of embarrassment, "A lot like my mother."

That night as Jack slept, I lay in bed picturing the Queen of Diamonds, her glossy image on the card, the diamonds in the corners worth more than the real one around my neck. I would remove the borrowed necklace as soon as I was home, before I could lose it like some pathetic Maupassant heroine. I knew I would never wear it again.

I wanted to be that woman on the card. And I wanted to have someone like that for *me*. I had no great "first love," no precious token to carry on my person. Just Jack's calling card on the bureau with those other cards, from the Rodin exhibit and the man on the train.

I told myself that maybe Jack could become that person for me. We had been together not even two months, but who knew, maybe we would fall in love. Maybe we were already falling in love. I didn't know what that might feel like and supposed this might well be it, even as I wondered why nothing felt clear to me.

As I lay musing on this, Jack began to talk in his sleep. There was something disturbed in his voice and I tried to follow along, but my French wasn't strong enough. Even when he repeated the phrase, it made no sense. I tried to break the syllables into words I knew, *a lac chou mal* . . . Or no, *harmalac* something. Jack repeated the words, adamant, and I chanted the phrase to myself as best I could, so that in the morning I could ask what it meant.

But that never works. In the morning I could barely remember what he had said.

A similar thing keeps happening now. The memories arise intact, but the moment I report them back to myself, they disintegrate. As if by recalling something, I have erased the original. The way an old elastic band cracks at the moment of release, or the yellowed pages of a book crumble under your fingertips. Delicate things secured in a boarded-up room, still there behind the door but too fragile to touch.

I know that's what I did, boarded up the room, sealed it all away. And I made it this far without looking back. Not at Kyra massaging the knots from her thighs, or Jack in the big soft bed, murmuring strange words in his sleep. Or Carl sweating, shaking, flinging my hands from his shoulders.

Our other housemates were out and Kyra was asleep. I thought if I woke him I could free him from his nightmare. Instead he bolted upright and knocked my hands away. Grabbed my wrists and pinned them down. Chest rising, his head so close to mine, I could smell his sweat. I saw him begin to understand that the person he was looking at was me.

Slowly he let go. Cold patches of sweat where his palms had been. Loud exhausted exhales.

I asked if he was all right. Looking down, he nodded, chest still rising and falling. Then our eyes met. I stood there, scared, thinking he might say something more. But he just watched me, his mouth tense, his face glistening. I managed to say, "Okay, good night."

He nodded again, his mouth still tight.

Shaken, I returned to the bedroom, where Kyra lay sprawled across my mattress. This was a new habit of hers, saying she was too drunk to climb up to the bunk, or too tired, kicking off her pointy boots, crawling into my bed and immediately falling asleep. Lately it seemed there was nearly always some reason for not going up: she had to pee in the night, or there was a draft, the air from the window chilled her, she was freezing up there.

Usually I didn't mind scooching over. I thought maybe this was what it was like to have a sister, to be that close. And though it occurred to me to wonder how often Kyra had been sleeping in my bed already, on the nights I was over at Jack's, the truth was, I liked waking to find her beside me. I hadn't felt that sort of kinship since back when Janet had French-braided my hair.

But that night I nudged her over, annoyed, and tried to fight away the awful thought that would not let me sleep. It was the sense that Carl and I had communed somehow. Shared some awful fear. I didn't even know what the fear was, just our commingling sweat. As if I had made some sort of pact with him.

I could still smell the residue of his sweat, feel the awful strength of his arms. I wanted Kyra to wake, wanted her to ask why I was trembling, what that sour smell was. When I tried to breathe, her hair was in the way. I remember thinking that, even unwashed, her hair never smelled dirty. It was the perspiration of healthy exertion, not the acrid sweat of Carl's terror. A phrase came to me: "the smell of fear." And with it the swift clarity of comprehension.

I waited until Carl and I were alone to ask him. He was in the living room, fiddling with yet another broken tape player, chewing a piece of gum. He didn't look at me, just said, "Hey," and continued with the repair. His whooping cough was gone, so that his usual little cough—the one that emerged when he laughed—now seemed a residue of illness rather than some instinctual ambivalence about the world.

"You've been in the army, right?" I asked. "Is that where you were before you came here?"

Without looking up from the cassette player, he nodded, cracked his gum. "I was ROTC. To pay for school. I still have a couple years of service."

I tried to act as if such things were familiar to me, as if my friends and I didn't find it nobler to pay eternal interest on student loans than to serve our country in time of war. The truth was, I considered myself a pacifist and had signed various petitions.

I asked where he had been based.

"Florida first. Then California. Then Saudi Arabia, and six weeks in Kuwait."

Of course. I'd seen photographs, my last semester of college. The bombed-out desert, and the oil fields on fire. The smoke-blackened sky.

"It was a good way to get through school," Carl said. "Just not the best timing." He gave his low cough-laugh.

"What did you do with your—gear?" I meant "gun."

"Stays at the armory."

I asked which branch he had been in. I suspected "branch" was the wrong word and felt ridiculous. Carl said he had been a platoon leader, a first lieutenant in a tank creeping along behind a mine-sweeping truck, praying to God all the mines had been cleared. In his duffel, I would later learn, were dog tags, a Kuwaiti Liberation Medal, and a Southwest Asia Service ribbon with a little bronze star. Instead of a fancy business card, or a girl's phone number, or the Queen of Diamonds, Carl carried a mandatory reference card listing the rules of engagement. Armor to armor. Air to armor. Artillery and air. I know because I saw it—not that day, but later.

"But you've never even mentioned it."

The look he gave was one of the crueler things anyone had done to me.

Already I was doing the math: While I was squirreling away pennies from my internship at the *Atlantic*, Carl was at an army base awaiting deployment. While I was deciding which clothes to pack for my semester abroad, he was trading green fatigues for tan-and-brown ones, for a chemical protection suit and gas mask. While I was out dancing *en boîte*, he was camped out in the sand waiting for war to begin. While I was flying back home for my final semester of college, he was rolling forward in a mine plow through enemy rounds.

While I read Sartre and Céline, Carl watched oil wells burning, black smoke swallowing the sky. Midnight at noon. Instead of *l'heure bleue.*

My cheeks burned. And I am ashamed of what I said next. "It's not like anyone would have held it against you. It's not your fault." And then, "Jesus, Carl, what did they do to you?"

He looked away.

"When do you have to go back?"

"I'm on medical leave." He held up a trembling hand, evidence. That low laugh again. But he still had two years of service left.

"I saw photos," I said. "Of the sky completely black. From the burning oil wells."

At first he just looked at me. He seemed to be deciding whether to say more. Very quietly he said, "The sound they made—it was like they were *bellowing.*"

There was a small twitch in his cheek, as if he wanted to continue. The veins in his neck pulsed. I waited for what he wanted to tell me.

But his eyes shifted away, and he turned back to fixing the cassette player and didn't say anything more.

push-ups

I wondered about Carl, who his friends were, if the men he worked with knew he had served in the Gulf. Maybe some of them had, too. Maybe they too startled at the smallest noise, and kept their eyes and ears on alert. I was noticing things I hadn't before, such as the exercises Carl followed in order to keep fit. He must have been doing them when none of us were home, though he no longer hid them from me. When the others were out, I witnessed the push-ups and sit-ups and deep squats, hundreds of them, Carl's face turning red and sweaty. The many variations of every drill—sit-ups twisting side to side, or push-ups that stepped the arms out and in, back and forth. He wasn't showing off; he was doing what he needed to do to keep his muscles tight and didn't care if I heard him grunting and panting.

One day when I had the afternoon off, Kyra and I came back from our deli lunch to find Carl home instead of at work; there was some electrical problem on-site, and the carpentry crew had been sent home. He seemed antsy, not sure what to do with the free time. He asked if we wanted to go shoot some pool.

"In the middle of the day," Kyra said. "How decadent."

Carl said, "Can't do crowds."

We went to a place on Houston, just the three of us, and for the first time I saw Carl at ease, not fiddling with something but simply playing—reaching over the pool table, adjusting the trembling cue. Kyra kept missing the ball altogether, and finally we gave up and ordered a second pitcher of beer. Carl told Kyra she had smoked too many cigarettes, that was why she kept missing. The nicotine made her hands unsteady.

"Well, I mean, look at yours." She lifted his hand, touched his fingers. Then, like some strange nurse, she kissed his palm.

It looked less like flirtation than like some kind of benediction. Carl's cheeks turned pink. Kyra asked, "What makes them shake?" I realized she must not know about his army service.

To my surprise, he answered her question easily. "It's the medicine." Prescribed by a psychiatrist, he said, to stop the nightmares.

"How long have you had them?" So she truly hadn't heard him cry out.

For a moment Carl just looked at her, and I wasn't sure if he would answer. "They started as soon as we left Kuwait. I don't know why. I was fine when we were there. Even when we were cleaning out the barracks, all those burnt bodies, I was fine."

"You were there." Kyra didn't seem terribly surprised. Maybe he had told her about ROTC but not about his days on the ground. "I saw photos," she said. "Of, you know, the 'Highway of Death.'"

Carl gave an impatient nod, yeah, yeah, hadn't we all. Kyra didn't seem to take it personally. In that matter-of-fact voice, she said, "That must have been hard."

These simple words did something to Carl. The vein in his neck began to throb, and the skin around his eyes twitched. I could see him trying to stop the twitching, trying to get hold of himself. Only when he had composed himself did he say, dismissively, "Yeah, that's what the shrink says."

Kyra was still looking him in the eye.

Carl gave his little cough. "We went over there months before anything happened. So we had all this time waiting for the war to start. All this time to practice." He looked down at his feet. "We totally had the protocol *down*. Hand off the ammunition, aim, shoot, reload. Any scenario, we had the whole sequence of commands, it was like second nature, who loads, who fires, we could do it in our sleep. And then things finally get going, second day of the ground war, three of us in a Bradley, we're behind the minesweepers, there's a line of Bradleys behind us. We go in, we've made it past the border, past the mines, past the trenches—and then this Iraqi tank fires at us.

"And we all just start screaming. 'They're shooting us!' I mean, we couldn't believe it—someone was actually *shooting* at us! My gunner's going, 'Shoot him! Shoot him!' Forgot the whole fucking protocol. We're just loading up and screaming, 'Shoot the fucker! Shoot him!'"

Carl was laughing, and I remember loving him in that moment, that he could laugh at himself. But then he coughed and I could tell from his face that something awful must have happened.

Which confused me. Wasn't this the war where we sauntered in and made toast of the Iraqis in no time? Where we dropped a bunch of bombs from far up in the sky, and that was that?

"You could see puffs of dirt wherever the rounds landed. But we made it through, and I thought we were all okay. But another Bradley was hit worse. One of the guys, Neil, took one in the head. There were just two of us who died that day. Neil was one."

Kyra said, "Well, and I guess a lot of Iraqis died that day."

Carl narrowed his eyes. "There were Iraqi tanks all over the place, aiming at us. Our orders were to shoot them." He was looking right at Kyra. "We shot them all."

I thought he might leave then, he looked so ticked off. Instead, he told us more. About Kuwait City, the burnt shells of bodies, carcasses picked clean by feral dogs. About Neil with his head blown off. The smell of the highway—burning metal with burning flesh. At first I wondered if he was trying to scare us. But then I realized what was happening. With each question, every nod of her head, Kyra was opening him up, drawing him out.

"The worst part," he said, "is that ever since then, anybody I meet, first thing I see—" He broke off. "The first thing I see is what they'll look like dead."

The image that whipped through me had been with me since I was ten. My mother at the very end, when she turned a horrible pale yellowish color and I grew afraid of her.

I tried not to imagine what death vision Carl might have of us. I didn't know what to say. The sky in the window had dimmed to a twilit blue. Our pitcher of beer was empty. The pool hall had become louder, crowded. So it took me a moment to realize that someone had stepped up close.

"Just leave while I'm at work." The man speaking to Kyra looked to be in his early thirties. "No explanation. No conversation. Just a fucking *note*."

Kyra's eyes closed briefly.

"That's it, then?" he asked. "You don't even have the nerve to say goodbye, do you?"

She turned away. "I thought I was sparing us both."

The man shook his head. All he said before walking away was "It's really time you grew up."

When I looked back at Kyra, she was crying. She said, "I'm such a fuck-up."

I didn't say anything; for all I knew it was true. Carl, though, looked oddly buoyed. I think he took this encounter to mean that Kyra was not attached to anyone, and that he might have a chance with her.

Because in just our time there in the pool hall, he seemed to have fallen for her. I was surprised at how swiftly it happened. I suspect that until that afternoon he had thought of her as just some rich girl playing poor, that only in receiving her compassion did he understand there was more to her.

But as the after-work crew grew around us, he became visibly tense. *Can't do crowds.* We decided to head home.

Outside, the temperature had dropped shockingly. I was tipsy from the beer, and my teeth were chattering. Yet there was a warm feeling as the three of us leaned into the cold air. I remember thinking that this was how friendships grew, in small bursts. With the beer in my belly, it seemed my life was on the right track. Yes, I still worked in a clothing store, but I had friends, and a lover, and a story waiting to be read by *Harper's*.

Even Carl with his trembling hands looked happy next to Kyra. I watched him light her cigarette and then his. Side by side, they made a handsome couple. I remember thinking to myself, yes, of course.

Just then a swell of teenagers passed by, one of them calling out to the others in a foreign tongue. I thought I recognized the words, and reached into my coat pocket for the notebook and stubby pencil, chanting the phrase inside my head.

Carl and Kyra realized I had stopped walking. They waited as I scrawled the phrase into my notebook, my hands still in gloves, my fingers barely able to move in the cold. Carl asked what I was writing.

I explained that I thought it was something Jack had said in his sleep. "I don't know what it means. I tried to memorize it so that I could ask him, but I forgot it."

Kyra bent closer to look at what I'd written. "Can you even read your handwriting?"

She was right. I was drunk and freezing and the words were barely decipherable. I tucked the notebook back in my coat pocket, and we headed home.

a fight

There was a day when Jack swooped in line behind me at the deli and kissed me grandly, just as Johnny was passing a sample of tuna salad over the counter, asking me to guess the secret ingredient.

I took a taste. "Cumin?"

Johnny's eyes crinkled at their edges. "No . . . you?" He nodded to Jack, but Jack didn't even try the sample, just shrugged. Johnny's dark eyes shone. "Sumac!" Then he pouted theatrically when I ordered my liverwurst, and winked at Jack to show he was teasing.

But Jack didn't wink back, didn't even smile, and Johnny quickly turned away. I was annoyed at Jack, and confused, since it was so against his nature. But I waited until our food was ready and we had found a table to ask why he had done that.

He pretended not to know what I meant.

"You were rude to Johnny. You rebuffed him."

Jack exhaled dramatically. "It must be my mood. I've had bad news from home. A dear friend of my parents has died."

I was surprised to see him so affected, since he rarely spoke of his parents. He told me the friend was the most intelligent person he had ever met. "A journalist. A real intellectual."

I told him I was sorry. When I asked what paper the friend had written for, he said, "Oh, you wouldn't know it."

That hurt me, that he didn't want to share his journalist with me. I said, "Still, you shouldn't take it out on Johnny." Then I asked how old the journalist had been. What I really meant, as we all do, was, How did he die?

Jack closed his eyes and gave a small shake of his head, as if to indicate some common disaster (cancer?) or avoidable tragedy (suicide?) too infuriating even to name. It wasn't the reaction I'd expected, and my annoyance fell away. I squeezed his hand.

But as we ate, I considered that he hadn't seemed upset when he swept in and kissed me in front of Johnny. I wondered if he might be jealous, if he saw Johnny's enthusiasm as flirtation. After all, Johnny too was, in his way, tall, dark, and handsome.

It tickled me to think of Jack being jealous. It seemed to me evidence that our romance was real, that we were growing closer. Even when I was home later that evening, playing Texas Hold'em with Kyra and Carl, I carried this little episode in my heart as proof of his affection.

a visit

In mid-March, Jack went to visit his family in France for spring break, and I couldn't help feeling left behind. Perhaps as consolation, Kyra invited me to join her on a jaunt to Rhode Island, where she was due to visit her mother.

She invited Carl, too, but he had some big renovation out on Long Island. I felt bad when I saw the disappointment on his face. Ever since our pool hall excursion, the three of us had been hanging out together. I remember curling up on the futon watching Adrienne's soap opera, Carl narrating, straight-faced, a newscaster-style commentary that had us laughing until we snorted. I remember that he called Kyra "K"—just the initial, spoken softly. At the time it simply seemed an affectionate diminutive, but now it strikes me as a show of restraint, as if saying the full name would have been too much. As if he didn't dare try to fully claim her.

So we left for Rhode Island without him. Somehow Kyra had procured a car—a big, shiny gray sedan with leather seats. When I asked whose it was, all she said was, "This guy who likes me."

No one ever offered to lend *me* their cars. But what I felt wasn't as simple as jealousy. I was still rooting for Carl and didn't want to hear of other contenders, especially not ones who could afford a swanky automobile. It had to do with what I wanted to believe about the world and about myself: that not just Carl but I, too, could be loved by anyone. That my upbringing, my family, my past, none of it mattered. That I could end up with a jet-setting Frenchman or whomever else—that I could sport off to Newport, land of mansions, manors, and gatehouses, in a fancy car with leather seats.

As we made our way out of the city, I remember thinking Kyra brave for navigating the streets so confidently, dodging taxis and the squeegee men with their sloshing buckets. Deep down I was still cowed by Manhattan, its noise and size and speed, and could not have imagined driving myself. Especially not on a Friday afternoon, everyone tired and impatient. As we inched forward in the mass of traffic, one of the squeegee men, very tall and reedy, carrying his sponge-mop like a pitchfork, approached us.

We had come to a full stop, so many cars merging. As the light turned red, Kyra shook her head at the man. Out loud she said, "No."

The man maneuvered his mop toward the car, and Kyra wagged her finger. "Don't even think of it." But the man reached over and smeared a big swish of dirty lather across the windshield.

Kyra slammed the horn so hard, the man jumped back.

"I said NO!"

The man gave a little shrug as if to say, *Fine, your choice.* He took his pail and mop and slouched away, leaving the dirty smudge on the window.

"That motherfucker." Kyra yanked on the hand brake so hard the veins on her hands bulged. The traffic light switched to green, but Kyra had flung open the car door. "Get back here!"

Instead the man straightened up and began striding proudly away as if to prove how unbothered he was. The car behind us had begun to honk. Kyra had hopped out and was going after the man, while I sat nervously watching.

"I'm talking to you, asshole!"

More cars were honking. This must have unsettled the man. He turned warily back, and Kyra pounced. "Get back here and finish what you started."

The honking was worse now, and the man looked frightened. He slouched back to the car and wiped the suds away, while behind us the traffic shifted bitterly into the next lane. Kyra looked like she might explode. Before taking her seat and slamming the door, she said, in a firm, furious voice, "You need to learn: when a woman says no, she means no."

"I got it," the man said, and slunk away.

It wasn't until Kyra had released the handbrake that I realized I was shaking.

She said, "Sorry about that."

"No, you were right." But I had to wonder why Kyra's generosity toward other unfortunates—like the men in front of our building—didn't extend toward this enterprising man with his mop. Well, it wasn't her car. Probably that had something to do with it. Or the fact that *he* had approached *her*, not the other way around. And he had disobeyed her order. She did have that imperial side. I began to laugh.

Kyra looked at me. "What?"

"What you said to him." It must have been the tension releasing. I was laughing hard.

Kyra grinned. "What can I say? When a woman says no—"

"She means no!" We both yelled it, together, and began laughing hysterically.

It was only afterward that I wondered why exactly she said that. One more thing I never quite figured out—though later we continued to employ the phrase, usually sarcastically, at opportune moments. At the time, it always cracked us up, tied as it had become to the squeegee drama. Now, though, it just sounds ominous.

Who knows what trouble Kyra might be in. If she's safe, or even alive. Meanwhile all I know is that she sent a package, that it's on its way to me.

On the drive to Rhode Island, I learned that her parents had divorced when she was in elementary school and now her father lived in London. "But even before that he was never really around. He works for Exxon and is always traveling. You know, six weeks in Bombay, five days in Texas, a week at home. My mom grew tired of it. Though of course that's where the money comes from." Kyra laughed. "I don't think they ever had much of a marriage. I mean, even before they got divorced—well, put it this way, I always had a lot of uncles."

It took me a moment to understand what she was saying. "None of them stuck around?"

"My mom just lives how she likes. She was a ballet dancer and was used to attention. I think she liked having admirers more than she wanted any one person. But after she quit teaching ballet, she let herself go, and after that, all the uncles just sort of fell away."

I told her about the time after my father divorced Janet's mother, when there had been a wild spate of dating. I still recalled the voices on the answering machine, the falsely jaunty messages, the diffident ones, their tremulous persistence. There was the day I arrived home from school to find a woman sitting on the doorstep, looking vexed and determined, smoking a cigarette. Seeing me, she raised her eyebrows in a way that did little to hide her surprise. She rubbed the tip of her cigarette into the slate of the step, said, "Your father's a real prick," then walked to where her car was parked, and drove away.

"From then on, in my mind I always heard 'Your father's a prick,' and I knew it was true. But I still wished some fantasy woman, or even *that* woman, or my ex-stepmother, would marry him, so that we could live happily ever after."

Kyra was silent for a moment. "So, you believe in love and forgiveness and all that?" Her tone made it seem I had said something naive.

"Well, I mean, who doesn't want to believe in love and forgiveness?"

"*Right*." She spoke slowly, deliberately. "But believing in it and having to do it are two different things."

I didn't know what to say to that. But she abandoned the subject, and soon enough we had arrived at our destination. A large house of gray stone, with a driveway of glittering white pebbles and a landscaped yard, the brave green tips of crocuses poking up from the dark earth.

This was where Kyra came from, who she had been: a debutante, member of the equestrian club, with manicured nails and coiffed hair and firm thighs from dressage practice. Cotillion classes and coming-out balls, embossed invitations overlaid with vellum. Facials at Elizabeth Arden. Prize ribbons from riding competitions. I saw the evidence, propped in picture frames and on the walls of her bedroom, and tucked into the corners of photo albums.

Like Jack, I remember thinking that evening as we sipped aperitifs in the plushly carpeted living room. That same crucial, random, inherited luck.

Her mother's name was Grace. One of those ballet dancers who as soon as she retires becomes fat. It was from denying herself sweets for so long, she explained at dinner, reveling in the pink steak with its juicy brown crust, the creamy mashed potatoes, the sweet glazed carrots, the chocolate ice cream she stirred until it became smooth. "You have to understand, they weighed us weekly. Always taking measuring tape to our waists. That kind of prolonged hunger, it can never be satisfied." A face oval like Kyra's, her lips somehow stretched, her neck comfortably ringed in fat. Her light brown hair, parted in the middle, came to her chin, framing her round cheeks. Small hands and feet, as if to prove that really she was still a dainty thing. I couldn't help but think of the short fat lady Jack and I sometimes saw at the café on Thirteenth Street, whom we had nicknamed "Profiterole."

The next day was mild, and Kyra and I took a long ambling walk along a path by the ocean. I remember the moist air on my face and the leisurely pace of our ramble. We took breaks to sit and look out at the water, and I tried to envision what it might be like to grow up this way, among the prosperous. Was that what gave Kyra her breezy confidence? Maybe I too would have the nerve to give up a scholarship to Oxford if I could afford frivolous mistakes and tenuous employment. Maybe I too would dare confront a squeegee man in the middle of moving traffic. But I could hardly conjure what that confidence would feel like.

We were sitting cross-legged on a bench facing the ocean when I heard myself say what had been rising in me. "Why am I so afraid of the future?"

Kyra looked alarmed.

"See," I said, "you don't even know what I'm talking about. Because you know the whole world is yours."

I wanted to think the same for myself—that I could be whoever I wanted, that I could fall in love and have a family and live a chosen life. Some part of me knew that might even be true. But just as I had spent my childhood pretending acute envy did not pierce me daily, just as I had tried to adopt the easy self-assurance of my college friends, I struggled even to believe in my dreams.

"I want to believe everything they told us at graduation. That I can go out and do whatever I set my mind to, be whoever I want to be. Sometimes I almost believe it. But most of the time I can't even imagine it."

In her flat calm voice, Kyra said, "*Can't* imagine it? Or is it that you're not *allowing* yourself to imagine it?"

That really annoyed me.

"Mim, you're a writer. You use your imagination all the time." She seemed to really be considering this. "It must be that for some reason, when it comes to your own story, you won't let yourself envision what you most want."

"It's not that I'm not *allowing* myself." Yet even as I said it, I wondered if she might be right. Somehow she seemed to see through everything.

Now it strikes me that I must have sensed this even in my very first glimpse of her, on the train: the no-nonsense part of her, the flat gaze. I think that frankness was what I picked up on—was perhaps the very source of her familiarity, the reason I thought I knew her. Really what I was recognizing was, I suspect, myself. That is, the possibility, in another person, of being fully, truly seen.

On the bench facing the ocean, with the salty breeze tangling my hair, I said, "I think it's because I lost my mother. I'm afraid of what other bad things might be waiting around the corner. Whereas you, you're brave, you aren't afraid to take a leap. I'm just not like that."

In a voice that managed to sound somehow hurt, Kyra said, "Bravery isn't just some personality trait. It's what you *do*."

I had never thought of it that way. I asked how I could ever do anything brave if I didn't feel brave.

"That's what I'm trying to tell you. Bravery is an *action*. It's there when you *act* on it." She reached for my hand. "You're just as brave as I am."

I felt no different than before. But because Kyra had said so, I was able for a few brief minutes to believe it.

When we arrived back at the house, Grace was eating another bowl of ice cream. She told us Roy had stopped by.

At my reaction, she said, "Kyra, you didn't tell her about Roy?" Eyebrows raised. "He and Kyra basically grew up together, they're like peas in a pod. Anyway, he's coming tonight for dinner. He's a total sweetheart. And so smart. He went to Harvard. Kyra, show her my favorite photo."

Away fell the sisterly feeling, the frankness of our conversation on the bench. Kyra mumbled that she had to go take a shower—but she satisfied her mother by plucking up a framed photograph and handing it over.

"This is from a few years ago," Grace said as Kyra left us. "Fourth of July. Roy took everyone out on his boat."

There they were, a whole clan of healthy young people, the girls in their bikinis, the boys in madras shorts and Adidas flip-flops, holding beer cans, grinning. "Here's Roy." With sandy blond hair. The most handsome of all.

He arrived for dinner carrying a dark bottle of wine and a little cake done up in colored cellophane. The look on his face as he handed them to Grace suggested that he, more than the cake or the wine, was the gift. "I brought that pinot you like"—but it wasn't the right year, they only had the '88. "That cabernet was such a disappointment last time, I don't know why I still trust them, but you know, we need to support the locals."

Kyra had come down from upstairs. "Hey." She was wearing a baggy sweatshirt, faded jeans, and thick socks, like a girl in a school dormitory. She draped an arm around Roy and leaned up to kiss him on the cheek, and the necklace with the tiny diamond trembled at her throat.

Roy kissed her forehead, tenderly, as one kisses a child's scraped knee. Even just the way his hand rested on her arm spoke of many such past reunions. When I held out my hand, he kissed my cheek, and a dismaying shudder of delight rushed through me.

Grace ushered us to the living room for cocktails. She had put on a big silky dress of a grayish blue that made her eyes shine, and as she sat next to Roy, the dress expanded in silky ripples around her.

Roy was asking lots of questions, and seemed genuinely curious, until Grace cut him off. "What about *you*, Roy? Fill us in."

"Where to begin?" The searching, anticipatory look of someone about to quote a poem. I glanced at Kyra curled up on the couch, but she didn't seem to find him at all ridiculous. "Business has been slow, of course, with the economy, so lots of time for other things." He had his own company—personal investing—and a boat he kept at a slip in Newport; there was a race he participated in each summer. He told us about old friends he had seen and a recent trip to London. He always stayed in a boutique hotel on Portobello Road; the West End had so much more character, he wouldn't stay in the center if you paid him.

I felt myself shrinking there on the sofa. The boat, London, Portobello Road . . . Things that to me were foreign everyone else in the room knew as normal. Or rather, *I* was the foreign one. Roy was casually leaning back on the sofa with his hands behind his head, his legs straight out, crossed at the ankles.

For dinner Grace had made coq au vin, with an endive salad, a baguette warmed in the oven, and her specialty, baked alaska, for dessert. A glow of affection hovered over the dining table, the palpable ease of friends having nothing to prove. I watched my companions trade light jabs and old jokes, shared tales of fantastic, inconsequential mishaps, of hilarity on sailboats and verandas. Roy sat across from me, next to Kyra. Something protective, almost proprietary, about his way with her. Kyra was quiet, hardly asking Roy any questions—not as if she didn't care, but rather as though she already knew everything about him.

When Roy inquired as to our New York escapades, I told him about Adrienne's soap opera and served up some comic moments from my job folding sweaters. Roy looked amused. "Yeah, I did time in the city for a couple years," he said. "You know, I'm just a quick drive away if you girls ever get into trouble. Any time you need me, just holler." He was twenty-six years old—a grown-up.

We drifted back to the living room to sip fruit cordials, Roy and me on one sofa, Kyra and her mother on the other. Grace had brought along a second helping of the baked alaska, the silky dress rippling around her like an enormous puddle. As she finished the last of her dessert, I had a thought that nearly caused me to laugh out loud. It was the sense that Grace had *become* a scoop of ice cream, melting.

Taking a cigar from his jacket pocket, Roy said, "I think I'll have a smoke on the porch, if it won't offend our hostess."

Some nearly imperceptible change of tone made me sense he wanted Kyra alone to join him. It was only in that moment that I realized something must have gone on between them. Some thwarted romance, or maybe a long-ago first love. I don't know why I hadn't realized it before. I hesitated as the two of them stood to leave the room. But Grace was shooing us out the door. "It's a beautiful night, don't mind me, you kids go bay at the moon." I followed uncomfortably behind them.

To be outdoors at night without a coat after so many months of winter felt like a small act of defiance. We were far from any streetlights, and the stars burned like flares. I couldn't tell from Roy's face if he was annoyed to have me there, but Kyra didn't seem to mind. She and I lit cigarettes while Roy set to lighting his cigar with what seemed to me too much attention. He leaned against the porch railing, asked Kyra about the dance company. "When do I get to see you in action?"

I watched him more closely. As confident as he was on familiar turf, he seemed somehow nervous to be suggesting he might seek Kyra out in New York. Kyra didn't appear to notice. When she told him she had a show coming up at St. Mark's Church, he said, "I'm there. Just give me the coordinates."

I remember thinking, Oh—then I'll see him again.

Kyra seemed pleased that he wanted to see the show, which in turn appeared to restore his confidence. "Look at that sky," he said, and slung his arm around her, so that the two of them stood as one unit, Roy pointing out the constellations as if they were among his own private collection. Stubbing out my cigarette, I announced that I was cold and heading back inside.

"Wait, I'm almost done with my cig." Kyra said it casually, so I couldn't tell if she didn't want to be alone with Roy or was simply worried about hurting my feelings. Even when she had finished her cigarette and we were all saying goodnight, exchanging goodbye pecks on the cheek, I wasn't sure.

In the car the next day, heading back to the city, I stole a look at the sparkly diamond hanging at Kyra's neck. I had only ever worn it that one time. "Is Roy the one who gave you that necklace?"

Kyra nodded, and I waited for her to offer up something more. "C'mon," I said, "what's the deal with you two?"

She said, "I guess I'm supposed to marry him."

I looked at her face to see if she was serious. "Do you *want* to marry him?"

An odd little sigh. "You saw what he's like. How can he keep living this way? He's so removed from the rest of the world. I mean, even his job. 'Personal investing.' He manages his friends' brokerage accounts!" I expected her to laugh, but she looked like she might cry. "I had a mad crush on him growing up. Then the summer after my freshman year of college, we finally got together. That lasted about a year. But he was already done with college, and then—" She gave a little rustle of her shoulders, as if shaking something off. "I don't know."

"Well, I mean, do you *love* him?"

"He's actually a really good person, Mim. Really kind and generous. I don't know why he has to be so . . . you know." She seemed

69

to become upset all over again. "That's the thing, he's so smart, he could really do something with his life, you know?"

In her expression I witnessed the acute pain of discovering some unbearable quality in a person you love. And for some reason, what I thought of next was Carl. That this Roy person might present more of a hurdle than I thought. Because I knew Kyra must really love Roy, at least a little bit, to be disappointed in him that way.

Back on the island of Manhattan, Kyra dropped me at our building, then went to deliver the car to whichever man had lent it. I checked the mail for word from *Harper's* and made my slow way upstairs, reluctant to return to our shabby existence.

"She's returning the car," I told Carl, at the look on his face.

I could see that he felt somehow caught out. He was sitting on the couch and seemed to be trying not to look disappointed. He looked tired, too, after his weekend on the Long Island job. As consolation I said, "We missed you." It was disingenuous, but I thought it would please him.

I told him about the fancy house with the circular driveway, and Grace and the baked alaska. Carl kept asking questions, and I recognized what he was doing, waiting for me to mention Kyra, for the small thrill of hearing her name. And so I sat there with him on the ratty couch and told him all I could—omitting the part about Roy.

I knew I was withholding information. But that wasn't lying, per se. And I didn't want to hurt his feelings. Also, I truly believed Carl might have a shot at winning Kyra's heart, and I hated to do anything to puncture his confidence. After all, what kind of competition was Roy, really? He didn't even live here.

Instead I told Carl about the scrapbooks and dressage ribbons and the photographs from coming-out balls. Carl shook his head and picked up one of the cushions from the couch and sort of buried his face in it.

70

It was probably the closest he ever came to stating his feelings. I wanted to console him, to show that I understood. I said, "The human heart is a mysterious thing."

"Kyra is a mysterious thing."

"I mean, you never know."

This seemed to encourage him, and we stayed up late talking and waiting for Kyra. But she had gone off with the car and did not return that night.

solstice

It was the first almost warm day, mid-March, my afternoon off, and I was arriving home from the Benetton. The homeless men were at their posts, coats open now that winter was beginning to thaw.

I wore my belts too tight. Yeah. It was the fashion, belted up in the middle. That's why the baby came out all wrong.

I recognized the voice, cigarette-hollowed, absurdly low, more frog than human. Huddled under so many coats, the creature with the long white braid and the red bandana had looked to me like little more than another cantankerous drunk. But now I saw that under all those layers was a hunched and wrinkled woman.

The baby, they showed me, he was pink like cotton candy.

I looked at her, this woman I'd never bothered to look at before. For a moment I just stood there. It was a mark of wretchedness that people like me couldn't even see who she really was.

I was still feeling shaken as I entered the dark vestibule of my building. Turning the little key to the mailbox, though, I immediately forgot all about the frog-woman. Among the bills and direct mailings was an envelope from *Harper's*.

Thin.

My entire future lay within that envelope. If it were a form letter, some curt dismissal, like the terse little notes we had used at the *Atlantic*—a firmly typed *Thank you but this is not for us* photocopied on little half-sheets of paper (so as not to waste precious supplies on the hopeless)—I would die.

I tore the envelope open right there in the grim foyer. The letter was folded in three, on thick creamy paper with the *Harper's* logo up top.

Dear Ms. Woodruff,

I thoroughly enjoyed this story, with its quirky subtleties and existential mystery. I'll be presenting it at our monthly fiction meeting three weeks from today, and we'll see if the others see a place for it at *Harper's*. Could you please call me before then to assure me the story has not yet been published? I'd also like to ask you about possibly changing a line or two in the final paragraph.

Sincerely,

_____, Senior Editor

I took the stairs two at a time. But I was superstitious and worried I might jinx things if I mentioned it to anyone. Though bursting inside, I decided not to say anything about it.

That night was the debut of Kyra's spring performance, and our entire household trooped over to St. Mark's Church. Carl carried the bouquet we had pitched in for, gerbera daisies wrapped in clear plastic, tied with a bow made of twine. Jack was with me, and as we settled onto cold, hard wooden risers, I was glad to have his warm arm around me. In my state of euphoria over the letter from

Harper's, I had decided it was time for the crotchless tights again, and Jack kept giving me spontaneous kisses, probably because he recognized the tights and was grateful.

Only Kyra, who sometimes saw him at the deli, had ever really spent time with Jack. Adrienne was always either performing, rehearsing, or waiting tables, and hadn't met him at all. That night she was looking dramatic, in a long velvet dress with a biker jacket and a choker necklace around her throat. Our med school housemate sat next to her with his new boyfriend, a stocky fellow with his hair streaked blond.

Carl sat to my other side, in his washed-out jeans and vinyl sneakers, the bouquet leaning against his calves. His hair had fully grown out by then, bangs swept to one side, so that he looked like a dreamy poet. He pushed up his shirtsleeves and leaned forward, arms on thighs. Even with the lights dimming, I could see the muscles in his forearms twitch. He shifted in his seat, visibly uncomfortable, and I wondered whether to explain to Jack that Carl didn't like crowds.

Yet he had braved them to come watch Kyra.

The first piece was a big cheery group number set to fifties pop songs, with Kyra leaping across the stage like a gazelle. The second was an intense male solo, danced in silence. The final piece comprised five duets, Kyra's couple the angry one, fiery and cruel and unable to stop hurting each other.

When the show ended, we all waited for Kyra in the front hall. Carl was still in charge of the flowers. And then I heard, "Hey there, Miss Miriam."

Roy, from Newport, holding an enormous bouquet.

In my excitement over the news from *Harper's*, I'd forgotten about him, and I think it showed on my face. But I recovered my manners and introduced him to everyone, feeling privileged to already know him. The bouquet he had brought was gigantic, lilies and orchids encircled by a big silk bow. He said, "Wasn't that amazing."

I recall their reactions: Adrienne's curious amusement at this handsome fellow with his treelike bouquet; Carl's surprise and hurt at my knowledge of a new suitor; and Jack's relaxed look of easy familiarity, which I put down to species recognition.

Roy stood there chatting happily. Carl was sort of chewing at the sides of his mouth. I knew he was angry with me. I felt rotten and tried to avoid his gaze.

At last Kyra arrived and accepted the bouquets. She was still glowing from the dance, looking surprised and pleased. When Roy announced that a table was being held for them at a restaurant a few blocks away, Kyra asked if the rest of us might join them—but the restaurant was sure to be packed, Roy said, it was one of those places where you had to wait weeks for a reservation. Kyra gave us an apologetic goodbye, but she didn't seem to mind either way. As they walked off, I could feel the heat coming from Carl beside me.

He turned away without saying goodbye, to head back to the apartment with Adrienne, while our med school roommate went off with his boyfriend. Jack and I made our way to the subway.

I was still feeling bad about Carl. About my own behavior, really, and at how easily Roy could snub us all. I asked Jack, "Why does everyone fall in love with Kyra?"

Without pausing to reflect, he said, "Because she doesn't wash her hair."

I turned to stare at him. "How do *you* know she doesn't wash her hair?"

"It has that nice glimmer," he said matter-of-factly. "Reminds me of the women back home. Americans have poufy dry hair. It's not natural."

"Is that it? Just don't wash your hair? And everyone will love you?" Kyra did have a lovely face, but her teeth were stained from cigarettes, and she wore all those sweaters. Either way, it seemed Jack truly saw no other possible reason to be captivated by Kyra.

Of course, she was no competition for the Queen of Diamonds traveling along in his wallet.

"No, really," I said, "what is it? It's that she's skinny, right?"

"Too skinny," Jack said, good boyfriend that he was. "Oh, good, here's the train."

mutts

One of the things the marriage counselor has taught us is always to apologize.

Not that we fight much. Nolan is more the type to brood silently than to cause a fuss. So it took some time for me to understand the little ways I sometimes hurt him—usually by focusing on my work, hiding away in my study without realizing I'd shut him out.

But back when I was twenty-two, I knew exactly what I had done to Carl. I could barely wait to tell him I was sorry the next day.

Adrienne was home too, though, when I returned to the apartment. She was pulling on her boots, about to head to rehearsal, and told me she had found Jack very charming. "That accent, subtle but sexy. And of course I love that he's a mutt like me."

That stopped me. "What's that supposed to mean?"

"You know, a *moo-laa-toh*." Adrienne always adopted a jokey tone when it came to what she called her racial "mélange." "I mean, he's part North African, right? Arab or whatever. Some kind of mix. There's a word for it, isn't there? You're the French major."

When she saw the look on my face, she burst out laughing. "You didn't know?"

Of course, now that she had pointed it out, I saw quite clearly. Jack wasn't simply tall dark and handsome; he was part Maghreb. The olive tint of his skin, and the thick hair and eyelashes. I made a quick calculation: his last name, Italian, came from his European side, in which case it must be his mother who was . . . what? Moroccan, Algerian, Tunisian. From some colonized state.

That I hadn't noticed these things, or simply hadn't paid attention, seemed more than naïveté. I was mortified by my blindness, my incuriosity. It seemed a comment on our relationship, on the sense I had of grasping at air where our two selves ought to have met. How could we ever truly connect when I had never really *looked* at him?

Even the fact that, for two days now, I hadn't mentioned to him my news about *Harper's* now seemed an aspect of my inattention. Probably there was something strange about my purposely keeping news of that sort from the man I was sleeping with. I couldn't help wondering if it was a sign of some sort of indifference.

Carl was watching us, while Adrienne shook her head and laughed. I thought of the dark-eyed Queen of Diamonds on the playing card. The girl who reminded Jack of his mother. I knew the xenophobia of the French, that colonial condescension, nervous glances on the metro at the Arab boys. Was that why Jack's parents had sent their son to school abroad? The confident rich boy demeanor was only part of who he was. Behind the crisp shirts of finest cotton, the big platinum wristwatch, was this other history.

"So *exotic*," Adrienne teased.

That was exactly the problem, I realized. With a single label—*Maghrébin*—Jack suddenly became someone "other." I recalled the French couple in the café, the way Jack had transformed before them, and his reaction at the deli to Johnny, who was probably Moroccan or Tunisian or Algerian himself. Probably beneath his untroubled nature lurked resentment.

Lightly, Carl said, "Funny he never mentioned it."

As if Jack had been lying to me. It did give me pause. "Do you think he thought I'd care?"

I liked Jack the way he was and didn't want him to change, not the way he had for the French couple in the bakery. I felt a tenderness and affront on his behalf. And anger at myself, for never having fully attended to him.

Adrienne, pulling on her coat, was still laughing. "You really didn't know?" Shaking her head as she stepped out the door.

I fetched my little notebook from my coat pocket and flipped to the page where I'd scrawled the words I now knew weren't French. "Carl, did you learn any Arabic while you were over there?" Saudi Arabia, I meant, and Kuwait.

Just a few basic phrases, he said. *Halt. Drop your weapons. I bring you peace.*

"What about this?"

Carl barely looked at the words. "How the fuck would I know?"

"Carl, I'm sorry about that Roy guy. Really. I totally forgot about him. I just didn't mention him before because, honestly, he was just some doofus from out of town. I mean, I didn't think it mattered."

Carl didn't say anything.

"I know you're mad. I'm sorry."

When he ignored me, I looked again at the words in the notebook. Jack would know what they meant.

He came by soon after, on our way to some party. Kyra, Carl, and I were the only ones home, watching the latest episode of Adrienne's soap opera. When I went to grab my coat, I heard Carl ask Jack, "So, part of your background is North African, right?" As though it had just occurred to him.

Yes, Jack said easily, and it seemed possible he assumed I had known. "My father is a *pied-noir*. Do you know that term?" As if having learned not to expect much from Americans.

79

Kyra stopped fast-forwarding the VCR. "The French settlers in Algeria." She turned to look at him with new curiosity, and I remembered she had been a poli-sci major.

Jack looked surprised that one of us knew something. Perched on the arm of the ratty sofa, he explained that his father's side was Corsican. Farmers who settled in Algeria in the 1800s; his grandfather had become a wine exporter in Oran. "But my father went to study law. He worked for the government and left during the war."

He still hadn't looked at me, and I decided he knew it was strange not to have discussed this before. That he was trying to act as though he simply hadn't thought of it.

"My mother's Algerian, also from Oran. From a long line of merchants." Dealers in olive oil, in nuts, grains, in raisins, dates, Barbary figs. Jack described a majestic house near the sea, with a marble patio and terraced gardens and a view of the peak of Murdjajo. In the courtyard, bougainvillea, fountains, pools reflecting the acacias.

It wasn't boasting; I understood, quite suddenly, that Jack had *been* there, that he knew and loved that house, that garden. That rarely could he share that love without judgment. But here in our apartment in New York he could describe the view of the sparkling ocean, and the trees studded with bright firm oranges.

Carl was nodding, slowly, slyly—yes, of course they were rich.

Kyra had come to sit on the floor at Jack's feet. Somehow even in that small motion I felt chided. My lack of curiosity I now saw as more than a commentary on my feelings for Jack. It was a moral failing, to never really have looked at him. To never have wondered who he fully was.

Kyra asked what it had been like for his mother, growing up in occupied Algeria.

"My mother's father was very progressive. He wanted more for her than, you know, the Koranic school, married off at age fifteen to some man she didn't know. It wasn't just a matter of education.

He wanted her to be able to wear what she wanted, to walk the boulevards in the center of town." Free, Jack explained, to have her photograph taken. To have a job, a profession. To say, *I love you.*

In his words I heard, *See, we are not who you think we are.*

"He sent her to one of the French schools, but the rest of the family was ashamed that she went around without the veil, dressed like a European. Women were supposed to be hidden away at home, to marry and have babies. I don't quite know how to explain how rare it was to be a woman like my mother."

He was speaking to Kyra as if I weren't there. I asked if that was how his parents had met, at the French school. I wanted him to look at me.

"No, it was when my mother came to study in the capital. Love at first sight. And absolutely taboo. There was almost no intermarriage then. Also, the fight for independence had already started. For my mother this was especially dangerous."

Kyra was nodding. "Right, if you were seen with the 'enemy,' you could be a collaborator."

"Yes, and she had nationalist friends. Her own cousin was a liberation fighter. He was caught and taken to Barberousse. The prison. He was beheaded."

"Beheaded!" I was horrified, but Kyra didn't look surprised. She said, matter-of-factly, "The guillotine."

"So you can see why my parents had to leave. It didn't matter that they believed in integration. Others did not."

"Well, no," Kyra said, "because it's not really integration when you have this small European minority dominating a huge Muslim majority." Her voice was plain yet firm.

I looked nervously to Jack. "True," he said, "though that minority allowed my mother a great degree of emancipation. But then the war started, and there was my father, working for the occupying government. They had to get out."

81

Crammed on a boat to Marseille. Migrants to a homeland they had never laid eyes on. "They had never been out of Africa," Jack explained. "In France they were always cold."

No one lent them their coats. No one welcomed them home. Instead of a honeymoon in Andalusia, there were the cool glances of neighbors—at this influx of strangers, their odd accents, and an Arab woman in the mix. "All her life my mother had been taught that she was French, a citizen of France. But after 1962 she was simply Algerian."

Jack must have felt that way too, I realized. That without the big gleaming wristwatch, the cashmere sweaters, he was just another son of refugees. A *Musulman* from Africa. "The thing is," he said, "my father, too, was viewed as 'native.' A *pied-noir*, uncultured, indigent."

He told us more: about his father's transfer to Paris, his mother's trust fund, visiting her family in Oran. All the while, he addressed Carl and Kyra, looking only occasionally at me, as if I already knew all his stories. I couldn't tell if he realized it or if he was consciously dissembling.

He explained that normally he would have gone to Oran for spring break, but it had become too dangerous. Just the previous month, a state of emergency had been declared.

In her matter-of-fact voice, Kyra told us, "The Armed Islamic Front is trying to overthrow the government. There was a first-round election and the militant Islamist party won—but to stop them from winning the next round, the government *canceled* the whole thing." She widened her eyes, and I remember thinking, quite clearly, that she would be a better match for Jack.

He said, "It's basically civil war. Do you remember"—he turned to me—"when I told you a friend of the family had died?"

"The journalist?"

"Assassinated. In broad daylight, stabbed to death. He's native Algerian, born and raised in Algiers, but he was educated, and a socialist, a supporter of religious freedom. So they killed him. Send a message to the public, you know."

Carl said, loudly, "I'm surprised you guys haven't been talking about it." And then, "Mim, what about that sentence you were asking about?" He looked at me with such false innocence, I wanted to clock him.

Jack asked what sentence.

"Oh, something I heard." I would not reveal that he was the one who had spoken it. That really would be an intrusion, to publicly expose what someone had said in his sleep. "I think maybe it's Arabic." I reached over for the little notebook in my coat pocket and showed him the words I had sounded out.

He nodded. "It means 'Allah would be ashamed of you!' It's very strong. You might say it to someone behaving badly."

That surprised me. I wondered what had prompted him to say that. Meanwhile Kyra was asking if he had been raised as a Muslim.

"My mother was laïque—unreligious. And my father was raised Catholic but doesn't go to church. You see, my parents have never really fit in. No matter that my father is successful and my mother wealthy. They still speak with an accent, people always know they're different." He paused. "It's the same for me, I suppose. In Algeria the other boys always knew I was French. They knew I wasn't one of them."

After a moment, he added, "Sometimes they were quite cruel."

I wondered if that was the source of his nightmares, what made him cry out in his sleep.

"We had better get going, hmmm?" Jack squeezed my hand and stood, pulling me up with him. I still wondered what he could have been dreaming when he spoke those words.

Like Carl and his nightmares. Perhaps the truth of who we are is something we say in our sleep, that we don't even know we've said.

carl's story

As the author of historical novels, I understand that it's easy to be swayed by hindsight. Nolan and I sometimes discuss this, when I share with him some tidbit from my research. To him, so many episodes from the past seem obvious, even preventable. But that's mere retrospection. Most of us would make the very same mistakes again if we had the chance.

I'm not saying this to make myself feel better. I'm simply aware, as a student of human nature, of the depths of human weakness.

Roy called, not long after the dance performance. I was the only one home, and we chatted easily, as though the call had been meant for me. I still hadn't told anyone about the *Harper's* letter, and I remember that for a split second I considered telling Roy. I suppose I thought it might impress him. But my superstitious side was strong enough to stop me. And a little charge of residual pique rushed through me when Roy explained that he had been trying to get in touch with Kyra.

He made it seem he was concerned for *her*: Was she okay, did I happen to know what she was up to, if she received the chocolates he had sent?

So that explained the fancy box in the living room. "Are they an apology?" I'm not sure what gave me the cheek to ask, just that it had to do with that photograph I'd seen in Newport, of the yacht and the bikini-clad girls—that guaranteed high life. People like that seemed to me impervious.

"Why would I be apologizing? Is she angry with me?"

"No, no." The truth was, she hadn't mentioned him at all. That too was for me a point of envy. As much as I found Roy ridiculous, it still bothered me that Kyra could take a handsome Harvard graduate for granted. I didn't have to like him to want him to like *me*. To want him to find me, too, alluring. No matter that I was perfectly content with Jack. It still gave me a little thrill to have Roy's attention.

So I chatted back and felt a small sense of accomplishment by the time we had ended the call. I don't think I realized yet that Roy would start checking in every so often. If Kyra wasn't home, and someone else answered the phone, he would ask for me. Probably it was a way to save face rather than look like a person whose calls were being ignored—but I still felt a small rush each time I was summoned to the telephone. I remember deciding that, since Kyra appeared to be through with him, Carl might have a chance after all. And if Carl could succeed with Kyra, I too could come up in the world.

It was in these two or three weeks leading up to the *Harper's* meeting—what seemed to me then the longest, slowest weeks of my life—that I found Carl in one of his trances. This time it was broad daylight, and instead of the futon he was lying on the sofa. Shaking.

It was my afternoon off; no one else was around. I don't know why Carl was home. When I softly rustled his arm, he bolted upright and in one swift gesture threw me to the floor.

I landed, hard, on my shoulder. At first I just lay there. For the briefest moment, I wondered if Carl had thrown me on purpose. But he was still shaking. Carefully, I sat up, aware that I too was shaking. My shoulder felt stiff, and my hips hurt where Carl's hands had grabbed them.

"It's all right," I said, but my voice was trembling and the words sounded unsure. "It's just a bad dream."

Only then did he seem to realize what had happened. His face crumpled, and he leaned his head into his hands. He began to sob. I reached up, but the movement hurt my shoulder. Carl's arm was clammy. Slowly I pulled myself from the floor and sat beside him. The sobs shook his shoulders.

I rubbed his sweaty scalp. The acrid smell was beginning to dissipate. Carl's voice, muffled into my shoulder, said, "I'm sorry. I'm sorry."

"It's all right."

"I'm sorry."

"Honey, it's all right."

"I'm sorry."

I held him, and my shirt absorbed the tears and sweat. Carl mumbled into my shoulder, "Please, Mim."

"It's okay. Don't worry."

"Please, Mim. Please."

"Please *what?*"

Carl lifted his head from my shoulder. "How can I stop seeing them?"

I let go of him then, to look in his eyes and ask what he meant.

It was the first day of the ground war. They were driving in over the border into Kuwait. This was before they had been shot at; Neil was still alive and making the vulgar jokes that were his specialty.

"We were in a line formation, mine plows first, then me and my guys and a line of Bradleys behind us. The path had been cleared, it's all going well, no one's being blown up, no one's being shot at. And then we see the trenches ahead."

He swallowed as if deciding whether to continue. "We know the Iraqis are in them, waiting. So we're bracing ourselves for attack. We're ready. But we get closer and closer and no one's shooting. Before we even get there, some of the Iraqis have come out. They're waving white T-shirts. They don't even have guns. They're skinny— I mean, hungry-skinny. We can see their ribs."

"You mean they were surrendering."

"Yeah, but we weren't supposed to take prisoners, we were supposed to keep going in. See, we still had to get past the trenches, because there were more of them down there. So we just kept going. Over the trenches."

When he spoke again his voice was very soft. "We drove right over them."

I didn't understand. "Over who?"

"The guys down in the trenches. They were crying and saying, 'Allah!' I could hear them. But we just rolled on over them, and the sand buried the sound." His face had become very pale. "When we made it past, I looked back and there was just sand. As if I'd dreamed all those voices."

I said, "Maybe you did."

"The tank has thermal sights, to detect body heat. I used them on the tracks we'd left." Now he was whispering. "Mim, our tracks were *glowing*."

I didn't know what to say.

"They keep telling me it was just the heat from the tires. But that doesn't change what we did. No one ever said anything about it. Everyone talks about the air war, all the tankers and bunkers we blew up. But, Mim, there were probably a hundred, two hundred, maybe three hundred guys in those trenches. Sure, okay, maybe that's not a lot—but we fucking buried them *alive*!

"No one mentioned it, just handed us our ribbons. See, they pin medals on you so you feel good about shooting a bunch of tankers—instead of thinking about the assholes you ran over in the sand. Or the crap you breathed in over there, or the pills they made us take. The fucking Iraqis standing there waving their T-shirts, begging us to pick them up so they wouldn't freeze to death. They were fucking *shivering*." He wiped his nose with the back of his hand. "You get a ribbon, so what, it just means you showed up." He was crying again, his face wet and shiny. "Waving their fucking T-shirts."

He cried so hard mucus ran from his nostrils. Then he wiped his nose with his shirt, wiped his eyes, and began to tell me more. About the Kuwaiti soldiers beating the Iraqi POWs until they cried, then kissing them on their cheeks, *You are our brothers!* The panicked Iraqi who, seeing Carl's tank approach, stripped to his underwear to prove he wasn't concealing a gun. *Standing there in the desert in his skivvies, waving an undershirt!* The starving soldiers trailing after Carl's tank, please, please, we surrender! Wanting only to be delivered from cold and hunger. *But we didn't have time to deal with them, we just kept going.*

He talked until his voice was hoarse. I don't know how long we sat there. In the window the light was shifting toward evening, a deep dense blue. When I stood to leave, my hip and shoulder ached where I'd landed on them.

an argument

At last, it arrived: the day of the *Harper's* fiction meeting. I was anxious even as Kyra and I sat in the deli eating our lunch. There had been a brief telephone conversation with the editor, and I kept giving myself pep talks, convincing myself my story was brilliant— but then I would think of Carl, those stories he had told me, and my own story would seem petty.

I wanted to do something for him, to stop the nightmares. I wanted Kyra to love him and put him out of his misery. For there to be proof of happy endings—not just for Carl, but for me too.

It did seem he might have a chance, now that Roy had pretty much fallen off the map. Just a postcard that week, from Bermuda, addressed to both me and Kyra, with a scribble about how much fun he was having windsurfing.

Sitting there in the deli, I wondered why Kyra and I never spoke about the men in our lives. Now I think I must not have wanted to know, not wanted to hear about her feelings. Or was it that I hadn't wanted her to ask me about mine?

I decided to raise the topic, and asked if she understood how Carl felt about her.

She looked at me. "I'm not *stupid*."

"Well, I mean, he's a really good guy, right? Smart and good-looking and—"

"And going back to the army. Eventually." She looked away, though, because we both knew that wasn't why she didn't want to be with him. Now it seems obvious to me that the same things that separated them, money and class, were probably what kept me from ever truly being with Jack. Kyra said, "Why are you suddenly being a matchmaker?"

"I'm not."

"Some people don't just go and sleep with people because they're handsome and exotic or foreign or whatever."

I narrowed my eyes. "What's that supposed to mean?"

She shook her head. "Nothing. Never mind."

That annoyed me. "Sorry I even brought it up."

"Whatever. Forget it." She took a sullen bite of her sandwich, and neither of us said anything. We focused on our lunches. But then Kyra exhaled loudly.

I put down my sandwich. "What? I said I was sorry."

She shook her head.

"Then what is it?"

"Why do you pretend to *like* that?" With her chin she pointed at my sandwich.

"You mean—the liverwurst?"

She nodded, as if unable to speak the word.

"I'm not *pretending* to like it. It's good. I mean, it's protein, it has iron, it's good for me."

"See, even you know it's disgusting!"

"Well, Jesus, Kyra, sorry, I didn't realize you were disgusted by my sandwich." I took another bite, to prove that I was eating it by choice.

"I'm not disgusted. It's that I can tell you don't like it!"

I stopped chewing. It was true I always added a lot of pepper to make it taste better.

"You lie and pretend you like it because you're too cheap to buy the stupid egg salad!" Kyra looked like she might cry.

She was right that the egg salad cost just five cents more. I swallowed and put my sandwich down. "Why do you even care? You're not the one eating it."

"Because you're a penny-pincher! And liverwurst is horrible! I mean, fine, if you truly think you can't afford anything else. But don't pretend to like it!"

"You're crying."

She wiped her eyes. "No, I'm not."

I pushed the remains of the sandwich away from me. She was right. I didn't like the liverwurst.

She said, "It's just . . . you're upsetting me."

"*I'm* upsetting *you?*" What had I done? Well, she did have a point, about my dissembling. If nothing else, I might at least have complained about the sandwich.

"It's not the food. It's your stinginess. It's no way to live."

"Some of us don't have a rich mommy to go visit on the weekends. To pay our bills when need be."

Softly, Kyra said, "There's no reason to pick on me."

"Oh, but *you* can get annoyed at someone for eating the wrong sandwich? For trying to make ends meet? While you get to follow your dream and be who you want to be, and magically live on a dancer's salary without some dumb day job like the rest of us."

"But you're not just trying to make ends meet, don't you see? You go beyond what's necessary. You're always . . . denying yourself."

I stared at her. It was true that I never spent a cent more than absolutely necessary. Not without great anxiety and guilt. Fear, even, at what greater losses might be set off by even the tiniest splurge. The very idea of spending money, of what such spending might unleash, frightened me. So much so that I could not allow myself to admit when I wanted something—not even the egg salad.

91

I heard myself say, "I can hardly stand how I feel when I spend money. It makes me feel like I'm losing control."

I thought she would be pleased at my agreeing with her, but she looked more upset. And an odd brightness coursed through me. The closest word to describe it would be joy.

I didn't understand, in the moment, why I should feel that way. I supposed it had to do with finally acknowledging the burden of the liverwurst and being liberated from it. Never before had I understood that my behavior went beyond what was necessary. That I hoarded little things. The slowly evaporating bottle of Jean Naté, which I had no reason to keep but couldn't bear to throw away. The refillable pen from France for which I couldn't find cartridges in the U.S. The T-shirt everyone had received at graduation, three sizes too large. As soon as I returned home that evening, I told myself, I would toss it all out.

Only after we had finished our lunch, when Kyra had left and I was back in the Benetton waiting on customers, did I come closer to noting what exactly had pleased me. It was that I was happy at having upset Kyra. Happy that she cared enough about me to be upset.

Otherwise, why would she cry like that?

I came home to find the answering machine blinking. The editor at *Harper's* wanted to let me know that the others had not been so enamored of my story and she was sorry to have to pass, but to please contact her when I had another piece for her to consider.

Just like that, in a few sentences, it was over.

I lay on my mattress but could not cry. Who cares, I told myself. Who cares about your stupid story?

It was silly. Trivial. Why, just think about Carl, the stories he had told me. Or Jack, his family, all they had been through, his parents fleeing for their lives. Even now, their friend—murdered!

Get up, I told myself. Stop moaning. I was alive, I had a future, a life to live!

I took up my spiral notebook. But every story I had begun seemed pathetic, even while I suspected, deep down, that they might hold as much truth as those other, darker stories. That some greater truth might, in fact, lie in the connection between them.

I waited, pen in hand, for something to come to me, something meaningful and real. And at last I heard a voice.

I wore my belts too tight—it was the fashion. That's why the baby came out all wrong. Pink like cotton candy.

resurrection

Easter came late that year. Jack jetted off to Corsica for two weeks, not inviting me along, and though I could not have afforded the ticket either way, I still felt abandoned. We'd been together a full three months by then, which I believed to be a long time.

He left on a Friday night. After kissing him goodbye, I arrived back at the apartment to find Kyra in the living room with Carl.

They were together on his mattress, sweetly entangled and fast asleep. Like a pre-Raphaelite painting, with Carl's pale skin and the swoop of his bangs and the way Kyra slept with her mouth slightly open. I tiptoed past them making quick assessments. Was this just one more bed for Kyra to sleep on when she felt like it? Or had she heeded my suggestion?

The truth was, she had been standoffish ever since our conversation at the deli. It occurred to me that she hadn't slept in my bed in the days since.

Maybe this was more than just tumbling onto someone's mattress. Maybe she did feel something for Carl. Wasn't that what I'd hoped for? Because surely she knew better than to toy with his feelings.

I crept past them and settled into my own bed, with a book I'd borrowed from the library. Camus's *Chroniques algériennes*. But I felt pathetic now that Jack had chosen to go away without me.

In the kitchen the next morning, Adrienne said, "Carl finally busted a move, huh?"

"Do you think?" He and Kyra were still asleep. They still appeared to be clothed.

I thought of Roy off in Bermuda, and of the men who lent Kyra their cars and whatever else, and I couldn't help feeling bad for Carl. And for myself too. Jack had abandoned me! Meanwhile everyone loved Kyra. Everyone let her sleep in their beds.

Everyone loved Kyra, and no one loved me.

Despondent, I did the only thing I could think of. I went to get a haircut.

"Short," I told the hairdresser, not realizing she would take it quite so literally. Dark hairs drifted onto my smock, and before I could protest, she was using clippers to shave the back of my neck. With a fluffy powdered brush, she swept the hairs from my face, then spun me round so that I could view her work from every angle. A pixie haircut, short as a boy's.

Though I've worn it short ever since, never has it elicited the reactions of that first time. Look at your cute ears, a man said as I waited in line at the deli. And in the theater where I went to watch one of Adrienne's plays, a woman in the row behind me tapped my shoulder. "The back of your neck . . . I'm so lucky to have picked this seat!"

I suspect it had to do with the way I carried myself, newly exposed. There was a reciprocal effect too. It was as if, with my hair out of the way, I could see more clearly.

At least, that was what I told myself. That I was no longer some silly girl writing silly stories, pining after some boyfriend who didn't love her—and whom, I was beginning to admit, I didn't even love. I was no longer trying to be Anna Karina, or Anouk Aimée. I was finally becoming myself.

There was to be a huge revelation on the soap opera. This was a day or so after my haircut, and we all squeezed in front of the minuscule TV—everyone except Carl, who had packed up and gone on-site for the Long Island job. He would be sleeping out there with the crew rather than traveling all the way each day.

No one else seemed to think it might be to avoid Kyra, now that she was back to her usual self. At least, no one said so. After all, Carl had stayed on-site before. When he told us, so casually, that he would be away for a while, we didn't discuss his reasons, but I wondered if he was feeling hurt.

So that night it was me, Adrienne, Kyra, the med school guy, and his boyfriend—who, I was only just realizing, had apparently at some point moved in with us.

On the soap opera, Caitlin realized she loved not her fiancé, Chad, but Chad's brother, and Bianca revealed that she had a mere six weeks to live. And just when we thought that nothing more could surprise us, Nurse Miranda at long last remembered what the comatose patient had said.

I have no recollection of what he said. I was thinking about Jack loving Clementina instead of me, and Kyra loving Roy instead of Carl. Caitlin loving Gavin instead of Chad. Switch the names around, it didn't matter. What mattered was that someone was always left out, and the wrong people were being pined after.

I guess I'm supposed to marry him.

That the world could be this twisted, our hearts so misguided, seemed to me utterly tragic. When the episode was over and we had all retired to our various beds, I lay on my mattress unable to sleep. I could hear the light, whispery breathing of Kyra in the loft bed, and I thought of Jack, away in a different time zone, and of how I wanted to love someone, and to be loved in return. Real, true connection, not the empty embraces I had offered Jack.

On my bureau, I still had the postcard he had bought for me at the Rodin exhibit. Ages, it seemed, since we had stood there in the gift shop. In my nightshirt I went to turn on the little lamp, and took up the postcard I had grabbed so hastily from the rack. Lovers, blurry and mysterious. The delicate promise of their tender gestures.

They lay horizontally, heads angled into a kiss, hair mere watermarks circled in brown. The woman, her hair piled in a thick bun, supported herself on one shoulder as she kissed her lover, whose plainly sketched face, I noted, was equally fine. I held the postcard under the light. The hair, too, was similarly voluptuous, thickly gathered into a kind of bun.

I rotated the postcard vertically, so that the heads were up top. From this angle it was clear that the second figure, too, possessed a bulge for breasts, and a rounded lower abdomen, and a smooth round pubis only partially shielded by one leg. I stood there by the lamp, trying to make sense of this new vision.

I had thought love came from this—nakedness, two bodies moving together, no need for words. And though I understood, now, that love was much more than that, I still couldn't speak my true feelings.

I placed the postcard atop the bureau. For a moment I just stood there. Then I turned and went to climb the ladder to the loft bed.

A thin glimmer of night sky came from where the blind didn't quite reach. Kyra was facing the wall, so that all I saw was her hair, lit blue from the window. I peeled back the covers and slipped in beside her. I wanted to say something, to whisper in her ear. Instead I placed my hand on her hip, swept her hair aside, and kissed the back of her neck.

With a tiny sigh, she let me do this, to kiss her shoulders, her back, to run my palm along her thigh. Then she rolled over and placed her hand against my cheek. She said, "Well, now, aren't you a beauty?"

To this day, I have never tasted a mouth so lovely.

With Jack, lovemaking had been a game, a thrill, all about pleasing and being pleased. With Kyra I understood a more primal instinct—to unite as one skin, for there to be no separation. I remember Kyra slipping out of her little cotton tank top as I tugged her panties from her hips. I remember laughing, from the simple joy of her mouth on mine. When I brought my mouth between her legs, I did not wonder at how swiftly this new urge had overtaken me, to hear her soft moans and take in her briny scent. When her hips began to shift, I held them firmly and was certain I had never known anything so wonderful as this girl's bucking at my touch. I remember thinking that we were meant for nothing more in life than each other.

This was nothing like Jack's gymnastics in bed, the showy satisfaction of a merely physical act. Already it seemed I knew every curve of Kyra's body, every angle of her face, understood the outer form as an extension of her inner being. I took in everything, the pale ovals of her fingertips, the knobby points of her knees, the tiny faint lines at the sides of her smile. Now it strikes me as obvious that I had already, long before that night, begun to love her.

And so began the weeks in which all we did, really, was fall in love. The selfish enchantment of new lovers, as though time existed only to deliver us to one another. I gave barely a thought to Jack or to Carl. Nothing was more urgent than being with Kyra, knowing: I *love* her, and she loves me *back*! We *love* each other! For this was love—I knew it without knowing how or why (though we had already, in the zealous haste of young lovers, spoken the word). I suppose that is love: some inner conviction, like religious faith, without proof or explanation.

Nor did I pause to contemplate the fact that I had never kissed a woman before. I had simply acted on instinct, allowed myself to claim what I wanted. I did not stop to wonder how long Kyra had been waiting for me to climb that ladder. Probably she had never in her life had to initiate a romance. Yet I was secure in the knowledge that I was different from the others, that I was the one she had been waiting for. I had never seen her like this, giddy, almost abashed at her happiness. And Carl, didn't I worry about him? No, he was out of town. As for Jack, I used his abandonment to guard myself from guilt.

It had been two weeks when Kyra stopped by the store to meet for lunch, her face still aglow from rehearsal, her jacket open to the spring breeze. Standing there, fingers interlaced, swinging our arms. Stupid grins and laughter. We kissed, right next to the summer cardigans.

"Bonjour, les filles!"

I turned to see Jack, back from his Corsican travels. At first he seemed tickled at this vision, Kyra and me swinging our hands together.

"You're back," I said, stunned. Though I knew he was to return soon, I had assumed he would head home first and call me, and that we would talk.

He said, "You've cut your hair."

I let go of Kyra's hand, but Kyra, stubborn, slid her slim fingers through one of my belt loops. I said, "I didn't know you'd gotten home."

"I arrived this morning. I thought I'd come find you." There was the slightest shift in his expression; I could almost see his thoughts rearranging themselves. Yet he came up to me and, in a gesture of such generosity it still amazes me to recall it, kissed my cheeks—

one, two—rather than my mouth, so that I knew he understood. Graciously, he did the same for Kyra, who still held urgently onto my belt loop as if I might run away.

"Was it a good visit?" I babbled. "Did you have fun?" Whom had I become that I could feel like a stranger to this man?

"Yes, yes—I'll tell you all about it." He was squinting at me, as if reassessing. "But maybe now isn't the best time."

"I can come over this evening when my shift ends," I told him. "Or meet you somewhere," I added quickly, for Kyra's sake.

"Let's meet at the café," he said. He meant the little place on Thirteenth Street with the chubby lady we called "Profiterole."

He managed to exit the store with considerable aplomb—so much, in fact, that I briefly wondered if perhaps Clementina had turned up on the shores of Corsica. Only later, at the café, would he tell me his feelings had been hurt.

But as I stood there in the store with Kyra and watched him leave, a surge of gratitude overcame me. After all, it was Jack who had primed me for this freedom, who had opened my heart to the possibility of love. It was he, with his schoolboy fantasies, who had taught me to indulge in that big soft bed, to trust someone with my body and with my soul. Jack at the carousel of postcards, saying, Pick one.

And I chose this.

the dinner

And then comes the part I never did manage to shut away.

It was a Friday, not long after my meeting with Jack. I had stopped at the Food Emporium for groceries and in the butcher aisle eyed the juicy steaks wrapped in gleaming plastic. Too expensive—but then I saw a price. Cheap. Too cheap. I looked along the shelf where the cost per pound was marked; indeed, the price had been miscalculated. I examined another steak, and another. They had *all* been stamped with the wrong price. I could eat steak for a month! I could store it in the freezer and eat it for a year!

I filled my basket with steaks and potatoes and broccoli, already planning the grand meal I would cook for my housemates. I don't know if I consciously thought of it as a kind of amends, but recalling it now, it seems I knew Carl was coming back that night, and that I wanted to smooth things over. The steaks would be my peace offering.

Even as the checkout girl tallied it all up, I was prepared for the butcher to run over from the deli counter, shouting, "There's been a horrible mistake!" But no one came running, and the steaks absconded with me.

Only then did another wave of guilt overtake me—that I should have been honest and informed the cashier. Though I assured myself it was *their* mistake, and that no one would suffer, shame tainted my elation, and a thought wafted through me: that I would be punished in some way.

But it was one of those nights when everything comes together effortlessly. For one thing, all of us were home, even Adrienne, so that when Carl arrived, there was an air of celebration. I could see that our welcome-home pleased him. And it really did seem, as we cooked together, that everything would be fine.

We made too-strong drinks, and soon we were all comfortably buzzed. Even so, I kept slightly apart from Kyra, wary of flaunting my joy. I remember Kyra seated across from me, wanting to touch her, not daring to do so in front of Carl. Kyra too seemed wary. But after dinner, in some euphoric moment as we all cleaned up together, she leaned over to kiss me, and Adrienne, accustomed to our little displays of affection, said, "Ah, lovebirds."

At the look on Carl's face, I understood that what I'd tried to convince myself wasn't true. And that our guardedness had just made things worse—as if we had all been in on a secret together, purposely keeping it from Carl. He pushed past us to the living room to grab his jacket, saying, "I'm meeting friends for a beer, thanks for dinner," and left.

I felt awful and wondered what to do. Kyra kept biting her thumbnail, worrying how we might make things right. When we went to bed, we felt too guilty to do more than hold each other before falling asleep.

The next thing I remember is someone shouting. I blinked into the hazy dawn light. Kyra wasn't in bed. She was shouting from the bathroom, saying to call 911.

The med school guy was already dialing when I hurried over. His boyfriend stood behind him shouting, "What do we *do?* Ask them what we're supposed to *do!*"

In the bathroom, Kyra was leaning over Carl. He was in the tub, blood in the water.

Adrienne had woken now and stormed into the bathroom. In one swift move she retrieved Carl's shirt from the tile floor and began tearing it into strips. "Get him out of there," she said, and Kyra and I tried to pull him up from the bloody water.

"He's too heavy." I touched his face. He was still breathing.

Adrienne shouted, "Guys, get over here and help us get him *out*! Kyra, go look through Carl's pills, see if you can figure out what he took."

The med school guy said, "They're on their way," but just stood there. I think he was in shock. His boyfriend was the one who helped us lift Carl out of the tub.

I had never lifted anything so heavy. Carl's skin seemed to have a blue tint, which I first thought meant he was dying but then decided was just the lighting. I held his shoulders even after we had set him down on a towel. I thought that maybe the warmth of my hands would reach through his skin and heal him.

"Press there," Adrienne ordered, pointing just above Carl's slashed wrists. "Apply as much pressure as possible." She began to wrap the first wrist tightly with a long strip of cloth. "Okay, you can let go."

I asked how she knew to do that.

"We did it on the show."

Remembering this now, it strikes me as evidence: that reality can be the opposite of what looks true. The real doctor isn't the one who will save your life. The person in the military-style coat isn't a soldier. And the guy with the bands around his wrists isn't the one needing help; it's the one lying right in front of you.

Kyra was holding two vials. "I only found these." When we heard the ambulance sirens, she said, "I'll go down." She looked about to fall over. But she insisted she ride with him to the hospital. Even in that rush, I remember telling myself that, after all the other awful things Carl had endured, surely we couldn't have caused as much pain as all that.

The ambulance drove off wailing. And then our med school roommate began to hyperventilate, and we had to go help him.

Before that night, the worst thing I had witnessed was my mother in the days before she died, when she turned a horrible yellowish gray. Now it was Carl, lying heavy in the tub. Only hours later did Kyra phone to say that he would be all right.

I asked the others, "What does that mean, 'all right'? He tried to kill himself!"

We were drinking coffee with scorched milk. I wanted Kyra with me and was aware of a kind of panic overtaking me, probably at the guilt I felt, or simply at the realization that I could need someone that way.

At last she came home, pale and gray under the eyes. Carl had been transferred, she told us, to the mental health ward. She said, "They took the laces out of his shoes."

I told myself that Carl hadn't necessarily wanted to end his life. I said, for Kyra's benefit, "Maybe this was just, you know, a 'cry for help.' Maybe he did it so he wouldn't have to go back into the army."

It was agreed that this was possible. But Kyra wouldn't look any of us in the eye. She went to the bedroom and closed the door.

I followed her there. She was lying on her back on my mattress. I lay down beside her and draped an arm around her. I told her, "I'm just as guilty as you."

She turned onto her side, away from me.

"Don't do that." As small as my voice sounded, I heard the panic in it. Something in Kyra had switched off. For an awful moment all I could think was that I never should have bought those steaks.

"Kyra, please." I kissed the backs of her ears until she turned to me. She was crying, and I kissed her wet cheeks.

At last we slept. When I woke and moved to leave the bed, Kyra rolled me back toward her, with her strong, wiry arms. She slid her hand against my skin and brought her mouth to mine, and I remember thinking that maybe everything would be all right.

For another month or so, I clung to that thought. And then came word that Carl, sent home to Ohio to recover at his parents' place, had managed to procure another weapon, with which, in that ultimate act of self-determination, he had succeeded.

blue

It was in the airport, on our way back from Ohio, that I began to doubt everything.

This was after Carl's funeral—the stunned, pale parents, the bewildered friends, the ROTC buddies in their military garb. The Southwest Asia Service ribbon and Kuwait Liberation Medal on the closed casket. Kyra and I were waiting for our flight back to New York, and she was in a horrible state. I was trying to comfort her. I even tried to convince her that Carl had escaped an unhappy future—of pills and nightmares and hands that wouldn't stop trembling. Of the shivering men waving their T-shirts. I kept saying everything would be all right.

She pushed me away. "How can you say that? Don't you understand anything?"

People had turned to see what was going on. Oh, what we must have looked like, two exhausted girls with red puffy eyes, one of us dropping to her knees, pressing her head into the other's shins, saying, "Please, Kyra, don't be mad at me."

"Stop thinking of yourself all the time!"

Already something awful was solidifying within me, yoking joy and love to death and disaster. I had given in to passion, and as a result someone had died. I don't know if it had occurred to me yet that Kyra must feel the same—that probably just to look at me made her think of Carl.

When we arrived back in Manhattan, she went straight to bed.

She stayed there the rest of the day and through the night, and the next day, too. When I tiptoed in, every few hours, to ask if she was hungry or would at least drink some water, she would mutter that she didn't want anything.

On the evening of the second day, I managed to get her out of bed, but as soon as she sat down at the table, her face became wracked. Tears streamed, fast and silent. It terrified me. I saw that Kyra was trying to sit up straight, trying to eat, but it was as if she were prevented by some other force. I had never seen anyone cry that way, as if the crying were from somewhere beyond her.

Kyra gave up and dragged herself back to bed. She still hadn't spoken, and as she lay there, I became frantic. It was more than worry. I was alarmed by my own powerlessness. That I could not help her, could not reach her, seemed a comment on my standing. All night I lay next to her, sleepless, panic growing inside me. I was out of my realm, beyond my abilities. I had no idea what to do.

So I called Roy.

He arrived the next morning, mere hours after my call. My desperation seemed to have energized him. He bounded up to the apartment cleanly shaven and smelling of Ivory soap, and I led him back to our hot, stuffy, dank room, where Kyra lay on her side.

"Kyra," I said, "guess who's here." I worried only slightly that she might be annoyed at my contacting Roy. He didn't know about us. I just wanted him to make everything right again.

He sat down heavily on the mattress and placed his palm on her arm. "Hey," he said.

Eyes still closed, she said, "Roy." She sounded surprised but not displeased. A strange feeling swept through me: relief that I had been right to call him, and dismay that Kyra could be so glad to see him instead of me.

He stroked her hair, watching her, saying nothing, looking concerned but not shocked. Knowingly, patiently he waited, while I stood there awkwardly. Kyra's shoulders began to shake, that same silent, unintentional crying that made it seem some spirit had overtaken her.

Roy bent closer and whispered to her. Probably he was just comforting her, but the whispering made it seem there was some secret between them. In fact, it seemed Roy might have done this before. And the more I watched, the more it became true, that Roy *had* done this before, that there *was* some painful story between them, one that Kyra had never told me. Something my jealousy kept me from wanting to know.

Kyra had opened her eyes and reached for Roy's hand. I left the room then. I had begun to feel ill. I went to the kitchen to prepare some food, since surely Kyra would eat now. I tried to tell myself that it was my hunger that had made me feel ill. That it was not because I was experiencing, all over again, what I had felt in Rhode Island. That opaque sensation of being shut out.

Of course she loved him more than me. Who did I think I was, that I could ever be enough for Kyra?

At last they emerged from the bedroom. Kyra's eyes were puffy and strange, but Roy looked spry as ever; he had saved her. Saved the both of us: damsels in distress. All at once I felt cross at Kyra— for being a princess, so precious she needed to be fussed over. It made her grief seem less from compassion than privilege, that she could afford to curl up in a ball and cry for two days.

How stupid I had been, to think I could be with a princess! Just as I had been silly to think I could be with Jack. That world was out of my reach. What Roy had with Kyra—that shared foundation—I would never have.

At once it became appallingly clear that it could never work out between us. That what I had thought was a great romance was mere puppy love, soon to expire. As we sat at the table and attempted to eat the dismal sandwiches I had prepared, I began to second-guess everything. I even wondered, suddenly and terribly, if the reason I had first gone and slept with Kyra was not out of love but because Jack had hurt me. That made me feel even worse, that what I had viewed as the love of my life was nothing more than a reaction to hurt and insult.

Now I see what I was doing: trying to talk myself out of my own emotions. But it didn't matter. Already Kyra was pulling away from me, turning back to Roy.

Roy who adored her, who would—could—do anything for her. Who knew how to be her equal, or at least how to get her up out of bed. Because it was true: she did love him.

After all, she was supposed to marry him.

I could feel myself shaking even as I sat at the table. Sick to my stomach and terrified. A plan was forming, if more from panic than a decision. Perhaps, in my frenzy, I was also trying to hurt Kyra the way it hurt me to see her with Roy.

Before I could say or do anything, Roy said, "I've convinced Miss Kyra here to come back home for a few days."

She nodded plainly. "I think I just need to be with my mom. For a day or two."

What I heard, between the words, was *without you.*

That was how I knew I would do it. That I could be selfless. That I could give her up.

As soon as Roy went to fetch the car, while Kyra tossed a few belongings into her backpack, I told her.

Her hand lost its grip, and the pack fell to the floor. But her face was blank, as if this was what she expected.

I explained that our relationship had run its course, that she was better off with Roy. My voice sounded so strange to me. "Don't worry, I'll find somewhere else to live."

At first she didn't seem to understand. She said a quiet little trilled "No, nonononono," as if it were some silly idea.

"Look," I said, "it's clear you and Roy are meant to be together." It took everything in me to say it without my voice shaking. For a moment I thought I might faint. But I took a breath and forced myself to say, "It's time I moved on."

That was when her face crumbled in on itself. I hadn't thought she would react that way. I was clenching my fists, telling myself not to give in. I waited, but Kyra didn't deny what I had said. She didn't say anything at all.

The intercom buzzed: Roy, live-parked in front of the traffic island.

I felt dizzy, everything spinning out of control. Kyra was silently crying, her face contorted, just gasps of air. That's how young we were—our bodies messy and flailing, like infants.

So I buzzed Roy up, still telling myself this was the only way. When he bounded in and found Kyra crying again, he didn't know that this time it was for another reason.

Like some storybook prince, he shouldered Kyra's bag, told me goodbye, and ushered her away from me. Just like that, with a last glimpse over his shoulder and a small nod of his chin. I watched only briefly as he helped her down the stairs. Then I shut the door, quickly, because already I had begun to hate him.

home

I went to stay with Janet, to figure things out.

I kept trying to imagine some other way, that somehow things would eventually work out. But whenever I closed my eyes, I saw Kyra's crumpling face. Whenever an ambulance moaned past, I saw Carl on the bathroom floor.

At South Station I took the T to Summit Avenue and headed up the hill to Janet's. All around were the bright neon greens of spring, branches erupting with blossoms. Near the crest, just before Janet's block, I looked out past the new foliage at the Boston skyline. I think I already knew I would move back.

Because how could I remain in New York without Kyra and Carl? How could I return to that apartment with its vermin, that city with its million daily miseries? Maybe in Boston I could find a job—a real job, not folding sweaters in some store. Coming back home wouldn't seem like a failure, then. It would look as though I'd seized an opportunity.

Janet was waiting on the stoop, reading a magazine. The bangles on her wrists jingled as she reached out to embrace me. Her face looked almost as it had before her accident. Just the nose and the top lip were a little different.

I hadn't yet told her all that had happened. I wanted to do so in person—had imagined confessing everything, and that she would dispense advice that might help me move on. Instead I found myself unable to begin.

I didn't understand what was stopping me. But then I heard myself say, "You never told me what really happened. How you fell."

Away from her I'd been able to ignore it, but now the feeling had risen to the surface, that she had purposely kept something from me. Janet began to repeat what she had told me, about falling down the stairs. I said, "Come on, Janet."

Her pale blue eyes shifted. "I really don't think he meant to hurt me" was what she said, and I had to look away.

"I really don't, Mim. We were fighting, and I wanted to just storm out of there, and he just sort of shoved me, you know? But in a way I provoked him—"

"Janet! Don't make excuses for him!"

"I'm not making excuses—"

"How can you say that? Who *is* this guy? Janet, no one gets to hurt you! Do you understand what I'm saying?"

Janet's eyes flashed. "Oh, like you know something about it. Little miss fancy pants with her prissy friends. You think because you moved to New York you know something. You don't know shit. You haven't even *lived*. You don't know what it means to love someone who hurts you. You don't know *how* to love! You only know how to leave. And you come here acting like you have something to teach *me*? Like there's something *you* can tell me?" She laughed, a mean laugh. "I can tell *you* some things!"

I wanted to tell her that I *did* know how to love, I *had* been hurt. But she spoke first. "So he hurt me, so he made a mistake. You want to hear hurt? You want to hear some bad behavior? You know your dad was cheating on my mom, right? You know—"

112

"I know that," I said quickly, to stop her, though I'd never really had any proof. "I don't care. He's a prick—"

"And that he was sleeping with my mom long before yours died, right?"

"It figures," I said, trying to sound nonchalant. "She was sick for a long time."

"Oh, so who's making excuses *now*?" Janet jutted her chin at me.

I wanted to say something smart, something that would shut her up: that I too had behaved despicably—that I had killed someone.

But I had begun to cry. Tears ran down my cheeks, and over my lips and into my ears. I was leaking tears. In my mind I saw my mother in her final days, when she became someone I no longer knew and who frightened me. I heard myself telling Janet from under the tears, "She—was all—yellow."

"Oh, baby." Janet reached over, the bangles on her wrist jangling. She held me, head close, the sweet smell of her hair. "I'm sorry." She was crying now, too, and with each small movement her bracelets tinkled faintly.

We cried for a good long while like that, and I told her about Carl and about Kyra, about my guilt and my love and my broken heart. That everything was tainted now, Carl's corpse lying between us. It didn't matter that Kyra had loved me. It didn't matter that I was the one leaving—that I was doing what I knew was right. I still loved her. If only Carl hadn't died, maybe there would have been a chance.

The crunch of tires on gravel startles me. There's the white FedEx truck winding its way up our driveway, steering carefully past lumpy patches of snow.

I wait at the door, shivering in the cold air. I have to steady my hands to sign for the package. It's one of those big cardboard mailers, like a flattened box. As much as I want to tear into it, I wait

113

until the van has started heading back down the drive. Then I close myself in my office and use a pair of scissors to slice the mailer open.

Inside is an extra-large envelope, the kind for mailing books or oversize documents. Across the front, written in all caps, is my name.

I slit the edge open to find a clear plastic sleeve thick with papers. Paper-clipped to the sleeve is a note—scrawled, the ink smudged.

I couldn't sleep last night, not sure why. But I realized something: if you never see these, I might as well never have written them.

Even rushed, the handwriting is familiar. Seeing it makes my heart turn over.

I slide the pages out. Here the handwriting looks more as I remember it, loopy and uneven. And then I see why it hasn't changed. The top page is dated June 20th, 1995.

Dear Mim,

I'm writing you from the airport in Kinshasa. Awful. Spend enough time in corrupt countries & you start to see how corruptness leaks into everything, I mean even some poor underling in his tiny shitty job. The guards at the customs desk pick through my luggage with fake suspicion so they can find my underwear & grin at me & run their fingers along the crotch. Then they shove everything back in a big mess.

My bag is one of those huge duffels you can wear like a backpack, but when I'm tired I carry it across my arms like a corpse. I drag it over to the next line, the next bully-underling, & watch him make the most of his one small power (to stamp—or not—my passport).

So I'm sitting here with time on my hands. I have to wait, you know, there needs to be some sense I could be detained indefinitely. So I've got time to write you.

I've been with the ICRC for a couple years now. Last year I was stationed in Colombia, got to use my Spanish. Two of my coworkers were kidnapped but we got them released. We were able to open a school in an area that had been overrun by guerrillas. Mim, the kids looked half their age they were so stunted. Missing teeth, stringy hair—malnourishment bleaches it blond on top & red underneath. First your heart breaks, then you start to get used to it.

Here in Zaire there's an election coming up, but who knows if it will happen. We could be in for protests, clashes, which is why my group's here. People live with so much hardship. Meanwhile my daily challenges are things like these customs guards with their nasty smiles & rusted rifles, or the intake official across from me right now, pretending to figure out whether I have some evil motive for wanting to enter his screwed-up country.

I know I sound awful. It's hard to stay upbeat when you see the truth so much.

Anyway, that's my news. Roy & I split up. Our marriage lasted about a minute. I felt like one of those stepsisters in Cinderella, trying to squeeze her big ugly foot into a glass slipper that wasn't hers.

I would've written sooner, but all I could ever think to say was sorry. For being weak when you needed me to be strong. No wonder you had to leave. But when I try to put what's in my heart into words it just comes out like a tangled mess.

115

Here comes the customs guy. He's whispering to his buddy. Will we let her in? Should we let her in? What is she writing on that pad of paper?

Oh, they're asking ME.

Gotta go—

Love, Kyra

It doesn't make sense. Why am I only receiving this letter now?

I peel the page away to see the next one. *Dear Mim.* Fan through the stack. Thirty, forty letters, maybe more. 1997, 1998 . . . 2002, 2004 . . . 2009 . . . 2011 . . . At the top of every one, my name.

Something is happening. My chest cracking open.

I sit down at my desk, grab hold of the edges. But I still feel the ground beneath me shifting.

Twenty years. All that time she kept me in her thoughts.

Love, Kyra
Love, Kyra
All my love, Kyra
Love, Kyra
Your loving Kyra . . .

No sign that the letters ever would have been mailed. Many are pages torn from notebooks. Others are written on tissue-thin air-mail stationary, the kind that folds to become its own envelope.

We're in Honduras, where the hurricane has left a real mess . . .

I'm in Blida, about an hour from Algiers, but even in the cities it isn't safe. If you speak French or are "intellectual." If you're a foreigner, or a European, or "liberal." If you have a "degree" . . .

116

So I'm in Atlanta for my dad's funeral. Melanoma. I knew it was coming but somehow I wasn't prepared. . . .

I'm in Uganda, working for AidNow; I left the ICRC last year. . . .

I'm writing you from London, where I'm being reassigned to who knows where. They cut short my post in Libya after our headquarters were bombed. I have to admit I'm glad my mom's no longer alive, so she won't hear about it & worry.

I keep wiping my cheeks with the back of my hand. I flip random pages, taking in scraps here and there, watching Kyra's handwriting grow smaller, less youthful, no longer loose and loopy. Year by year, her world expanding—while mine was shrinking smaller and smaller.

I want to read all the pages at once, scan them for the things I've wondered so long. The questions that never let go of me. What did I mean to you? Why did you let me leave you? Was it just some youthful love, or would it have grown into something lasting?

I tried to do what everyone wanted but I'm not meant for that life. I need you to understand what I'm doing here and

Mim, I just read the article in the Times—*about your play! There it was in the care package my mom sent, along with the usual copies of the* New Yorker *&* People.

because I'd never felt that way before. You made love easy.

The Vows *article mentioned you'd written a book. You've gone ahead & done all these things, while I shuffle from place to place but never get anywhere.*

or maybe it's fear that stops me from putting these letters in the mail. The more time passes the more I can't bear to know what I've missed.

made a whole life for yourself, while I've been telling myself some fantasy. Like a little kid who believes in unicorns.

I keep trying to slow down, to stop my frenzied scanning of pages. I have to remind myself why I have these letters: Kyra must have thought if she didn't send them now she might not get the chance to later. There's a reason she felt she ought to do it before heading off to wherever she's gone.

Flipping to the end of the stack, I find the final letters. Three of them dated within the past few weeks, each written in fine-tipped pen, on paper so thin the ink has bled through. It's possible they might shed some light on whatever has happened.

The first is dated December 7th.

Dear Mim,

So I'm at our base in Jalalabad & my colleague Anne is here in the courtyard reading YOUR BOOK—in Dutch! Your name in big letters on the cover. Ever since Libya I can't ignore these coincidences (that's what I would have called them before). I've become "spiritual" or something. Anne says No Known Remedy was a bestseller in the Netherlands. She's impressed I know you.

As if I do after 20 years. Would you answer these letters if I sent them? I guess I've always thought of them more like a diary. Always writing in a mood or when I'm lonely. Selfish, I know. But you're the only reason I ever think to write anything down.

There are ten of us on the assessment team. Four from AidNow plus six locals. The main project I'm coordinating has to do with land disputes (a big cause of violence here). It's mundane & pedantic & involves lots of folders stuffed full of old papers in no clear order, many signed with no more than a thumbprint.

We lead a very confined life. It's not safe to go outside the "security zone." We have a nightly curfew plus Anne & I are supposed to have a male chaperone if we leave the base. I wrap myself in a scarf but even then I get stares. I understand why so many women, even the ones dolled-up & in high heels, choose to wear the burqa. It's gets tiring being stared at all the time.

The good thing about being foreign is the rules don't always apply. Since Anne & I are Western & "corrupt" we aren't really women, more like some in-between gender. So we're allowed extra liberties & aren't always so strictly separated from the men.

There's electricity every night from 5:30 to 11 pm, & from Sunday to Thursday we have a generator. My younger colleagues party in a bomb shelter every Thursday night when the weekend starts. I don't drink anymore, which works well in a Muslim country. Plus I'm down to 2 cigarettes a day, crappy Chinese ones, makes them easier to resist.

Jalalabad is surprisingly lush, though the mountains are snow-covered. I'm told they'll be that way until May.

Love, Kyra

ᥴᠵᠵᠵᠣ

January 4, 2012

Overhead sometimes I see planes with no markings.

They fly very slow, in circles. I wonder if they see me. If they wonder what I'm doing here.

I wonder what I'm doing here.

My liaison officer resigned. He said I was disorganized. Well I am, though I try not to be. It's just me & my assistant in the office while Anne & the agronomists do their projects. The only people I can really communicate with are the NATO guys at the base not far from here. But AidNow is supposed to be "neutral" so we're forbidden to fraternize with them.

But Mim it just feels so good to be able to *talk* to someone!

One of the NATO guys told me about a place where expats gather. A "secret" bar run by a Canadian. So that's a possibility.

It's awful to be in a country where everyone is basically just waiting for you to leave.

Love, Kyra

Footsteps echo in the hall. For a moment I'm utterly confused. Nolan, home from work.

"Almost done," I hear myself call out. I don't want him to see me in this state.

He calls back, slow and easy, keeping outside my office; he knows I like to put in a full day's work. His solid footsteps move toward the kitchen, and I hear the clang of pots and lids being unstacked from the dish drainer.

Though I long ago told him the story of Kyra, I feel duplicitous behind my half-closed door. I can hear him whistling in the kitchen, some sweet loopy tune, and it just confuses me.

Just one more letter left. If Kyra had any last thing to say to me before she scrawled that note, it will be on this thin leaf of paper. And once I've read it, I'll have to head out of this room, into my life, and tell Nolan what's happened, and what it is I need to do.

January 8, 2012

Mim, I went to that bar. More like a speakeasy, sort of hidden behind a guesthouse, & guess who was there? Jorgen—my old colleague from way back. He doesn't work for the ICRC any more. He was "let go" for unorthodox techniques. He's too hands-on for an organization with so many rules. Now he has his own scrappy little operation, totally outside the wire.

I hadn't seen him for so long, it made me wonder what it would be like to see you. I used to think I couldn't bear it. But now, Mim, I think you'd be proud of me. Proud of the choice I made. Proud of the work I've done.

For the past year Jorgen's been working with villages in the mountains, helping get solar power up. It can be dangerous for foreigners to stay out in villages overnight, but Jorgen says the only way to accomplish anything is to be out in the field.

Yesterday I went to a village with him. A drone had crashed nearby (or was shot down, who knows) & the worry was kids would play in the wreckage or people would scavenge & get hurt. Since Jorgen is so trusted, he was the go-between for the Americans to coordinate with the village "commander"

& recover what they could. Quite a sight, a U.S. base commander with an Afghan warlord!

There's still a lot of animosity. The local police chief hates Westerners & kept stopping by to "oversee" the project. He wasn't in uniform (often the police out here aren't) but I could tell he had some menial power. They say he moonlights for the Taliban. They say that about a lot of police, though. At first I thought his face was dirty but then I saw he had these tiny dark moles all over his skin.

Jorgen's an inspiration. In Jalalabad he's been working with teachers at a girls' school to set up an internet computer network. He showed me photos of the students—all these bright smiling girls with headscarves over their uniforms.

Jorgen calls them his "ninja warriors."

Love always,
Kyra

Part II

THE DESERT

a landlocked country

The letters, with their distantly familiar script, lie in their plastic sleeve inside my backpack. I keep rereading snatches of them, trying to keep calm.

All I've shown Roy are those final three, from Jalalabad, written just last month. As soon as I'd read them I called him. I was still huddled in my study, hadn't yet told Nolan. I asked if Kyra was with that Jorgen person, if he was missing too.

Roy said, "Or maybe he abducted her." Accusatory, as if this were all my doing. A new wave of worry crested over me. Roy was putting forth more theories, and even as I told myself not to panic, I was still adjusting to this new reality. One in which Kyra had been writing to me for years, and where some sort of trouble—or a premonition of trouble—had caused her to finally mail those letters.

Already Roy was working out a plan. As if it were no different from his business trips, simply a matter of hopping over there, powwowing, exerting some pressure. The first step, he explained, was to let AidNow know we were on our way. "Light a fire under them" was how he put it. "They need to know we hold them accountable. That they can't let up even for a second." His secretary was already looking into visas and flights—visas would be straightforward,

125

given the U.S. presence there. No time to waste. No time for hesitation. It didn't appear to occur to him that I might not come along.

But who else was going to do it? Most people here don't even want to have to think about that country anymore, let alone go there. I explained to Nolan that Kyra doesn't have anyone else. No parents, no siblings. No one to advocate for her. I told him, "If Roy and I don't go, no one will."

Nolan sometimes does this thing where he raises his eyebrows and narrows his eyes at the same time. "So you're suddenly a detective who can go off and find a missing person?"

I explained that we were just going to grease the wheels—meet with the authorities, make sure the right people are on her case and doing all they can, that it doesn't end up on the back burner. "Like when I go to New York to meet with my publisher." He knows that's a trip I make only infrequently, when I sense my overburdened editor might need me at her side to give my book the extra push she's fighting for. He knows what happens when I don't go.

"Except that you're not going to *New York*. Mim, you know what the situation is there."

"That's right, I do. I'm going to be in a city of three hundred and fifty thousand, where people lead lives and go about their business, just like we do here. Nolan, people go to Afghanistan all the time."

"'Right, 'adventure travelers.' Mercenaries. Terrorists—"

"And businessmen and doctors and journalists and whoever else. People live there, Nolan, they work there. Fall in love and raise children and live their lives there."

"You're not a businessman. You're not some journalist. You're a woman, and you're white."

"So that's why I'm not supposed to go there?"

Nolan just shook his head and left the room—a habit our marriage counselor has tried to wean him from. Even so, I called after him: "Wouldn't *you* do the same for *me*?"

126

That was over a week ago. Since then he has barely spoken to me. I know it's just that he's worried. Yet here I am, guiltily installed next to Roy in a fancy convertible seat on a plane nosing its way east. Business class, with complimentary pajamas, real linen and silverware, and a porcelain cup for my coffee. At Dubai we'll continue on to Kabul, where the AidNow director has arranged seats for us on a U.N. flight to Jalalabad.

Roy, though, has little faith in AidNow. "My college internship was with a nonprofit. Those places don't know how to get anything done."

He has no patience for scrappy do-gooders. He's even hired his own private consultants. While part of me is grateful, another part distrusts his confidence, his global-traveler swagger—the ease of a businessman accustomed to handing over an AmEx card and getting his way. His money belt is thick with cash. Anything we need, he tells me—information, help, ransom—he can pay for.

He makes it sound so simple, not messy at all. Like his brand new scuff-free hiking boots, and hi-tech polyfleece sweater, and fancy travel pants with many hidden pockets. Along with his Rolex watch he sports a scruffy last-minute attempt at a beard. Stuffed into the overhead bin are an elaborate backpack and one of those astoundingly expensive parkas I've read about, with the patch logo on the sleeve.

My own jacket, a fleece thing of "state-of-the art" fabric, is pricey enough. They say the weather this time of year can range from hot in the sun to below freezing in the mountains. I can't help thinking of Kyra in her many sweaters. I hope she isn't cold. I hope she's alive.

"The problem with Sandrine," Roy is telling me, "is she won't look at the bigger picture. She knows perfectly well I'd never do this if I thought it could cause the slightest problem for our girls." For some minutes he has been going on about a fight with his latest ex-wife.

He has mentioned her multiple times, always with the besieged expression of a man who's had poor luck. I have to admit, it's not what I expected. The dashing prep school boy is now a twice-divorced father of two, with crow's-feet and heavy cheeks. Though at first glance he looked as I remembered him, up close I see small changes. He has had the good fortune of keeping his hair, but his neck is thicker, his eyes less cheerful. They're a hazel color, with faint gray circles below. Probably he hasn't slept much since hearing about Kyra. Neither have I. Also, he keeps grinding his teeth, though I'm not sure he realizes it.

"The simple fact is," he says, "Kyra needs me. I would never *abandon* my children! It's just that Kyra needs my help. Which I can't do from afar." As if he's the knight in shining armor and I'm merely along for the ride. "That's the thing about Sandrine," he adds. "She only looks at how things impact *her*. The opposite of Kyra, really."

Something tells me this sort of commentary could be what led Sandrine to choose ex-wifedom in the first place.

Roy takes a gulp of his scotch. "What about you? Did your husband make a fuss?"

I don't mention the very last thing Nolan said, in his steady, low, slow, calm voice: that if I go ahead and do this, he really has had it with me. "He said I should think of our son, what it would do to him if something happened to me. That what I'm doing is careless and foolish."

I can still see his face as he said it. He's a man of few words, which means that in the rare instances when he does show anger, in that same low voice but with his face reddening, I find it terrifying.

Roy looks up from his scotch. "You have a son."

"Yes, and believe me, Sean would be absolutely fine if anything happened to me." He's a tough one, in more ways than one. Also, I wrote him a long letter, explaining everything, in case I fail to return.

"How old is he?"

"Nineteen."

Roy's look of surprise is a common enough response, though the older I get, the less frequently it happens. He says, "You started young."

"By the time we adopted him he was already eight years old. Long story. Short version is, we were foster parents. Now he's in college."

"Which school?"

I say the name even though Roy won't have heard of it. "It's very small, sort of offbeat. Well, it's the students who are offbeat. Sean was never into sitting at a desk. He's got too much energy, always needs to be moving around."

In his expression I see Roy beginning to sense the truth, that Sean is one of *those* kids, the troubled ones, sent to penitentiary-style summer camps, or roughing-it-in-the-woods rehab programs, who leave a trail of bulging file folders as they skip from this school to that one. Well, yes, that is indeed the case, although we were lucky to find a great program for him a few years ago. After that, things eased up. So, yes, Sean has been trouble, but in the past year I've finally begun to relax—to believe we're through the hard part and the worst really is behind us.

Roy has pushed up the sleeves of his sweater, revealing fair downy forearms. As he asks more questions about Sean and tells me about his twin daughters, I sense that, like me, what he's really doing is trying not to think about Kyra. To prevent himself from imagining what might have happened to her.

Each time my imagination starts up, I grasp at other thoughts. Kyra dancing, her tremendous strength. But then there's Roy with his enormous bouquet, and Carl holding the gerbera daisies, glaring at me. Kyra leaping across the stage like a gazelle.

There used to be times when I thought I saw her. They started after I returned to Boston. Momentary glimpses, in crowds, or coming toward me on the sidewalk, or just in the flick of someone's hair. My cheeks would go hot, and then I'd scold myself for having thought any of those strangers could have been Kyra.

I didn't know yet that it hadn't worked out with Roy. That she had gone off to a whole other life.

Mim, do you know what all refugees, no matter the country, have in common? I mean besides suitcases tied with rope & plastic garbage bags stuffed with food & donated clothes that don't fit right. It's that they squat. Sit on their heels, or on suitcases, elbows on knees, head in hands. It struck me just the other day: that's why we say "squatter's camps." Nowhere to sit, nowhere to rest. Perpetual waiting.

I've already lost weight from worry. Not just about Kyra. Tucked into my backpack along with her letters are the telltale trappings of a nervous traveler: ibuprofen and intestinal remedies, little tubes of antibiotic ointment, an emergency kit with bandages and wipes soaked in iodine. I also have a big thick pashmina shawl, a tiny but powerful flashlight, and lots of American dollars, which Roy says are as good, if not better, than afghanis. I've installed an international SIM card in my cell phone and uploaded a travel guidebook, which I keep trying to read, to distract myself.

The guide is written in a firm, impatient tone I particularly like. *Located in Central Asia, Afghanistan is* not—*despite the mistaken impression of many Westerners—part of the Middle East. Afghans are* not *Arabs, and they do* not *speak Arabic.* The author explains the difference between Pashto and Dari, between Sunnis and Shias, between Pashtun, Tajik, Uzbek, and Hazara. I peruse the images of traditional dress: Kuchis in their colorful gypsy clothes; pakol hats like thick berets; wound turbans known as lungees, and the payraan tumbaan—matching long shirts and pants like elegant pajamas. I review the basic chronology: multiple British invasions; a decade of

130

war against the Soviets; five years of civil war among mujahideen; Taliban control for another five; then 9/11 and the U.S. Army, NATO reconstruction, and Taliban insurgency ever since. Poppy crops, government elections, roadside bombs. Coalition forces are to leave by 2016.

What most engrosses me, though, is the least practical of information. Phrases of Persian poetry. The symbolism in Pashtun jewelry. Elaborate carvings in wooden furniture from Nuristan. The stern proverbs:

The sun cannot be hidden by two fingers.
If you deal in camels, make the doors high.
Storing milk in a sieve, you complain of bad luck?

The truth is, I hate to travel. Since moving out to the Berkshires I've never wanted to leave. Each year I allowed myself to settle in more deeply, the gray stone borders of my land becoming the borders of my life. And though I've seen myself referred to as a "recluse," I really don't see it that way. It felt right to set down roots and ignore the hubbub. Even back when my career began to take off, I never cared for the promotional jaunts to whichever city I'd been dispatched to. I no longer fancied myself some worldly American with passable French from my stint abroad. I was able to admit the truth: that what I wanted most was to be at home on my own patch of land, with its thatch of woods and one distant neighbor down the dirt road.

Yet here I am studying a travel guidebook, memorizing standard greetings in a language not my own. "Peace be with you" and how to ask where the restroom might be. Each time reality stalks back—each time I consciously recall why I'm on board this flight—I have to tamp down the panic all over again. It's still roiling there even as I peruse the photographs: the black-red-and-green flag with the circular emblem of the Islamic Republic of Afghanistan, land of brown mountains and parched earth—and olive trees, green valleys, and winding, icy streams. I try to picture Kyra among these images, but all that happens is that I panic again.

The photographs provide a flash history of the past fifty years: Early 1970s Kabul, an urban metropolis with men in business suits and women in dresses, miniskirts, heels. Red Army tanks a decade later, mujahideen with their Kalashnikov rifles, and amputees at a Red Cross tent. Then the Taliban with kohl-lined eyes and beards long enough to be held in a fist. The mandatory burqas like blue shuttlecocks. George W. Bush in a gray suit and bright blue tie, shaking hands with Hamid Karzai in his triangular sheepskin cap. And now, a grinning boy on a skateboard. Village girls in headscarves and tunics and plastic sandals, kicking at a soccer ball.

One image shows two men praying. I thought I knew what Muslim prayer looked like, kneeling and bowing toward Mecca—but the picture reveals what an active posture it is. The men press their palms to the ground on either side of their heads, their feet flexed, heels up as if to push the scalp more powerfully into the earth. I realize I have always considered religious submission passive, but what I see here is active supplication.

Roy keeps looking over. I catch the slight movement of his chin, the flicker of his eyes. I suppose he's doing the same thing I am, taking in little glimpses, assessing this strange new version of someone who was, until now, a memory.

I keep my eyes trained on the guidebook. But I still feel Roy watching, until it dawns on me that he is waiting for me to look up. That there's something he wants to say to me.

I don't look up. If I do, if I catch his eye, he might ask some question I'm not prepared to answer. Perhaps the same question I want to ask, the one making me feel I might burst. *What happened?*

So many things I want to know. What Kyra told him, and did she understand why I left? Did she too see Carl sometimes, lying blue under the fluorescent bathroom light? But if I ask, I'll have to think about my mistakes.

I think, perhaps, I made a terrible mistake.

I am practically glaring at the guidebook. Still I refuse to look up. The fact is, I resent Roy—for winning Kyra and then losing her. Just like I did.

But when at last Roy speaks, what he says is, "My wife, ex-wife, Sandrine, she reads all your books."

Of course it pleases me to hear this. But for some reason the question that comes to me is whether Roy was surprised to see my name. If he said, *I used to know her*. I don't flatter myself with the thought that he might have actually read one of my books.

But before I can say anything, Roy says, "How did you break into the business? How do you know what to write about? Do they tell you how many pages it should be?"

I always try to be patient with such questions. And it's easy enough to give Roy my usual spiel, about how I got started, writing in the off hours while working for the cooking magazine. . . . Yet even as I speak, the feeling is bubbling up: the questions I want to ask, and fear that I can't bear to hear the answers.

Already Roy is bunching up his sweater, shoving it under his head. My publishing saga clearly bores him. Before I can say more, he has fallen asleep.

barbed wire

The Jalalabad air base is sun-bleached and sand-colored. With the pashmina wrapped round my hair and shoulders, I follow Roy down from the plane, squinting into the noisy brightness. A helicopter is lifting off, loud and clunky—propellers squeaking, thumping the air, spraying dust everywhere. In the distance loom mountains so enormous the lowest seem mere sand drifts, the taller, rocky ones all clefts and gullies, each snowcapped peak layered over the next. Their crags and crests look like crumpled brown paper, folded and stretched out again.

Waiting for us is the local AidNow director, a surprisingly young woman named Nadira. Brisk and chic, in black slacks with a tunic-length business jacket and a long green headscarf. Dark eyeliner on her upper eyelids. She has the refined posture and Oxford English of someone trained in a finishing school, and informs us that our driver is waiting. All around us, servicemen and aid workers hurry to waiting Land Cruisers. Most are men, some in payraan tum-baan, others in business jackets and jeans. Some of the Westerners sport diplomat-wear—khaki slacks with shiny-buttoned navy-blue blazers—or desert-safari getups à la Indiana Jones. Some appear to be carrying assault rifles.

"Is that even legal?" I whisper to Roy as we follow Nadira to the car. I keep seeing posters with drawings of guns and a big X over them. But Roy just strides along as if here on a routine assessment.

We have come to a white hatchback, its windows rolled down, its driver, a young fellow with a goatee, deeply involved in some game on his cell phone. Seeing us, he mutes the sound, while Nadira gestures for Roy to take the front seat and joins me in the back, explaining that we have just a short drive to the AidNow offices; otherwise we would travel in a convoy. "Our compound is not in the city proper. That would be too much of a security risk."

I try to ignore my resurging panic. Focus on the asphalt road, smooth and flat, the air almost balmy, even as our tires send up puffs of brown dust. All around are rocky hills and hard brown mountains like mounds of rubble, with thatches of green here and there. Tall skinny pines and big-leafed succulents and poplars whose pale leaves are just starting. And in every direction, poking into the blue sky, cell-phone towers.

Right: my guidebook said that with so few landline connections, many areas here have excellent cell-phone coverage. We pass broad pale green fields, and tawny brown slopes dotted with clay-colored houses. And I hear myself thinking: Kyra saw this.

Kyra saw the brown hills and slender green trees whose upward-pointing branches seem vacuumed up by the sky.

Kyra was here.

Is here, somewhere.

"We've asked for the help of the police, of course," Nadira is saying, "since there is little more our organization can do at this point. It is really very unfortunate."

Her tone is tinged with annoyance, and who can blame her? Here's one more meddlesome American, good intentions that just end up causing trouble. I have to wonder if Kyra has gotten into trouble before. I also wonder how much the Afghan police can really do. I've seen the photographs in the newspaper, new recruits with their pants tucked into shiny new combat boots, in their jumpsuits of custodial blue and their boxy, high-brimmed caps.

"What about the CIA?" Roy asks.

"It is the FBI that handles kidnappings of Americans abroad. But we do not yet know if this is a kidnapping. It is true that Kyra has not returned, but no one has claimed her. Therefore she is still a missing person."

Perhaps not even alive. Two weeks since anyone has seen her. I've clenched my hands so tightly my nails sting my palms.

"And if she *has* been kidnapped?" Roy asks. "Then the FBI steps in?" Even from back here, I can see his shoulders tensing.

"To what extent it can. There is only so much anyone can do, depending on where she has gone. Even the FBI. It is simply too dangerous."

Not that I can tell, with the casual bustle along the roadside. Lots of makeshift kiosks, some with thatched roofs. I glimpse hanging sides of meat, skinned and gleaming, and wheelbarrows heaped with pomegranates, oranges, lemons. Young boys peddle fish that dangle from lines of string. There are stacks of firewood and piles of scrap metal and bulging sacks of I don't know what. Then we are heading along the river, where hills climb away from the road to become brown rocky cliffs. Flat rectangular houses blend into the land like slabs of stone. Just a few new green leaves. We pass more rectangular stalls with tarp roofs and then the high walls surrounding hidden houses. Some of the walls have razor wire at the top.

"I can assure you," Nadira says, as if hearing my thoughts, "our compound is well within the security perimeter."

Like many buildings we have passed, the AidNow headquarters turns out to be a concrete structure hunkered behind an enormous wall. The wall is topped with concertina wire, and solar panels line the roof, where an Afghan flag, flicked by the wind, twitches on its pole. At the gate, our driver shows his clearance pass to a rail-thin security guard, and once we are in, another skinny guard treats Roy to a full, enthusiastic pat-down.

With no female guards here, Nadira and I aren't searched at all.

We head through a big thick metal door to the main building, down a long hall and out to a sunny courtyard. Nadira has loosened her scarf, letting it drape her neck; I do the same, the sun warming my face. Roy is looking round, nodding like a supervisor on a visit from the main office. As we take our seats around a table set for tea, I wonder if Roy has any of the thoughts I do: that Kyra must have sat here, too, maybe in this very chair, with her own scarf loosened, her hair absorbing the sun.

Over glass mugs of steaming green tea, we are introduced to Nadira's coworkers: a young fellow named Rashid with a neatly trimmed beard, and a youthful ponytailed woman named Anne— the Dutch coworker Kyra mentioned in her letters. Both speak fluent English, and as we exchange greetings Anne manages to slip in a quick, breathless "I love your books," quickly readjusting her expression for more serious matters.

The last information Kyra gave, she tells us, was that she would be traveling with a male companion and would return that Saturday. "She left no indication that she would not be back. We put out an alert as soon as she missed curfew. Her cell-phone records show no activity after Thursday, the day she left."

All I really want to know is whether or not they think she is alive.

Roy asks if anyone has established whether Jorgen is missing. We've already made sure to inform AidNow about Kyra having reconnected with Jorgen.

"We have no confirmation that he's been seen since her disappearance," Rashid tells him, "though no one has officially declared him missing. It seems he was on his own and made a habit of remaining at his work sites for days at a time." Disapproval in his voice. "Outside the wire."

"A rogue operation," Anne puts in.

Nadira tells us authorities have spoken with the U.S. base commander we informed them about—from the letter about the fallen drone—as well as the schoolteachers Jorgen has been working with, but neither had much information.

I think of the list I made of all information I could cull from those final letters. "What about Kyra's project here? She said it had to do with land disputes. Could that have something to do with where she went?"

Rashid is the legal aid on the project and doesn't consider it related to her disappearance. "Well, except that it can be frustrating work, and also somewhat boring." Mainly paperwork, he explains, things like fake deeds, rarely a clear or easily executed outcome. "Kyra often said she wanted to work with people, not paper. She wanted to feel more directly engaged. Possibly she thought she could achieve that by going somewhere else."

"That drone we read about in her letter," Roy says. "It was near a village where Jorgen had been doing work. Do we know if he's been there since?"

"It is unclear," Nadira says, and Rashid, perhaps sensing our impatience, hurries to explain all that has been done so far, who has been notified, the small bits of information gleaned. "And we are keeping an eye on all news reports. In case of related news."

Roy looks unimpressed. He asks if we can see Kyra's quarters.

"Of course." Nadira quickly adds that the room has already been thoroughly examined.

Anne nods. "Her laptop and email too. We checked everything."

Our hosts lead us into the next building and down another hallway. Roy strides ahead with Rashid and Nadira, asking question after question like a boss grilling his employees. Anne and I follow behind, and as Roy peppers Nadira and Rashid with more questions, Anne leans toward me.

"The girl in *No Known Remedy* reminded me of Kyra. I was thinking about that just yesterday. Even the way she moved. Where you described her sitting at the table sipping her tea, the way she draped one leg over the other, I kept thinking it was just like Kyra."

A lump in my throat prevents me from speaking.

"There's that gentleness to her. I didn't think of it right away, but now the resemblance seems uncanny. She's this light that shines on everything."

But I didn't have Kyra in mind while I was writing it. At least, I didn't think I did.

"I have to admit I was crying at the end," Anne continues. "I told myself maybe she never did get on that plane. Maybe Benjamin found her in time after all."

All I can do is nod. We have come to the end of the hall, to Kyra's door. I take a long breath before entering. A simple room—the sparse look of a life free of baubles. A sheer white curtain hangs loosely over the window, emitting a dull glow. On the desk are just a cell-phone charger, a USB cord, and a pencil and blank pad of paper. An internet cable snakes along the wall. I search for something clearly Kyra's, but it has been so long, I don't even know what that would be. The room could be anyone's, with a jar of skin lotion and a few hair elastics on the table next to the bed, and a flimsy pair of reading glasses.

"We'll leave you," Nadira says gravely, as though allowing us to pay our final respects.

Roy immediately begins touching everything, sweeping aside the curtain to peer out the window, tugging open the bureau drawers. As if to get to everything before I can—though of course I'm silly to think that.

"Even the insides of the drawers are dusty," he says. "I remember when Kyra was in Pakistan she said it was like this." Somehow even this comment bothers me, not just his tone of judgment but that Roy has remained part of her life all this time. Now he is peering into the open niche that serves as a closet, snooping through Kyra's clothing like some sort of spy. In my mind I hear Nolan's scolding voice: *So you're suddenly a detective who can go find a missing person?*

"What are you even looking for?" I don't mean to sound snide.

"Trying to see if there's anything they overlooked. My guys said any new information could help." By "guys" he means the consultants he's hired.

But it doesn't seem right to rifle through everything, or perhaps I'm simply overcome. I sit down on the bed, launching a fine puff of sand-dust. I touch the covers, the pillowcase. If Roy weren't here I would hold the pillow to my face, to see if I might recognize her scent.

Next to the bed is a small bookcase. On a low shelf are an English-Farsi dictionary, a Pashto phrasebook, an imposing-looking tome of Afghan history, and a paperback edition of my latest novel. *No Known Remedy.* The reviews weren't as kind as before. Some said it was time I stopped rehashing the same old theme—what one critic called the "rich girl, poor boy, Superman" love triangle. Others found the ending too open to interpretation. Even so, a core group of readers swore it was my best yet. Now I can't help thinking about what Anne said. It certainly has happened before, Kyra sneaking into key characters. But it's too much to contemplate. I look away, at the sparse furniture, the dusty bureau.

There's something atop the bureau, a tangle of purple. Up close, I discover a small pile of rubber bracelets. I pinch one between my thumb and forefinger, hold it up to the light. They are a version of those yellow wristbands popular in the States—the rallying cries for so many struggles: cancer, epilepsy, anything. These are purple, imprinted with the words DATA = POWER.

There are at least ten bracelets. I wonder if Kyra wore them.

In Pashtun tradition, according to my guidebook, *bangles symbol-ize womanhood and beauty.*

But these are rubber. Knowing Kyra, she would have bought them to support whatever cause.

Roy sighs. "I don't think there's anything here." He sounds tired. I return the bracelet to the pile, drawing a line in the dust. Then I touch the knob of one of the drawers. Just to touch something Kyra touched.

"She knew it wouldn't take much for something to happen to her here," Roy says, and sits down on the bed. "The fact that she planned for that possibility doesn't necessarily mean she thought it would happen when it did." He runs his fingers through his hair, grabbing it by the roots.

"Do you think we got her in trouble by telling them about Jorgen and all that?"

"She got herself into trouble." He's still tugging at his hair, like a character in a Chekhov play. Then he lets go. With his hair mussed, he looks suddenly younger. Boyish almost. A flash of when I first met him, full of promise there on Grace's doorstep.

As if sensing this, he abruptly rustles himself. "Someone knows where she went. Or who she went with." He stands so quickly the bed shifts. "Look, let's not waste any more time here. Ahmed's going to pick us up soon, and then let's get some rest, so that we can go out later and find that bar."

honored by the visit

There were a few years after moving back to Boston when I would go out to bars. Usually with friends from work—be social, meet people. Flirting with anyone, just to prove I was up to it. I even went on a series of hopeless dates. I tried going with women, but they weren't Kyra. When men asked me out I said yes, but it always felt like a chore. Still I kept at it: workdays at the magazine, happy hour with whomever, and long stretches of solitary writing at home. And then, when I'd been back about three years, a panicked call came from my father's wife.

He had suffered some sort of infection or severe allergic reaction—Amelia wasn't sure—and it had put him into cardiac arrest. Stabilized, he was still in the hospital, with lingering damage.

I flew to Houston and went straight to the hospital room where my father lay heavily under a thin blanket. He was unshaven and looked very tired. He didn't seem surprised to see me. Apparently he thought himself on his deathbed.

"Just pull the plug, Mim, I can't take it anymore. Please, I'm begging you, pull the plug."

"There isn't any plug. You're not hooked up to anything."

He had never been a good patient, was one of those men so rarely sick they find even the most minor illness an affront. Now he said, "Mim, I always wondered how cripples and people with handicaps and things like that went through life. Now I know. With reluctance and resentment."

"Oh, so now you're crippled, too?"

"I was strong, Mim. Now look at me, I can barely sit up in the bed."

It was true that he was lying there like some beached creature, his head awkward on the pillow, too big for his body, it seemed. He had been in the hospital one week and already had adopted that hopeless stance that hospitals bring out in people.

He said, "The food here is crap. The nurses aren't even pretty. Did you see that thing who brings the tray in? Enormous."

"Don't be obnoxious." I sat in the plastic chair and fiddled with the zipper of my cardigan. Why had I come? Did I care if he was sick, if his voice sounded strangely small and impoverished? Well, I did note that at last my father was having a taste of helplessness. Maybe now he would know what my mother must have felt.

"The restaurant, I should have known something was up. Everything drowning in sauce." He took a short, wheezing breath. "My pork was so spicy, how could I tell if it had gone bad? We get home and I don't feel right, and then my entire chest is heaving and I'm praying to God I don't die on the bathroom floor. They say my heart has permanent damage."

I felt sad that he'd had to go through that.

"Amelia wants to sue the restaurant. She already spoke to a lawyer."

I sensed something in his expression. "Do you want to sue?"

"Nah." He tried to shake his head but didn't have the strength. "Amelia keeps saying, 'They poisoned you!'" He made a weak attempt to roll his eyes.

"Well, I guess, if your heart has permanent damage—"

"I'm not suing, Mim. I have my reasons."

Maybe by "reasons" he meant guilt—about my mother, the girl-friends, whomever else. His eyes had a depth I hadn't seen before. Even though I still thought he was a prick, I felt warmer toward him at the thought that he too could feel guilt. At least we had that in common.

Not that I had told anyone other than Janet about what happened with Carl. It still hurt too much. But a year or so earlier, on a night when I couldn't sleep, I listened hard for Carl's voice, and everything he told me came right back: The stunned affront of being shot at, and rolling across the trenches hearing the cries of dying men. The whine of missiles diving, blasting, dimpling the earth into cruel hollows.

I wrote it all down. I was still writing monologues then. Adrienne had even auditioned using the one about the homeless woman; she was getting parts in off-Broadway plays and the sorts of films that opened at festivals, received glowing reviews, and then went immediately to video. After the homeless woman monologue, I'd written one based on an article by Camus, about famine in Algeria, and submitted it to a contest. Though mine didn't win, I was approached by a theater agent, who sent out "No Man's Land," "The Thistle-Eater," and "Crossing Over"—the one about Carl—as a triptych titled *Displacements*. Thanks to a series of lucky breaks, the play ended up being performed off-Broadway, and when one of the actors was nominated for a Tony—for a different play, but it meant my own was suddenly popular—the run was extended. Amid this unexpected success, I found myself being referred to as a "playwright." Really, to my mind, I had never actually written a play. I hadn't yet found my voice; I simply wrote down those other voices that would not let me sleep.

"I should let you rest."

"Eternal rest would be good. I mean it, Mim, if they try to do anything to extend my life, anything at all, pull the plug. Give me your word, will you?"

"Okay, okay, stop already."

But even that seemed to buoy him. "That's my Mim. You know what to do."

Through a professional acquaintance, Roy has arranged for a guide to help us.

"You'll see, he'll know how to handle everything," he says as we wait for Ahmed to fetch us. An Afghan American, born in Jalalabad, raised in Weston, Connecticut. "Not like those goody-two-shoes at AidNow. Ahmed went to the B-School, he used to work for Goldman Sachs. Those guys know how to get things done."

I raise an eyebrow at his faith in Goldman Sachs. Roy makes a *what?* face back at me. But even as I shake my head, the truth is, I'm glad to have Roy taking charge. It makes me feel safe knowing he has things under control.

And sure enough, Ahmed arrives right on time. He looks to be in his early thirties, fit and tan and preposterously handsome, with gray eyes and thick shining black hair. He's dressed Western-style, fitted jeans, a button-down shirt, a maroon pullover, and Puma sneakers. Sideburns but no other facial hair. "Hey," he says, shaking our hands as if we've already met. I find his relaxed confidence reassuring. In my mind I tell Nolan, *See? All kinds of people live here— even Wall Street whiz kids who could live any place they like.*

"Well so listen," Ahmed says as he helps toss our backpacks into the back of a big shiny Jeep. "No use beating around the bush. I need to fly to Berlin for a business thing, it just came up and I can't put it off. But I've called my cousin Asim, and he's going to take care of you."

Roy just stares. He looks awfully warm in his expensive coat.

"Asim's a good guy, you'll see. Totally up for being your guide. And frankly, he can use some money. I assured him you could pay."

Every atom of my exasperation comes swooping back. I should have known Roy would hire some creep from Goldman Sachs.

"Anyway," Ahmed continues, affecting not to notice Roy glaring at him, "I told him you could have lunch together, since I've really got to get going. The restaurant's not far from your guesthouse."

I don't want to go to a restaurant. I want to help find Kyra. "I thought—"

"I'll drop you there, and then I really have to run."

Roy manages to refrain from saying anything. Which just makes things seem worse, that he doesn't even think it worth putting up a fight. Looking sullen, he takes a seat in the front of the Jeep while I settle into the back, Ahmed making smooth chitchat all the while, never a pause, never time for us to complain about the change of plans. Even as he drives, his stream of small talk never lets up. I stare out at the streets, at men in turbans and pakol caps and payraan tumbaan in every shade of brown, some with dark waistcoats or long padded coats, others wrapped in the pale brown man-shawls my guidebook calls patu blankets. Lots of the younger men are hat-less, with jackets over their tunics, or Western-style pants, or jeans. Everything else is brown—the baked bricks of buildings, the dust-covered earth.

Then the road broadens and we're in a district of boxy multistory buildings. Big windows, lots of tall green palms. In a park faintly green with new leaves, boys are playing volleyball. When I roll down my window, the air carries a barnyard smell. From this angle, the mountains seem very close, a wall of brown knuckles.

Then the road feeds into a sort of roundabout, a messy inter-section where we become involved in a big tangle of traffic. Lots of three-wheeled moto-rickshaws clattering by, bright with shiny trim and painted flowers. Honking minivan taxis, heads protruding from every window. Motorbikes with riders clinging to each other in clumps. Mustached policemen standing round, and bicyclists weaving in and out of the crowd. Men zigzag their way through the traffic to hawk phone cards. From somewhere in the crowd, an enormous bouquet of balloons bobs along.

Ahmed nudges the Jeep past the roundabout and pulls over at a street of tightly packed storefronts. On foot we follow him past more hiccupping scooters, more rickshaws spitting exhaust, more boys on bicycles weaving round. The breeze teases up swirls of dust and litter. A woman wrapped in a black robe sits on the ground pressing a child close to her, a palm held out. We follow Ahmed briskly past her to a busy pedestrian area of open-front stores one after the other. Each is very narrow, all sorts of things hanging from the ceilings. Vendors call out, many wearing small boxy round white brimless caps that look to me like a sort of miniature fez. Rubber sandals over their socks. So many shoppers with plastic bags. Men chatting, laughing, arguing with each other.

And so the blue stands out. Slow-moving. Faceless. No hands, no mouths.

"Yeah, lots of burqas in Jalalabad," Ahmed says, noticing our stares. "Younger women especially. They find it easier. Underneath they can wear jeans, dresses, whatever."

Even with the mesh across their eyes, some women shift their gaze when we pass—though the thicker netting is so dark, I glimpse nothing behind it. Nearly all wear blue, though I also glimpse white and black. Some burqas seem to be cut shorter in the front, with matching loose pants; others have side slits revealing long skirts. I watch a woman lift the front hem to use her hands to pay a vendor— yet on her feet she wears wedge-heeled, open-toed sandals.

I know I stand out in my corduroy pants and hip-length jacket. I feel people noticing me, and wonder if this is how it was for Kyra. Always looking away, trying not to meet anyone's eye. The urge to be invisible. I try not to be self-conscious as we make our way along the tiny storefronts. Past old men sitting on a mat with their shoes off, playing cards. Past beggars missing legs, missing arms. Past a U.S. Army GI in his camouflage, buying apricots.

"This is the place," Ahmed announces. Men in white caps turn kebabs on grills right out on the street. Blue smoke reaches up, a heavy scent of roasting meat. Some of the men sit on low stools, meditatively stirring big woks heaped with gleaming rice. A few wooden tables have been set up for lunch, and from one of them a young man with short wavy dark hair leaps up.

"And there's my cousin Asim."

Asim saunters over in jeans, a gym jacket, and a fringed scarf tied round his neck. He's smiling, and now that he's before us, I see the other side of his face. A thick scar stretches from his jaw to below his eye—a fat row of shiny knotted bumps. The scar pulls at the corner of his mouth, making his smile off-kilter. The other side of his face is pristine, with a smooth, round cheek.

He and Ahmed are hugging and laughing, a long back-and-forth, as if this reunion were a complete surprise. Roy and I dole out the salaam alaikums that are all we know—Roy, like me, pretending not to be jarred by the mangled face. Asim is pumping Roy's hand, speaking very fast. "Are you well? Is life well? How is your health? How is your family?"

"Asim has been working as an interpreter for quite a while," Ahmed cuts in, as Asim repeats the questions to me in a rush, eyes averted, touching his hand to his heart. When I repeat the questions back to him, Asim conveys that, thanks be to God, his family is *awesome* and his life is *totally cool*.

Ahmed says something terse in their language. A brisk conversation ensues, the clipped bargaining tones of business.

To Roy I say, under my breath, "I don't think these guys are cousins."

Roy huffs through his nostrils, and Ahmed turns to us. "So listen, I've got to run, but it's great to meet you." He pumps Roy's hand, "Okay, see you," and breezes off.

Asim says simply, "Come eat—this restaurant is awesome."

He has an easy, confident walk. Inside are more wooden tables, more men eating kebabs. No women. The entire room rattles softly with the steady humming sound of a power generator. Asim quickly orders for us while a waiter pours hot green tea into glass mugs. Clearly he senses Roy's annoyance. I try to make conversation, ask whom he usually interprets for.

"Contractors. American dudes. Security dudes."

Risky work. I've read the news stories, interpreters killed for "collaborating" with coalition forces. For Asim, even just sitting here with us in our Western clothes is a risk. But it must mean good money for him. Who knows what that guy Ahmed said we would pay.

Asim says, "Yeah, those dudes taught me a lot of words," looking pleased.

Roy is frowning. I want to point out that already Asim has produced more in English than the two of us together could in Dari or Pashto. I want to remind him that we all sound odd when we stumble around in a foreign language. What matters is that Asim is local, that he can negotiate for us and help us find Kyra.

The thought sets my heart tumbling again. I hate the images that rise up, of Kyra lying in a ditch, or wandering, lost, in a gorge, or handcuffed under a blanket in the back of some truck.

Asim has to raise his voice over the hum of the generator. Roy nods along, and I can tell he is trying not to be rude, not to take out his anger at Ahmed on this unfortunate "cousin." He cheers up when our food arrives. The kebabs are tender, the flatbread still hot from the oven, the greasy rice glistening with sliced onions and carrots. Asim tears pieces of bread to scoop up each bite, and I follow

149

his example, quick and ravenous. Roy uses a fork rather than the bread, but who am I to blame him.

Asim stops chewing to ask, "You are husband and wife?"

I nearly choke. Roy gives a little "ha!"

"Ah, you are brother and sister."

I'm still swallowing and can only shake my head. Stiffly, Roy says, "Old friends."

Asim looks at me with new curiosity. "Your husband he allowed you to travel without him?"

I sigh. "Not really."

Roy cuts in, "Look, Asim, there's a place we need to find. A bar where Westerners hang out. It's imperative we find this place as soon as possible."

Asim's eyes light up. "Yes, yes, I know it. At the big hotel. No problem." He gives a thumbs-up, and the glimmer in his eyes almost distracts from the scar.

"No," Roy says, "I don't think this is a commercial establishment. It's where international development folks go. Run by a Canadian. A sort of private club. For foreign aid workers, that kind of thing."

"I see. I will find out."

Asim's confidence buoys my spirits. "What about you?" I ask. "Are you married?"

"Soon. We are very in love. She is beautiful and very learned. A schoolteacher." Before they can marry, he explains, he must raise the money. The "bride-price," he calls it. "Because she is so very learned and beautiful, the bride-price is very high." He had planned to go to Iran, to earn the money faster. "But with this job for you now, I will soon have enough."

Roy squirms a little at that. I ask the girlfriend's name.

"Fareshta. Our families they are friends a long time, ever since we are small children, and Fareshta and I too are good friends a long time. And then we fell in love." He looks somehow surprised—the way true love always manages to surprise us.

Roy looks suddenly overcome. Of course: it was the same with him and Kyra. Neighbors and family friends, and then came love and marriage.

But I'm the one who sent her back to him. Probably Roy blames me for that too. Well, depending on what Kyra told him. No wonder he resents me.

By the time we step back outside, the sun is lower, the breeze cooler. Pale sand skittles along the ground, and the market no longer bustles. Hard not to step on the animal droppings and tiny discarded banana peels. Children forage for leftovers and, seeing us, swarm over. Asim tells us not to stop for them.

Along the next street, children more fortunate are heading home from school, a cluster of boys in identical brown pants and tunics, no coats, just their backpacks and sneakers. And now comes a line of schoolgirls trailing after a woman in a yellow headscarf. The girls wear black uniforms with white scarves over their heads. Behind them follows a group of taller, older girls—young women, perhaps, draped all in black.

Jorgen calls them his ninja warriors.

The black-clad girls have not quite passed us when one purses her mouth and produces an enormous pink chewing-gum bubble.

When we arrive at a pocked, dented Toyota Corolla, Asim opens the door to the backseat. "Here you go, sister." He and Roy take their seats in front, and I check my cell phone for a message from home.

Nothing. Asim turns the key, attempts to rev the engine. Tries again. Again. And then the engine coughs back to life and we putter off toward the guesthouse.

stone borders

I was twenty-seven when next I heard from my stepmother. She was calling to tell me my father had died.

It turned out he had left me some money. Nothing extravagant, but for the first time in my life I had a cushion. So I took a reckoning of my life. My ex-stepsister Janet had married the manager of a big sports chain; their children were spoiled and I could not quite like them. I had no parents, few friends, and no lover. I basically just slept around. Waking up in the morning with some man's arms around me, the requisite meal at some brunch place, the rote lines I employed to make the future utterly clear: "Good luck with your project." "Have a great semester." "Well, so long." I did not miss love, or crave love. Love could be snatched away.

One curiosity was that I still heard every so often from Jack. I assumed this was due to professional ambition, though it may simply have been one more aspect of his good nature. Every other year or so a letter came, via my theater agency, in which Jack updated me on the progress of his dissertation. That year—the year my father died—the book itself arrived. *Parallel Voices: Colonial Dominion and Sexual Domination in the Literature of the Maghreb.* I read a chapter but neglected to write him back.

As for my own writing, I had somehow parlayed my success as a "talented young playwright" into an advance for a first novel: a quirky tale of love and espionage during the First World War. Buried underneath the Great War trappings was—I realized only when proofing the galleys—a second attempt to write about Carl. In this new guise, he was a midwestern boy carrying the torch for an elusive upper-crust Londoner. Without a monologue to hide behind, I was starting to find my own voice. And though the book sold only a few thousand copies, disappointing the publisher, it found a small, oddly devoted readership.

Meanwhile, *Displacements* was still being licensed, and not long after my father's funeral I was invited to see a production in the Berkshires. Driving along a pitch-dark country road, I looked out at the farmhouses glowing in the fields and thought that if I lived in one of those houses, I could make a new life. Start fresh. Property there would be cheap, and I had the money from my father for a down payment; if I kept my work at a decent clip and lived meagerly, I could survive on my thrift, if not my writing. It would be an escape from society, no expectation to go out on dates or to plays and readings. I would be far away from all that.

Two days later I made an offer on a house not far from Stockbridge, with four acres and a view of the mountains. The nearest neighbor was a half mile down the road.

For the first time in my life, I felt I had made a wise decision. No doubt or apprehension as I followed the rutted road through the woods to where my little yellow house sat atop its hill, surrounded by sugar maples, pines, and birches. I stood on the patch of overgrown lawn (on which, I would soon discover, the neighbor's horse liked to graze) and looked out across the valley to hilltops green from rain, and knew I had found it at last. My very own country.

The realtor had explained that if I walked deep enough into the woods, I would come to a line of stones demarking my property.

The very day I moved in, I set out to find the stone border. From the sunny green patch of lawn where hummingbirds sipped at bright flowers, and fat bumble bees rumbled in the bushes, and nuthatches and phoebes (though I didn't yet know their names) relayed urgent news, I stepped into the woods. Instantly the air was cooler, the ground mossy. Everything seemed strange, magnified, the sounds of leaves rustling, of brush underfoot, of life in every niche and nook. Really the great whirring of an enormous engine was simply treetops rustling in the wind, and loud quick enormous footsteps turned out to be a chipmunk scurrying through dead leaves. Even the hollow tap-tap of a woodpecker high above, and the reedy, metallic whistle of a wood thrush, seemed gigantic. From all around came the cracking and squeaking of branches moving imperceptibly in the breeze. I told myself not to be so jumpy, and continued making my way until I found the long, low, gray stone wall.

A deer was standing there. It froze when it saw me, eyes wide and dark. I too held still, alarmed at how close we were, each of us startled by the other. We held each other's gaze, and in that split second I thought: Kyra.

The dark, staring eyes. The taut stretch of muscle and bone. The narrow shins and high arches. I thought I had escaped her. I had thought I was starting anew.

I said her name aloud. "Kyra."

The deer kicked up its heels and leaped away, quick arcs in the air, the fluff of its white tail in bright retreat. The surprising sudden quiet in the woods as she fled.

Late afternoon, streetlamps lit, smudges of light in the musky air. We've driven to a bleak neighborhood of cinderblock houses with open sewers alongside, and high courtyard walls of flaking masonry, and children filling pails at water pumps.

A thought occurs to me: "That guy Ahmed said our guesthouse was near the restaurant."

"No, no, is right here." Asim has pulled over onto a quiet, cobbled street and parks alongside another high, decrepit wall. Rotting bricks peek out from crumbling stucco.

In his businessman voice, Roy says, "This is not the place Ahmed arranged."

Asim is already stepping out of the car. "This place is much better!"

"Now, look, Asim—"

"Just wait, you will see, much better here."

Roy is too tired to put up a fuss. Or perhaps he thinks it not worth the effort. I decide not to ask if we are within the "security parameter."

Instead I follow them up to a tall wooden door, into which Asim inserts an enormous, rusted key. The door swings open to reveal a courtyard full of large clay pots overflowing with bright flowers. Two tables, many wicker chairs, and a veiled woman hunched over a short-handled broom. When she looks up, she lets out a yelp and tosses the broom aside.

She rushes over, rattling off a long string of greetings that Asim echoes back. She has a plump face with soft-looking skin. Asim introduces her to me as "Auntie," and to my great surprise, she kisses me energetically on my cheeks, three times, smack-smack-smack, her skin warm against mine. "Hi!" she says, and "Thank you!" and continues to repeat these phrases.

A thickset, big-bellied man has emerged from the house, his pants and tunic topped with a knit cardigan. In stubby English he welcomes us, asking how we have fared on our travels, if we are tired, if we are well, how is our health, how is the family. Roy and I smile and proffer up our poor salaams, and Auntie nods back,

Thank you! Hi! Asim is grinning, the shiny scar pulling at his cheek. Then, assuring us he will return later tonight, he runs off.

Amid our flailing salaams, I've already forgotten the names of our hosts—who, having exhausted their repertoire of spoken English, have switched back to their own tongue. The husband speaks incredibly fast, barely a breath, no physical gestures to help us understand. Probably Asim told him we *could* understand. He addresses Roy in easy, confiding tones, chortling here and there, the wife interjecting her own commentary. Exclaiming something about *chai*, she disappears back into the house.

The husband's monologue is full of murmured asides and wheezy laughter and continues as we follow him inside. At the door we pause to remove our shoes. The husband wears his moccasins as slippers, the backs stepped on so that they fold down beneath his heels, but Roy and I have to unlace ours. From the other end of the building comes the tinny sound of a radio or television. Maybe the wife is there, preparing the tea. The husband is still chatting as he leads us down a narrow hallway to what I am made to understand will be my room.

Plaster walls, a clear shiny window, and a cot with a fleece blanket. The spotless tile floor is partially covered by a beautifully patterned red carpet. Unlike the leprous walls outside, all appears in fine condition, neat and clean like the courtyard.

Just seeing the cot reminds me how tired I am. Dropping my backpack onto the floor, I tell Roy I'll join them for tea after I've had a rest.

When they have left, I open the window to the late afternoon sky and find a canister of what appears to be mosquito repellant. Under the cot I glimpse a rolled-up mat. For prayers. I set my alarm and plunk myself down on the cot.

Before I close my eyes, I pluck a random letter out of the sleeve in my backpack.

August 21, 1996

Dear Mim,

I'm sitting here thinking about Carl. I used to hear his voice really clearly but now it's faded. I didn't realize that could happen.

I thought because I never actually "did anything" I hadn't led him on. Now my behavior seems criminal. I see how people can live their entire lives convincing themselves they haven't done anything wrong.

I meant to tell you, Mim: I'm in Algeria. Things are still horrid. In the villages there are massacres. They shoot & stab & fucking decapitate them. Women, children. Babies. Some people think it's actually the army behind these things—that they do it so the Islamists will look really awful & everyone will decide to support the government instead.

Our mandate is "to protect and aid victims of conflict." I try to believe that even if I make one person's life better, that's something.

Little things give me faith. Last night we went to hear some Andalusian music at a café in town. It made me want to dance.

Yours always,
Kyra

I keep thinking that if I read her letters closely enough, look hard enough, I might figure out what it was she was running from. Why she had to go so far away.

Not that I doubt she's in earnest. But I can hear the heaviness in her voice, and it reminds me of the things I wondered about: the lovers she had before me, the joyless flitting from one man to the next. Roy whispering to her as she lay on my mattress. Who she was before I met her, and who she became.

I've already begun to drift off when a sound startles me. The harsh electrical screech of a loudspeaker. And then a voice rises up. Raspy, rippling.

Never up close have I heard a muezzin's call to prayer. Now there seem to be three, four voices, issuing from multiple directions at once. One sounds tinny and far away, while the closest is gruff and not particularly melodic. Quavering voices crossing the air. Their words float past me, and I plunge into sleep.

the ministry of virtue and vice

As soon as night falls, we behave like any desperate infidels in a godly country. We try to find the bar.

Our goal, Roy says, is to speak to everyone possible. Get the word out, see if there's new information to glean, or even just someone to help us keep the investigation on track. But first, of course, we need to figure out where exactly the bar might be.

With Asim's help, this is accomplished fairly swiftly. One of his "dudes" knows the place Kyra described in her letter and agrees to accompany us there. He's an Australian of about fifty, with a kaffiyeh scarf draped round his neck. A veteran of the Australian Air Force, he says he's here "on contract." I don't ask what exactly that means. Mercenary, bodyguard. He sits up front, Asim at the wheel, with Roy and me seated behind them. Their conversation is loud, boisterous. I close my eyes and watch Kyra leap across the stage. Try to remember. Kyra rolling me toward her on the mattress, her arms strong and wiry. Next to me in the Benetton, hanging onto my belt loop. But then Roy is there, shouldering Kyra's backpack, ushering her out the apartment door.

I look at him beside me. Leaning back, eyes closed, his beard somehow already fuller. I'm trying to remember what he said when he phoned me, about forgetting the past. Or was it "forgiving"? Fatigue has muddled my thoughts. And then I hear myself say, "What exactly did Kyra tell you? About the two of us."

Roy opens his eyes. "That she was in love with you." He says it so plainly, with such lack of emotion, I know at once he doesn't believe it. "And that you loved her," he adds, "but then you left, because you blamed her for your friend's death."

"I didn't blame her! She was the one who was so torn up she couldn't get over it, you know that. That was the reason I called you in the first place."

Roy doesn't seem to care either way. Why should he? And why should I? It was so long ago—we were children.

"I had to leave," I tell him, "because the person she really loved was you." Even as I say it I'm waiting—I can't help it—for him to protest. To say, *She loved you more. She told me so.*

He nods. "A lot of young women go through a phase like that."

I stare at him coolly. "A *phase?*"

"Thinking they're, you know, lesbians."

I realize I'm making that face Nolan sometimes makes, where he raises his eyebrows and narrows his eyes. "Fuck you, Roy."

"Well, then, what would you call it? It's only natural. She was confused. Happens a lot to girls that age. I mean, you ended up with a man, too, didn't you?"

"Honestly—" I don't let myself finish. Roy shrugs. Up front, Asim and the "dude" are joking, as if nothing were the matter and Kyra weren't missing, or lost, or dead.

I want to scream. I cannot wait to get out of this car.

Somehow I stay quiet for the rest of the drive. As soon as we've arrived, the moment Asim has parked, I hop out, into the cold night, away from Roy.

I keep my distance even as we follow Asim and the Australian to the club, or speakeasy or whatever it is. Tucked behind a guesthouse is a one-room building pulsing with candlelight. Over the entrance hangs a square banner with hand-stitched letters:

MINISTRY

for the

PROMOTION OF VIRTUE

and

PREVENTION OF VICE

The room is basically a big square with a poured concrete floor. In the candlelit darkness I glimpse wooden tables and benches and a dozen or so men and women standing around chatting, holding cans of beer. Everyone looks up when we enter. They're Westerners, mainly white, in jeans, sweaters, and fleece jackets. Most of the men look to be in their forties, short-bearded, with Afghan scarves loose around their necks. The women look younger, with down vests over their sweaters. A noisy boom box emits a familiar song. Michael Jackson. *Billie Jean*.

At one end of the room is a big stone hearth, golden flames hissing and leaping. Along the room's periphery, narrow countertops hold abandoned hats, fanny packs, flashlights. In the center of the room, to my great astonishment, is a tiki bar.

Like something out of a budget travel package: bamboo stalks propping up a thatched roof above a meagerly stocked counter. Kyra must have laughed when she saw it.

We're introduced to the bartender—a young woman with a German accent—and then the Australian makes a beeline for a brunette warming her hands by the fire. Roy shows the bargirl the posters he has made, with Kyra's photograph: somewhere outdoors, her face partially in shade. It was the most recent picture he could find. The sunny part of her face looks as I remember her but for the crow's-feet. "Could I post some of these?" Roy asks. "And I'd like to speak with anyone who might know something."

161

A young man with an ID lanyard around his neck has stepped over to sling his arm around the bargirl. She tells him, "They are the friends of Kyra."

"And my colleague, Asim," Roy adds in his businessman voice. Asim, the only Afghan here, shakes hands with the man and they relay their greetings, *Are you well? How is your health? Are you tired? How is your fine family?* From the man's accent, I gather this is the Canadian of Kyra's letter.

"We're trying to find out about Kyra," Roy explains, "and the friend we think she went away with. We think his name is Jorgen. I'd like to speak to everyone here, if that's all right."

He heads off without asking for my assistance. Fine—probably we're more effective each on our own. Still I'm anxious as I make my way from patron to patron. There's a Dutch engineer who launches into a lecture on solar energy, a French doctor who works with amputees, and a Swedish Red Cross worker tracking down Afghans arrested by U.S. forces to help connect them with their families. Among the Americans, I meet a weary-looking journalist with a collection of shot glasses on his table, a probable missionary flashing her engagement ring, and a young fellow from New Mexico who, as far as I can gather, is on the run from the Taos police.

Pretty young things, repeat after me, say na na na na!

Asim has hunkered down with two buzz-cut men shouting over each other's beers: a security contractor and a "private consultant." Former Marines here on six-month contracts. The security contractor tells me he works for a helicopter transport company. I don't know what the private consultant does.

The others keep their distance from these two. A sort of invisible, unspoken divide. None of that matters to me. No one has anything helpful to share. The buzz-cut men speak in expletives and shorthand, call Jalalabad "J-bad," and talk of skirmishes at the "Af-Pak" border. The tired journalist offers me a shot of "horrid

Uzbek vodka" and tells a gruesome story involving a three-year-old child and a three-decade-old landmine. The fellow from Taos touches my thigh and tells me he has always had a thing for small-breasted women.

On the wall is a big cork bulletin board busy with business cards. Among the addresses of de-mining companies, fixers, translators, aid organizations, and defense contractors, Roy has posted the flyer with Kyra's picture. *MISSING*, and a number to call.

Across from the bulletin board is a large whiteboard, a message written in red pen at the top:

HUMANS NEED TO COMMUNICATE

Directly beneath it are multiple labeled columns: *Roads. Water. Internet. Incidents.* Roadways are listed as "passable" or "mudslide" or "gunfire" or "IEDs." People have written the names of villages with clean wells, or where they are lacking. They've listed internet hotspots, cell-phone recharging stations, and projects in progress.

One of the girls from the fireplace sidles over and nods at the poster of Kyra. "She your friend?" She sounds American, maybe from the south.

I nod back.

"I only saw her once," she tells me. "I spoke to Jorgen here a few times, though. Good guy. But I got the sense he'd had it with official regulations and bureaucracy and all that. I think he purposely didn't tell anyone where exactly he was working."

"Do you have any idea where?"

She shakes her head. "A few different villages. He was heading outside the wire and didn't want to give the wrong people a heads-up. I'm getting another beer, want one?"

Having slept through dinner, I don't want to drink. But I follow her to the bar and accept an apple juice from the German girl.

"You know," the American says, "there *is* someone who might know where they went. Ismail. He basically knows everyone."

"Ismail!" The bargirl's face lights up. "Of course!"

The Canadian nods. "I forgot about him. He hasn't come in here for a while, come to think of it."

"He kind of keeps to himself," the American girl says, "but he's lived here longer than all of us combined. He's met everyone at some point."

"He fought the Soviets with the mujahideen," the bargirl says, and her boyfriend raises his eyebrows. "Well, he has done so for one year, and then he has returned to London." She gives a defensive shove of her chin. "To finish his degree. He is a PhD in Persian literature."

"I didn't realize you were part of the Ismail fan club," the boyfriend teases.

"His mother was from here," the American explains, "but his father was English. His real name is George or Roddick or something."

The bargirl says, "Ismail is his nom de guerre."

Her boyfriend rolls his eyes.

"He had a wife here," the American says, "an Afghan, but she died in childbirth. The child didn't survive either. He's lived alone ever since. He says every time he tries to go back to England he feels pulled back here."

I ask where we might find him.

"*That* might be a little tricky," the boyfriend says. "I think he sleeps somewhere near town, but he's always out in the villages where he has his projects. He's a sort of a one-man NGO. Goes out into the field and sets up teams of locals. I don't know who funds him, even."

I tell them it sounds like this Jorgen fellow was trying to do something similar.

"Yeah," the Canadian says, "they were friends. But Ismail has a good twenty years more experience. They say he'll walk into a room and suss out everyone—tribe, politics, ethnic ties. He goes into a village and by the time he walks out can tell you who's pro-government, who's Northern Alliance, who's Taliban or al-Qaeda, and who's not."

The American girl calls to the gray-haired journalist with his collection of shot glasses. "Michael, do you remember where Ismail was working?" To me she says, "Michael has an elephant's memory."

The journalist wades over, hands tucked into his rumpled pockets, and names a village he says is east of here. "I *think* that was it." His words are slow, sodden. "Last I heard, Ismail was helping them set up a grid for power lines."

"Can you spell the name of the village for me?" I hand him the little notepad I always carry, and he writes something out with great drunken care.

That's when I notice, atop the bar, a small pile of bracelets. Rubber—purple. I say, "Kyra had those."

The bargirl smiles so that her dimples show. "That is our motto. Data equals power. You give us info, we give you a drink!"

Her boyfriend says, "That's why I started this place. The whole point is to share information." He points to the whiteboard on the wall. "We call that our 'data-hub.' Because there are all these aid organizations but not a lot of coordination between them. I figured one thing everyone has in common, wherever they go, is they're going to look for the local watering hole. So we've turned that into a way to keep on top of basic stuff like which roads are safe, which towns have water, etcetera. Knowledge is power. Data is power. Sharing is power. We're all about open source here."

I dangle a bracelet from my forefinger. *In Pashtun lore, bangles are also secretly useful; a man follows their sound to find his lover.*

"Here you go." The journalist hands me back my little notebook. I look down at the shaky writing and, though I have no idea where this village may be, feel hopeful.

But seeing Roy approaching with Asim, I shove the notebook back into my pocket. With all this "outside the wire" talk, I'd better first talk it over in private with Roy—though right now I really don't feel like speaking to him at all.

Say you wanna be startin' something, gotta be startin somethin' . . .

It seems we've lost our Australian. "He went home with that brunette," Roy says, petulant. Asim narrows his eyes, says, "Yes, he is very much with the ladies."

I too am ready to leave, and say so. We wish everyone goodnight.

Hard to tell from Roy's face if he has any leads. In the car he leans back, eyes closed, while Asim drives us to our guesthouse—in good spirits, because tonight, he tells us, he has learned a lot of new American words.

a rapprochement

I wake to a screeching sound—the public address system from the nearby mosque. Loud crackling of amplifiers, and then voices crossing the predawn sky. One close by, the others farther afield, echoing each other. Beautiful. Through the window, the sky is a deep hazy blue.

The voices weave into my sleep, into my thoughts, my wondering what Sean and Nolan are doing right now. I've lost track of the hour back home and feel guilty at even that small treason. I hear the marriage counselor asking if I truly meant to reconcile, asking, "Am I right, Mim, that you tend to guard yourself? That you keep yourself at arm's length, as a mode of self-protection?"

But that doesn't mean I don't love my husband. When we went through our rough patch, it was the normal drifting apart that can happen to any couple. I just drifted too far, shut down too much. But we patched it up. At least, I thought we did.

When I try to turn on the light, the electricity is out. Since my window faces west, I have to use my flashlight to find my clothes. I dress quickly: corduroy pants, a loose long-sleeved shirt, my fleece jacket, and the pashmina to cover my hair and upper body.

Then I unhinge the lock on my door and find my way down the corridor.

In the courtyard, Auntie greets me like a long-lost relative. "Hi! Hi!" and three warm kisses on my cheeks, and then comes the volley of questions as we inquire about each other's health, family, sleep, life. The sun's lemony glow washes over us. At a table draped with a maroon cloth, Auntie lays out dishes of yogurt and the round, flat bread, and pours the scalding tea. Her plump fingers have perfect oval nails, like shiny glass pressed into dough. When I gesture for her to join me, she just bustles back inside.

And now here comes Roy, checking his cell phone. We must be the only guests here. Flopping down into one of the wicker chairs, he gives me a tired look and says, "Hello, my sweet bundle of joy."

It feels good to laugh. I know he wants to diffuse whatever might be left of my anger from last night. And we both feel better now that we have a lead. I ask if there's any news.

"Just an angry message from Sandrine."

He must have told her our plans. We've decided to go there, to the village where Jorgen's friend Ismail has been working. Roy's consultants say it's a "friendly" one—our allies—and not far. But it does mean venturing out of the city. I told Nolan I would be staying strictly in Jalalabad.

I've messaged him with the name of the village. No reply. But I explained that it's a vetted decision, that Roy's advisers have given the go-ahead. I don't mention the reason we're going ourselves—that AidNow refuses to leave the "security parameter." I've simply made clear that if indeed this Ismail person knows where Jorgen went, we'll be one step closer to finding Kyra. Now that we're here, so close, there's little question of *not* going.

I might hesitate if I hadn't written my letter to Sean. A long one, in case something should happen to me. In it I explain everything.

That maybe one day he might have a similar chance—to rise to the occasion, to do the right thing.

It's no different, I told him, from how I felt when I turned back around in the courthouse and asked how one became a foster parent. Then, just like now, I knew what I had to do.

I was paying our property taxes and thought I'd stop by my sister-in-law's office; she works in the same building, and we were coordinating a surprise party for Nolan's birthday. I looked into her office, but she was on the phone.

I waited in the hallway and slipped a *New Yorker* out from my bag. There was a long article about brain surgeons. Reading, I became aware of someone near me. A child, maybe five years old, with tan skin, straight brown hair, and big dark eyes. Moons of fatigue beneath them. He was wearing pants that were too short and a ratty T-shirt much too large for him. When I looked over, he said, "That a comic book?"

At first I was confused. Then I realized the magazine had one of its cartoon covers. "Oh," I said. "No, not really."

"What about superheroes? Are there superheroes?"

I thought about the brain surgeon article. "Well, yes, but they look like regular people and wear regular clothes."

This was not sufficiently compelling for the boy, who went over to a nearby vending machine and began to press all the buttons. I wondered where his parents were. Then he kicked the machine and said, "Fuck you."

I was shocked to hear that. "What, did it eat your money?"

A look flashed across his face. "Yeah." He was lying but hopeful, and gave a dramatic, if not very convincing, sigh showing he expected me to make up the loss. "Do you have some money?"

"Not for little boys who lie." I felt horrible as soon as I'd said it.

He muttered something and kicked the machine again.

I said, "It's not the machine's fault."

He gave me an exasperated look that said, *What do you want from me?*

Who could blame him? I didn't know why I was acting that way. I think it was because I sensed, already, that this child was bright and, like any child, deserved better than some meager dream of a free candy bar. Also I was starting to worry about the fact that there were no parents in sight.

I asked where they might be.

He shrugged.

"Here." I gave him some coins to feed the machine, and together we watched the candy tumble awkwardly and land with a sad thud. The boy reached his hand in under the flap to grab it, then tore open the wrapper, took a bite, and said gleefully, "I'm not supposed to take candy from strangers."

"Right. Shoot." That was not so bright of me. But now I saw through the office door that Holly was hanging up the telephone. I tore off the cover of the magazine and gave it to the boy so he would have something to look at. Then I went into Holly's office and asked who that little kid was.

While we wait for Asim to arrive, Roy puts in a call to AidNow. "Keep them on the ball," he says, as if they don't confront calamity daily. I watch him pacing the courtyard, speaking in even, professional tones. He doesn't appear worried.

It's strange what prolonged worry does to the body. I'm no longer on high alert; probably I've run out of adrenaline. Now when I think about Kyra the worry is more like a dull piercing sensation.

As Roy strides back and forth across the courtyard, I reach into my pack for the sleeve holding Kyra's letters. With a small tug, I catch the top of a page.

and I realized something, Mim. I think I married Roy as a type of penance, for what I did to Carl. How hateful is that? And to Roy of all people. I don't even think I knew there could be such a thing as a happy marriage. I mean, I never had a good model. You know who has a perfect marriage to me? The couple in The Mercy Years. All those intimate jokes you gave them, how they tease each other but never in a cruel way. Did you know a couple like that, or did you just dream them up and

"Still no news." Roy flops himself back into the wicker chair. I sneak the letter back in with the others. But Roy sees. He gestures at my bag and says, almost peevish, "I still don't understand about those letters."

Already I feel some protective flare go up inside me.

"I mean," he says, "why did Kyra send them to *me* if they were meant for *you?*"

"I suppose she didn't have my address."

"Takes two seconds to look you up on the internet. Your publisher and website come up right away. She could have sent them to your literary agency. That's how I found you."

I consider this. "I think maybe she was in a rush and didn't have time. Or maybe she just felt better sending them directly to you and not some business address. She knew she could count on you to reach me."

Roy nods, but I sense that's not the answer he wants. Maybe what he really wonders is why she wrote them to me instead of him. Sounding distinctly annoyed, he asks, "Do you think she thought I'd open the package myself?"

"I don't think so. She's always trusted you." But now that he's asked the question, I too wonder. Did she care whether Roy read them or not?

Maybe this is Roy's way of asking to see the rest of the letters. He's drumming his fingers on the table, checks his watch again. In the daylight his forearms are lightly freckled. "As soon as we find her," he says, "I'm taking her out of this hellhole."

This surprises me. Not just that he thinks Kyra would do what he wants, or that she might view this land as he does. I hadn't quite realized he still thinks he can win her back.

Well, why wouldn't he think that? As far as he is concerned, Kyra's love for me was a "phase."

But the fact is, Roy's confidence buoys me. Because if he thinks he can win Kyra back, that means he believes she's alive. And that we can do this. We can figure out where it is she's gone to.

a short walk

Midmorning by the time Asim comes to fetch us. The scar on his cheek manages to surprise me all over again, these two very different sides of one face. We swap tidings, Asim allowing that he is well, thanks be to God, his health is good, his family is awesome, God is great, very well, thank you. But when Roy hands him the piece of paper with the name of the village, Asim shakes his head.

"You don't know it?" Roy asks.

"I know it. But it is, like, too far."

Roy frowns. "How far?"

"Twenty, thirty kilometers."

"That's nothing!"

"The road is dangerous, man. I will need more money."

"Oh, so money makes it less dangerous?"

"A risk fee." Asim stands his ground.

Roy takes another bill from his money clip.

"Very dangerous," Asim says, shaking his head. "Bandits. Taliban. Police."

Roy raises his eyebrows, though surely he's read the stories of two-timing warlords, of crooked policemen, of improvised explosives at the side of the road. At the same time, I tell myself Asim must be exaggerating, given the assurance we've had from Roy's "guys." Probably it's for the bride-price.

"We're Americans," I remind Roy. "It's a risk for Asim just to have us in his car."

Asim nods. "Taliban have a new offer. You help them to kill a foreigner, they give you a motorbike."

"Fine," Roy says, and shoves another bill at Asim.

"Taliban pay two hundred dollars per month."

I assure myself this is all in the name of love. Roy grimaces, peels off another bill. "That's it. Now let's get going."

We head out to the sad little Toyota, where Asim opens the trunk and extracts a bundle of fabric. Unfolded, the material becomes the ubiquitous Afghan scarf and brownish patu blanket. For me he has a black robe much larger than my pashmina.

"Better this way," Asim explains, handing us the clothing. "For checkpoints."

The garment covers me completely. I wrap it tightly, along with the scarf over my head, while Asim has Roy remove his glasses. What about Roy's stiff, clean new boots, I want to ask. Surely those give him away. But I suppose no one will see our feet in the car.

Asim's shoes are slip-on rubber things molded to look like sneakers—even the laces, tongue, label, everything molded onto one continuous piece of rubber.

"No, no seatbelt please," he says when he sees Roy and me buckling ourselves in. That too could give us away.

And so we head off to the village, seatbeltless, in our new clothes. At first the street is cobblestone and quiet, with walled houses of cement, lots of crisscrossing electricity wires, and clotheslines draped with drying laundry. The next street is busier, men chatting in klatches, some in waistcoats topped by patu blankets, some in V-neck sweaters.

Unlike the men, the women never linger. In their burqas or black veils or scarves wrapped round head and shoulders, they keep moving, watchful, deliberate, staying close to the walls. One turns a corner and the fabric of her burqa parachutes behind her.

Soon we've neared an open square, a large concrete building at one side. Perhaps a clinic, or a government office; women have formed a queue there, squatting as they wait. All wear burqas, some bright and others faded. I wonder how long they've been waiting. With their faces covered, it's unclear if they're weary, anxious, impatient.

Something about this frightens me. I look away, at the crumbling brown walls, at the squeaking hand pumps where children catch precious water in tin pails. Beyond us, the hills are great dark humps.

The main road, although recently paved, is already pocked with holes; with all the reconstruction projects and heavy military equipment, Asim explains, the thin asphalt ruts quickly. Soon we're bouncing behind buses reeking of diesel, following grumbling, brightly painted trucks, their many little bells jingling, their windows decorated with tassels and curtains. In the distance loom wide brown hills and pleated mountains, their peaks tinseled with snow.

Asim tells us he grew up in a village south of here. He is twenty-seven years old, the seventh of nine children. His father was a raisin washer. "He hoped for his children to be learned, but this was during Taliban time, lots of Koran in school, not much else. My brothers now are bricklayers, but I did not want that. I studied more English."

He first studied when just a boy, in secret, "from the most learned man in the town. He had a lot of books of English. But then the Taliban they found the books. My lessons stopped." Since 2002, he tells us, he has been learning from "American dudes" and "security dudes." "They gave me music. Bruce Springsteen. Led Zeppelin.

Rolling Stones. I read the words of the songs on my phone. I can't get no satisfaction!"

I can't tell if his joke is genuine or a standard line for our benefit.

Fareshta too, he adds, likes rock music. "Man, her English is better than mine."

That's when I spot a mangled truck abandoned at the side of the road. Burned and blistered, with brush growing up around it.

"Oil tanker," Asim says so matter-of-factly it's hard to tell what his feelings about it might be. And though it's clear this happened some time ago, I still feel a cold spider crawl up my spine.

Roy says, "I can't see a thing without my damn glasses."

I wish he were here in the back with me. I don't know where exactly that thought comes from, perhaps just the strangeness of traveling without Nolan or Sean. When we slow down to navigate past a gypsy-looking crew complete with sheep, donkeys, and a skinny-legged camel, I fight the impulse to call out, the way I would at home, *Look, guys, look at that!*

The gypsies are like something out of a travelogue, in bright spangled clothing, purple, pink, orange, the camel adorned with tinkling bells and piled with heavy sacks.

Nomads, like Kyra, her life squeezed into a backpack.

Carl, his duffel lying in the corner of the living room.

We ease our way past, and the glittery sound recedes. Asim lights a cigarette, holds the pack out to Roy. "Good ones. American. *Smoking kills.*"

Roy shakes his head, and Asim rolls his window down to disperse the smoke. I try to lower mine, but it's jammed.

Gradually the traffic fades away. I lean back and watch the world outside, the hills like dark cracked skin. Like Jonathan Swift's giants. And then I see, ahead, a chain pulled across the road. On one side, a concrete bunker with guns pointing out, and uniformed guards with rifles.

"Do not talk," Asim says. "Keep eyes down. Do not look dude on his eyes."

I don't ask why. I've read that soldiers sometimes detain foreigners at checkpoints. The chain is at the height of our windshield. I watch as a jalopy ahead of us is half-heartedly searched and waved through.

At our turn, the officer peeks briefly through the window. Even with my head down I glimpse the gray fleece uniform as Asim hands him something. And just like that we're on our way. There has been no questioning, no exchange of words at all.

"I suppose that was part of the 'risk fee,'" Roy says flatly.

"There are tolls," Asim says.

Rocks line the road, big gray-brown ones and enormous sharp-edged boulders, and small ones strewn like rubble. Every so often, some that have been painted: red to one side of the road, white at the other. "Landmines," Asim explains. From the Soviets. White stones mean that side of the road has been cleared; red, mines are still there. After a moment Asim adds, "That is how I injured my face. A mine killed my friend. Some parts hit my cheek."

"How awful!"

But Asim says, "I am lucky! I still can see from my eyes. A lot of people they lose feet, hands, legs. But I have two feet. I have two hands."

"Some luck," Roy says. "Though I suppose, considering the Taliban penchant for amputation—"

"Jesus, Roy," I murmur.

Asim says, "Yes, justice punishments. But Taliban use anesthetic."

Roy harrumphs at that.

"And the ambulance it was right there at the stadium, to bring dudes to hospital to sew up. That is sharia law."

Roy says, "There's some cold comfort."

"For head-cutting they had meat butchers to do it right. Heads are not easy like hands and feet—"

"Okay, okay," Roy says, "enough already."

It's not clear to me if Asim is teasing or simply chatting. I hate not being able to see his face from here. I feel like a child, relegated to the backseat. We seem to be heading toward giant gray mountains that never grow closer. Just when I am beginning to think we must be lost, I spot, at some distance ahead, a shallow valley bright with the faint yellow-green of almost-spring, and tucked into the valley, like a pea in its pod, a walled compound the color of clay.

Though the rational part of my brain knows Kyra won't be there—that it's the Englishman, Ismail, we're looking for—a flame of hope flares up. That this Ismail person might confirm that Kyra's with Jorgen, know where they've gone, what they're doing, even know, somehow, that they are all right.

It takes some time until we've entered the valley. Asim drives right up to the village gate, a massive wooden door in a high adobe wall. Roy replaces his glasses. I remove the long robe but keep the scarf round my head and shoulders, and we step out into air that smells of manure. Asim clacks the big heavy metal door knocker.

For a long while we are made to wait outside the wooden door. From the other side of the wall come voices and the snorting of animals, and the gull-like cries of young children. So, they know we're here, waiting. I'm starting to wonder if they've decided to simply leave us here. But then the enormous door opens, revealing two thin men in payraan tumbaan and open waistcoats.

The older of the two wears a white skullcap that matches his beard. He stands very straight, neck long, chin held high. A face from antiquity. The younger has darker skin and light, golden-brown eyes.

The exchange of greetings ensues, while Roy and I smile dopily, nothing to offer but our feeble salaams. The men nod at Roy but don't look me in the eye. Faces look out at us from the village gate, people gathering in the mud courtyard, watching. There's a donkey that keeps braying, and laundry hanging from a network of lines.

Apparently the older man is the village leader. Narrow-boned, his face impassive. Roy says, "Please tell him we're looking for the Englishman."

"They are inviting us to tea."

But Roy won't have it. "Please, there's no time to lose."

"But we have not—"

"We can have tea afterward. It's a matter of life or death."

When Asim explains, the men answer briskly.

"Not an English dude," Asim translates back to us. "There is a Spanish."

"Spanish! Well then please ask if they know a foreigner named Ismail."

Their expressions show this to be a matter of speculation. The younger man, to my surprise, takes a cell phone from his waistcoat pocket—an old flip phone, with punch buttons. He dials a number, here in the middle of nowhere, and a brisk conversation ensues.

Asim shares what he has learned. "He says there is a Spanish in the next village."

"We don't want a Spanish!" Roy yelps. "We want an English. IS-MA-IL."

The two men stare at him.

"They say the next village it is just two hours walk," Asim explains. "They will walk us there."

Roy hangs his head. He seems to understand that we've come all this way for nothing. But then he turns to me. "We might as well."

It was one thing to drive out to this village that Roy's consultants had vetted for us. We know nothing about this other one. "They didn't even recognize his name," I say. "Why should we go there? And how do we know we can trust them?"

Asim doesn't seem worried. "Pashtunwali. Hospitality code. We are their guests, they will protect us."

Roy mutters, "Unless that's a bunch of hogwash." He looks like he might cry. All at once I see—with surprise, for some reason—how desperately he still loves Kyra.

"Look," he tells me, "no one else is going to come out here. This is our only lead. I think we should go with them."

I regard the men, their placid faces. Just because someone looks sincere doesn't mean I should trust him. But now that we've come all this way, it does seem a waste not to follow the only lead we have.

Roy says, "We're just walking to the next village. That's all. They'll look out for us."

I hear her voice, then. Kyra next to me on the bench in Newport. Looking out at the ocean, reaching for my hand.

"All right," I tell Roy, "let's go."

Asim is conveying our decision to our hosts when a frazzled man in grubby clothes comes running at us. Skinny, barefoot, yelling, pushing his way past the crowd. His words come very fast. I ask Asim what he's saying.

"He is calling you donkeys," Asim says matter-of-factly, as the man continues to yell. "Now he is asking for money. Now he is calling you donkeys. Now he is calling you infidels."

The two townsmen just sort of swat him away.

"Now he is calling you stupid donkeys. He is saying you owe him money. He is asking if you will give him a radio."

Roy says, "Can't someone give this guy a pill?"

"Now he is calling Mr. Roy a donkey. Now he is hitting him. Now he is—"

Pointing a handgun. He has whipped it out from his waistband, waves it round. Roy steps back, hands up, but I freeze, while the village men yell, and the younger one lunges and snatches the gun,

180

shoving the skinny man and kicking him in the shin. Then he tucks the gun in his own pants and turns back to Asim, while the village leader, if I am reading his expression correctly, calmly apologizes for the interruption.

The frazzled man runs off, still yelling. My whole body is shaking. Yet the men barely seem perturbed. Even Roy seems hardly to have registered danger. "Can we go now?" he asks.

And as though nothing odd has occurred, our small group begins its walk.

All I can think is that the man was a warning, that we're not safe, ever, no matter how we might convince ourselves.

The village elder leads the way. A little boy too has joined us— the elder's grandson, Asim explains. We follow them along a trail that appears to curve up out of the valley toward the mountains. I'm still shaking from the man with the gun.

"Spanish!" Roy is muttering. "Christ. All the way in that crappy car . . . I can't believe there's no drivable road between villages . . . That lunatic could have killed us."

"You're the one who said you wanted to keep going," I grumble back.

"You have a better idea?"

I stop to look at him. "We wouldn't even know about this village if it weren't for me. I'm the one who found out about Ismail in the first place."

Roy continues walking. Under his breath he says, "For all we know this Ismail guy doesn't even *exist*."

"Then why are we even bothering to go there?"

He just mutters "Christ" again and keeps walking. He's directly behind the younger of the two village men. I've had enough of him and hang back with Asim and the older man and his grandson, watching Roy's figure grow farther from mine. The little boy keeps pointing out this and that for Asim to translate:

181

This is where we stoned the poisonous dog.

I lost my boomerang there.

A Talib was hiding here.

This is where the wolf ate my baby brother.

"That's awful!"

The old man murmurs something, and Asim says, "Correction. That is not true. This boy does not like his brother."

The sun is high now. I'm hot under the pashmina, my armpits sticky, sweat above my lip and at my hairline. I wish I could remove the headscarf. We seem to be following a highland path. Spindly brown trees stand like strange statues, and shale shifts under each step. Then there's a flat gray river we traverse by stepping gingerly across a bridge made of tree limbs laid crosswise over logs.

I'm glad for the thick soles of my walking shoes and wonder how Asim is faring in his rubber sneakers. As for our three guides, they wear plastic shower sandals over bare feet. The men do not talk. Roy keeps hurrying ahead and then waiting impatiently.

Already an hour has passed. No sign of fatigue on the men's faces. Even the little boy shows no sign of slowing, though the sun throbs above us and our stomachs grumble. My headscarf has plastered itself to my forehead. My feet fumble over tree roots. And now here come three boys who look to be in their teens. When the older man asks them our question, they point higher up.

We turn onto a narrower path, the terrain suddenly steep. I try not to look down; I've always had slight vertigo and can't afford for it to affect me now. The rocks are slippery with fine sand that seems to have come from out of nowhere. Luckily we don't have to go far before coming upon a half-dozen men at work laying a path of pipes.

"The Spanish!" Asim announces.

A man turns to us—a grizzled Afghan with hollow cheeks, dark graying hair, and a gray wool pakol cap. Dressed like the rest in baggy pants and tunic and afghan scarf, he has a prominent nose, leathery skin, and startling, deep-sunk blue eyes.

Roy asks if he is Ismail.

"Indeed I am!" A strong English accent, the kind that to me always sounds slightly offended. "Has the law caught up with me, then?" He laughs. He has pushed up his sleeves, revealing strong dark wiry forearms. Deep wrinkles begin just below his eyes, reaching to his cheeks. "How can I help you?"

Roy introduces himself and asks if he knows Jorgen.

"Yes, of course!" And then, seeing our faces, "Has something happened?"

"They're missing!" I tell him, but it comes out as a sob. Ismail has dropped the piece of pipe, and I see that this is the first he has heard of the disappearance. I press my lips together to stop myself from crying.

"When? Who's 'they'?"

Roy tells him all we know, asks if he might know which village Jorgen was working in. "We think it may be the last place they were seen."

Ismail pauses to think. Nods, says a name. "I've been there myself, know the village elder. No more dangerous than here." He seems to be contemplating. "If they didn't have someone to look out for them, though, or if someone tricked them—"

"Look," Roy says, "We've come all the way from the U.S. We'll do anything to figure out where they might have gone."

This is the first he has put it that way. Perhaps it's the first that he's realizing it. That I'm realizing it.

Ismail pulls off his wool cap, uses it to wipe his brow. "We'll do more than that." He tugs the cap firmly back on. "We shall find them."

183

the village

It's been a long time since I've felt the need to seek someone out. The desire, the pursuit. Nolan's the one who first did that to me. That I could feel some form of love again, and not just the physical urge to love—that I could feel curiosity and appreciation of another being's subtle mystery—was an amazement for which I remain grateful.

I first saw him at the hardware store in town, a twenty-minute drive from my house on the hill. I'd lived there six months by then. I was buying mousetraps and poison, desperate purchases.

"Or you could get a cat," a man in the same aisle said, his voice cool, deadpan. He looked to be my age, late twenties, maybe thirty, lean and broad shouldered, with messy brown hair. "My sister's cat just had a litter, if you want to take a look."

"Ah—a salesman."

"Oh, she'd give you the whole bunch for free."

Matt, who runs the hardware store, was looking over from the counter and laughing. "Nolan, you're not really looking for moth traps. You came here to hang out in the extermination aisle and try to get rid of them cats."

"You found me out." But Nolan took down two boxes of moth traps. He said, "My sister's out on Slage Way, if you have any interest. You could follow me there."

Matt said, "Oh, you're a quick one!" Still laughing. "Kittens!"

I ran my fingers through my hair, suddenly self-conscious. I still wore my hair short, though it was an effort to maintain and not for some time had anyone complimented my neck or earlobes. In fact, this conversation was the most I'd spoken with anyone in days. Within me I felt an ancient, familiar rustling.

I told Nolan I'd take a look. Really I'd never owned a pet before and was terrified of being responsible for another living creature. But I followed his pickup out to his sister's, the first visit I'd made to anyone since my move. From a whole litter of kittens in a barn out back, I chose the littlest one, a soft gray puff. I hoped its smallness meant it would be spritely and adept at catching mice.

Nolan asked what I would name her.

"I'll have to get to know her first." I held the kitten in my palm and watched her toy with the little cloth zipper of my jacket. "Peanut," I said. "Maybe." Then I looked at Nolan and asked, "Who are you? Where do you live?"

Right down the road, in a log-cabin-style house he had built from a kit. "You just follow the directions, like Legos." I liked the way he cleared his throat before speaking, as if, like me, he hadn't spoken this much in a long while. He had grown up in town, had gone to college in Amherst, then lived in Northampton but returned when his father became ill. He worked in IT for the gas company. His father had died six months ago.

"My father died too."

We stood there playing with the kitten. Despite Nolan's low quiet voice there was something firm, solid, in his comportment. The kitten fell asleep in his palm.

I didn't want to leave, not just because I liked Nolan but also because I had no clue how to take care of a kitten. Nolan asked his sister for a box and poked some holes in the lid. "Come here, you sweet clueless thing"—and he placed the kitten inside the box. "Your life has just been saved."

He handed me the box ceremoniously, and I tried to find the courage to ask if he might like to get together sometime. But I was shy and thought he should be the one to ask. All he said, somewhat awkwardly, after walking me back to the car, was "Well, see you round."

So there I was, back in my house, alone but for a kitten that over the next five days would find all kinds of inventive ways to nearly kill itself—tangling her neck in the straps of a tote bag, swallowing my vitamins, playing dominos in the cupboard with the few wine glasses I owned. When Friday night arrived, I left the kitten to some new disaster and went to find Nolan.

Not that I admitted I was doing this. I drove to the one pub I could picture him at—there were just two in town—and strode over to the bar, telling myself that for once I was being a normal twenty-something, going out on a Friday night. And sure enough, as I cast my gaze across the room, I saw him. Sitting at one of the little square tables, with a woman.

She was dressed too nicely: dangly earrings, a glittery scarf around her neck. It had to be a date. Nolan nodded politely as she spoke. Then he noticed me watching.

With anyone else I would have quickly turned away. But I couldn't move—or smile or wave or nod. Even my breath seemed to have stopped. Nolan let his gaze rest on me for a moment before looking back to his date.

I felt despondent then. But I made myself finish my beer, and chatted with the regulars up at the bar, so that I could pretend to myself that this was all I'd wanted, a little socializing on a Friday night. Then I went to the restroom and tried to work up the courage to say something friendly on my way out the door.

The restroom was off a short dark hallway with a pay phone tucked in the corner. I was heading back out, just past the phone, when I saw Nolan standing there.

He spoke in a low voice. "We made this date a week ago. A friend set us up, I couldn't cancel. I didn't know what to do."

I just nodded. Another woman squeezed past us, and I stepped aside to let her by. Maybe Nolan thought I was leaving; he reached for my hand. At the warm grasp of his fingers, something came over me. Desire, and despair—that I would love him, and lose him, and that I could not bear it.

Yet I stepped closer, pressing my hip against his. I could smell the detergent scent of his shirt. His lips brushed my cheek, my jaw, and I turned so that my mouth would meet his.

I miss him horribly, actually.

I think this must be the longest we've gone without speaking.

The moment we're back in range of a cell tower, on our way back to Jalalabad, I make the call. I'm not surprised when there's no answer, just the recording, his voice low and contained. All I can do is leave my message: I miss you, I'm sorry about all this. I hope you'll let me know how you are.

I also tell him the name of the village we're to travel to—the one where Ismail believes Jorgen was working. I spell it out for Nolan, letter by letter, just so that he knows.

We have to wait until morning, since the road isn't safe at night. Also, Roy is still finalizing our plan with the specialists he's hired.

The village, they tell him, is generally safe—though I have to wonder what that really means. Roy makes it sound straightforward: first we will positively locate Kyra and Jorgen's whereabouts;

then, if it turns out they're being kept against their will—or if the situation is too dangerous, or beyond our capabilities—Roy's "guys" will negotiate for us and, if necessary, bring in local reinforcements.

This is what we came for. This is why I'm here.

Bravery is an action. It's what you do.

∽⌇∼

September 21, 2001

Dear Mim,

I'm thinking of you, of everyone back home, keep running through my mind if there's anyone I might have forgotten. I'm in the Philippines & can't check email as often as I'd like. I've gone every day this week & each time brace myself for some message about someone I know. Each time I think there must be someone I'm forgetting. Who I assumed wouldn't be there but for some fluke reason was.

My coworker Pablo knows someone who worked in Tower One but she was home sick that day. The TV kept showing the towers crumbling. Standing & falling, then standing again, so that even hours later I still thought of them as standing. It wasn't until the next day that it truly hit me they were gone.

I remember in New York every time I came out of the subway, that first moment on the street when I would wonder which direction to walk. All I had to do was look for the towers & I knew which way was south.

How will everyone find their way now?

Really hoping you're okay,

Love always, Kyra

Barely dawn when I meet Roy in the courtyard. He doesn't seem nervous, just sits in one of the wicker chairs and checks his phone, exclaiming with faux annoyance at the many messages flooding his in-box. I look at mine in vain for word from Nolan. Roy is still bushwhacking his way through his messages when Asim and Ismail arrive.

Asim is to drive, although I wonder if we need him now that we have Ismail. But he needs the money—the "bride-price." We toss my daypack into the trunk, and I rewrap myself in the long black robe. Roy once again removes his glasses, since there may be more checkpoints.

"*May* be?" Roy says testily. "I thought you guys knew where we were going."

"Depends on the day," Asim says.

"Even the time of day," Ismail explains. "The police give some hours over to warlords, make deals with them, to let them make some money, let some trucks pass, you know."

"No, I don't know," Roy grumbles, and I realize he must be as anxious as I am.

Ismail seems to understand this. He simply hands Roy a thick soft wool pakol beret just like his own. "This too, please. There you go." When Roy has tugged it on, Ismail helps him roll the bottom up, forming a thick band around his head.

Asim takes the driver's seat, Ismail next to him, Roy and me in the back. As we head out again on the new, already rutted road, I ask Ismail how he came to live here.

"I was in my twenties when I first came over, during the Holy War. I'd grown up with romantic notions about my mother's home-land. She spoke to me only in Dari, told me all kinds of tales. I came back again not long after I finished my doctorate in Persian literature. Learned Pashto, fell in love, married." He pauses. "After I lost my wife and child, well, this is how I stay close to them. I worked with Afghan Aid for years, but now I have my own team, all locals. In fact, we've been discussing collaborating with Jorgen. Tricky, of course, in the places we're trying to do work. The tribal areas are the most volatile."

"By 'volatile,'" I cut in, "I suppose you mean 'dangerous.'"

He swivels to look back at me. "I mean that these are the places where progress comes more slowly. So many people living beyond the law . . . But you have to understand, the villagers want good lives for their children just like anyone anywhere. They believe in education just like us. It's not hopeless."

Roy asks, "Why did those guys yesterday think you were Spanish?"

"Did they?" Ismail laughs. "I suppose because there were Spanish troops here once. Or a Spanish aid worker. Possibly someone thought it means something like Western, or European. Usually the word is *amrican*. When I first started in the region people kept saying I was American no matter how many times I said otherwise."

Asim has slowed the car, so much so that other vehicles are now passing us. When I ask why, he gestures toward a white Land Rover some distance ahead.

"U.N.," he says. "And police behind them." A green Humvee.

"Yes, they always travel with police protection," Ismail says. "Best to hang back a bit."

They are targets, that's what he means. NGO workers, U.N. personnel, Afghan police—collaborators with U.S. and NATO, always in danger of retribution.

So we hang back and soon are the only automobile in sight. Asim lights a cigarette and offers the pack to Ismail and Roy. Smoke swirls overhead.

Asim passes the time by asking questions:

"What does it mean, 'Back in Black'?"

"What is 'a bustle in your hedgerow'?"

Roy and I do our best with explanations. I look out at mountains strewn with boulders, the enormous rocks that never end. A stark beauty like nothing I've ever seen. A flock of dark birds crosses the sky like a cape.

We turn onto a smaller, desert road that crosses a dried-up creek full of stones. As far as I can tell, we're headed toward a vast moon-rock landscape marked by cell towers and nothing else. Until at last I spy, on a rocky hillock of scrappy greenish brush, a settlement of clay houses.

The first person I spot is a goatherd urging some goats along with a stick. Then there are two women carrying jugs atop their heads. They wear bright dresses over their pantaloons and shawls around their heads and shoulders. They pause when they hear our car. The settlement grows closer, with colorful laundry flapping in the breeze. Little girls play in bright skirts and sweaters, no head-scarves, while little boys in Western-style pants and sweaters appear to be conducting a game of slingshots. Now, though, they've heard us, and stop to watch our approach.

Anyone in this village might be able to help us, might know where Jorgen, and Kyra, could be.

As soon as Asim has parked the car, I remove the robe, since the women seem not to wear them. I step out onto the dirt and pebbles and scuttling sand to find our car covered with dust. Children gust toward us as the rest of the village sifts out of the mud-brick huts.

Stepping forward to greet us are four ancient men with approximately nine teeth between them. The oldest, most shriveled of all has recognized Ismail and slowly lifts both hands toward him, pronouncing a toothless greeting.

When I was a little girl, a favorite treat was the processed dried meat that came packaged like licorice sticks—a sort of cheap sausage, dark and hard and wrinkled. This dried meat is what I think of when I look at this man, everything about him dry and tough. Ismail, with his lined face and grizzled hair, could be a younger version of him.

Ismail bends forward as if in an effort not to be taller than the old man. The rounds of politesse continue, no need for a translator. One of the little boys is given orders and hurries off.

I keep listening for the name Jorgen. The village elder turns and, hobbling on buckled legs, his bare feet in the ubiquitous shower sandals, leads us into the main courtyard, the children trailing behind us. Just as Ismail explains that we've been invited to tea, the little boy returns with a grandmotherly figure, her headscarf tied loosely beneath her chin. It's as I'm handed off to "Auntie" that I realize the men are about to go off without me.

"Wait—" But they follow the ancient hobbling man into one of the mud-brick huts.

Already the children have surrounded me. Some wear sweatshirts with logos I recognize from home: an appliqué of SpongeBob SquarePants; the words *I'M A STAR* in peeling letters. I'm furious at the men for having left me but try not to show it. The old woman's face is beautiful in the way the old become beautiful again, eyes all the brighter for being surrounded by delicate crumpled skin. Then she smiles, and I see her broken teeth.

She leads me to an outdoor space near one of the mud-brick huts, where a cluster of women sit around a smoky fire pit. They sit on their heels, their skirts tucked under their knees, chatting as they chop potatoes, and pluck feathers from scrawny chickens, and sift stones from lentils, and scoop rice from a large sack into a large copper pot. An open-air communal kitchen. Then they see me, and their voices drop away.

The children hover behind me. The fire hisses, and smoke creeps out from under the embers. I'm handed a small bowl of watery green tea. Some of the women continue to eye me, curious, wary, but most return to their banter, and soon enough their voices are lively again, a bright back-and-forth I wish I could join in. All I can do is wonder if Kyra came here, if these women saw her, if they know where she is. I feel utterly useless, sitting cross-legged on the cold, dry ground, sipping tea, gray smoke wafting over us as the women continue their work.

The youngest looks to be fourteen or so, with gold-blond hair tucked loosely under her headscarf, her skin spotty with acne. Like the others, she wears plastic sandals, and a loose dress over pantaloons. She glances at me for just the briefest moment. Stunning eyes, greenish-brown like a cat's. One eye blinks every few seconds, as if of its own will.

All the while the little children hover nearby, giddy at my strangeness. I feel them watching—but when I look up, they flock away.

There's a hut just across from us and, slumped against the lumpy clay wall, a boy. He looks to be in his teens. He wears a baseball cap, and a fringed scarf around his neck. Even from here I can see there's something wrong with him. His expression is vacant, the bone structure of his face somehow lopsided.

"Farid," one of the women tells me, following my gaze, and with a small movement of her head indicates some sad story. At this, the girl with the cat's eyes tosses down her stirring spoon. It clangs loudly against the copper cauldron. The other women, chatting, ignore her.

That's when I decide to speak. "*Amrican*," I say. "Jorgen. Kyra." I point out at the hills.

The girl with the cat's eyes glances at me. Her left eye twitches. The other women busy themselves with their cooking, while the old woman manages to communicate that they have no answer for me—and then says something brisk to the girl with the cat's eyes.

The girl stands and takes up two copper gourds with wire handles. A furtive glance my way. She heads away from the fire pit and its steaming cauldrons, away from the mud houses, out toward a sandy hummock. At first I just watch her. Then I decide to follow her.

I don't care if I'm being rude. I think she has something to tell me.

Sand dust creeps along the ground with the breeze. The girl has a tough, don't-mess-with-me walk. But she slows down to kick at a small rock, keeping it in front of her, like a tiny soccer ball, with each step. She must be aware of me behind her, just as I am of the train of children following me. Together we form a strange parade, the girl, then me, and the children behind us, until the girl turns and snaps at them. The children scatter. The girl gives a hard kick to the rock she has been punting along, sending it away.

The sun is higher now and strong. I feel at once hot and cold—the sun burning my skin, the air chilling it. The girl keeps her gaze down, but I sidle up to her, point to myself. "Miriam."

Still not quite looking me in the eye, the girl stops to set down one of the copper gourds. She points to her chest and slowly, clearly, says, "Meena Gul."

"Hello, Meena Gul."

Her left eye twitches. "Hello, Miriam." She pronounces my name easily, eyes still looking away from me. I wonder if it could be hunger causing that left eye to twitch, or maybe a nervous tic. I try to look her in the eye, but she takes up the gourd again and walks ahead—firm, purposeful steps crossing the dune-like hills.

In the shade of a stunted tree, Asim is partaking of one of his "Smoking Kills." He crouches, Afghan-style, on his heels, his arms draped over his knees.

"Asim," I call out, "why aren't you with the others?"

He stands. "They, like, do not need me."

"I'm trying to find out if Meena Gul knows anything about Kyra and Jorgen."

Asim says, "Better to first ask other things."

194

That frustrates me. But he joins me to follow in her footsteps, keeping at a respectful distance, Meena Gul turning her face away when I introduce him. I decide to ask how old Meena Gul is. When Asim inquires, her reply seems much longer than necessary.

"She is sixteen. She has grown up here and never has left the village."

I'm sure she said more than that, but I don't press him. We have come to a scruffy area punctuated by mounds of dried clay. "And what are these humps?"

"Graves."

There are no monuments to mark the lumps, just rocks and dirt. And though some of the mounds are large, most are quite small.

Asim explains, "Many babies, they die."

No markers to read, no flowers. The cemetery appears untended. Asim must sense my thoughts. "Their spirits are not here," he explains as we pass. And then, as if to clarify, "They flew away."

We've reached the well and still Asim hasn't asked about Kyra. The strong muscles of Meena Gul's arms flex against her sleeves as she lowers the first gourd and then draws it back up. Asim carefully lifts it. Only when Meena Gul has filled the second one does he at last ask my question. I can tell because of how quietly he speaks.

Meena Gul hesitates, then answers. Asim tells me she has not seen Jorgen these past weeks. "But that is not unusual. She says he was not always here."

I suppose that makes sense, since Jorgen had projects in Jalalabad too. Even so, I'm sure there was something she wanted to tell me. "Asim, she knows something. There was a look she gave me back there. I think maybe it's why she's so nervous. Or sad, or angry, I can't quite tell. I think maybe it has something to do with Jorgen."

"She is engaged," Asim informs me. "To a dude in the next village. Bad guy. She does not want to marry him."

Meena Gul is carrying the other full gourd, and the three of us turn back. "That is why she is angry," Asim continues. "Her family, they owe money to this dude's father. But there is, like, no money. So they give Meena Gul to the man's son instead."

I lock eyes with Asim. He shrugs. "She says she will run away when they send her. She says maybe she will kill him."

I don't doubt it. Even though I know this sort of barter exists, I can't help asking if there isn't some other way to pay the father back.

Languidly, Asim repeats my question to Meena Gul. When she answers, he tells me, "They already have given him the carpet."

Back at the outdoor kitchen, lunch is ready. Asim has left to rejoin the men, and the women carry the platters of food to the door of the hut. Trays of stew and paneer are passed like trophies through the doorway. Steaming cloths full of fresh naan are brought out. Only after the men in their hut have been served do we sit down to our own tea and stew and bread.

The stew is chewy, with only a bit of chicken swimming among the onions and potatoes. But I gladly scoop it up with the naan. Meena Gul too eats ravenously, though as soon as she has swallowed the last of her stew she stomps away.

The faster we finish this meal, the faster we can go find Kyra. But when at last the men reemerge from their hut, I can tell by Ismail and Roy's bearing that they've had no more luck than I.

"They don't find it strange that Jorgen hasn't been round," Ismail tells me. "Seems he was often out and about. On call, if you will, with more than one project." I recall Kyra's letter, the computer network for the school in Jalalabad, the village with the fallen drone. I wonder if that village was near here. I wonder if we'll ever find them.

After turns at the toilet—an open dirt culvert behind the settlement—we trudge back to the car, my mind racing to come up with some next step. Our clothes smell of smoke, and my skin is covered in goosebumps and sweat. Dust has collected at the corners of my mouth. Half the day gone, and no lead. Ismail looks especially downcast, with those tear-wrinkles down his cheeks.

"Here you go, Miriam dear." Ismail opens the door to the backseat of the car. I hunch in and cover myself with the robe and pashmina. Roy slides in beside me, and we begin the drive back to Jalalabad.

We've left the village when a checkpoint appears—in a spot where there wasn't any before.

A mere piece of string looped round a tree at one side of the road, pulled taut all the way to the other and tied to a chair. A stocky man sits atop the chair, a rifle resting on his lap. Seeing us, his posture changes. He approaches us.

"Remember," Asim whispers from the driver's seat, "no looking dude on his eyes."

Roy and I keep our heads down. Ismail too sits silently as Asim rolls down the window and answers the man's questions. Paper bills pass from his palm to the man's.

But the questioning continues. Asim is answering politely, calmly, but I can see the tension in his neck.

Under the long wool wrap, I feel a cold bead of sweat run down my side. Next to me, wrapped in his patu blanket, Roy barely seems even to breathe. And then, beneath the many folds of the wrap, a warm hand touches mine. Roy grasps my fingers. His skin is hot. I can feel his pulse. That's how I know he's as scared as I am.

In my peripheral vision, the man continues to pelt Asim with questions. And then, to my horror, he leans in, angling his head toward the backseat.

I stare into my lap, aware of the head poking in. Beneath the many folds of my wrap, I cling to Roy's fingers.

That's when Ismail speaks, his voice confident, chatty. As the guard listens, I allow myself to glance up.

The man has many tiny moles all over his face.

I try to slow my breaths. I'm thinking of Kyra's letter, the man she mentioned.

Whatever Ismail said must have sufficed. The man unties the string and we are allowed to continue on, our car pulling away slowly, as if to hide our relief. Roy lets go of my hand, shifts away.

"I think I know who that was," I say as soon as we're out of earshot, and tell them about the local police chief from Kyra's letter. "She said people thought he was working with the Taliban. Ismail, what did you tell him?"

"I said you were Nuristani, that was why you didn't understand him."

But I'm still thinking about the fact that the man turned up in the first place. Someone told him we were in that village. "He knew to set up that checkpoint. He knew to wait for us."

Roy is nodding grimly. "And if someone snitched on us, someone probably snitched on Jorgen, too."

Someone in that village knows where they went. Or who they're with. But they all kept quiet. An entire village.

Asim says, "Someone has them below his thumb."

"Look," Ismail says, turning to look at us, "you have to understand, these villages are completely separate from the cities—the government, I mean. No matter who's elected or who's in uniform, it's the so-called 'commanders' who run the show. The regional warlords. And the villagers do what's necessary to protect themselves." After a moment, he adds, "It's also possible that the people we spoke to truly didn't have any information for us."

"You know, I wouldn't have even recognized that police chief if I hadn't looked up. Asim, why do you keep telling us not to look anyone in the eye?"

"Very rude to look on his eyes."

198

"Well, and it's also a safety measure," Ismail explains. "A way of assuring people you haven't really seen them. That you couldn't identify them if someone forced you to."

Just like the villagers today, no one knowing anything.

That's when Roy's cell phone pings. We must be back in range of a cell tower. He checks to see if his "guys" have anything to report.

I check my own phone. Nothing from Nolan.

Roy takes a short breath, tells us there's been activity on Kyra's debit card. Online purchases. "As recently as yesterday."

That means she's alive. I realize I'm shouting. "You need a PIN number to use a debit card, right? So she's alive."

Roy's frowning. "Or someone forced her to give them the code."

I ask what the purchases were—if it seems she was the one using it, or someone else.

Roy peers into his phone. "Huh."

"What is it?"

"Cell-phone minutes." He continues scrolling. "For a whole bunch of accounts."

"Then it's been stolen." My heart sinks. I ask if we might at least track the cell phones to their owners, but Ismail shakes his head. "Probably burner phones."

But I'm desperate and suggest we might track the signals to where the phones were last used.

"Yes, they've done that," Roy says, still reading. "Seems they were in . . . Kunar Province."

Ismail says, "Yikes."

"North from here," Asim says. "Many mountains."

That just confuses me. "Cell phones work in the mountains?"

But Roy is still reading. "No, wait, some were here in Nangarhar Province. Others show signals from Kunar."

"The next province," Ismail says. "Northeast of Nangarhar."

"Right." Roy nods. "Says here, *Part of the N2KL region. Tribal area along the Durand Line.*"

"Bordering Pakistan," Ismail explains. "Bit of a Wild West sort of place."

"*Lower Hindu Kush,*" Roy reads. "*Majority Pashtun. Also known as 'Enemy Central' for its many insurgent groups.*"

"Al-Qaeda dudes they live there."

"Yes, it's al-Qaeda's main area of operation," Ismail says. "A comparatively small province but lots of caves and forests and secret crossings. Good for hiding out. So, plenty of drug smugglers and criminals of that sort."

"And Talib dudes," says Asim. "Hezb-e-Islami dudes. Lashkar-e-Taiba dudes. Tehreek-e-Nafaz-e-Shariat-e-Mohammadi dudes—"

"Jesus," I hear myself say. What if those people have killed Kyra and are using her card?

"U.S. Army, too," Asim adds, brightly, as though to make me feel better.

"Actually, I believe the U.S. abandoned their base there," Ismail says. "Kept getting attacked."

"Right," Roy says, still reading from his phone. "*One of the most dangerous provinces in Afghanistan.*"

Who could blame AidNow for not wanting to go to a place like that? I wonder if the village today was on that route. "Why would Jorgen and Kyra ever go there?"

"They wouldn't," Ismail says. "Not by choice."

I have to wonder if she's trying to help somebody. "Maybe she bought all those cell-phone minutes herself. Maybe that's why nobody's claimed to have kidnapped her." Even as I say it, I know I'm tricking myself into some kind of crazy optimism.

Roy says none of this means that she and Jorgen are in Kunar Province. "All we know is that, of the cell phones that were tracked, some seemed to be near cell towers in that region. According to this message, my guys are no longer able to track them."

Probably they've used the phones and tossed them, or removed the batteries. Or just changed the SIM cards so that no one can follow them. I picture Kyra's letters, her handwriting maturing, growing closer in time. "That police chief. If he knew about us from someone in that village, the same thing probably happened to Jorgen and Kyra. And I know you said the men you spoke to had nothing to say, but you didn't even speak to the women."

The more I work myself up, the more I'm convinced that someone in that village can help us. Someone just a little braver than the rest. Or simply defiant.

"Meena Gul," I hear myself say.

"What's that?" Roy asks.

"I think some of the women might be willing to tell us what they know. We just have to try again."

"Meena Gul," Ismail repeats. "Beautiful name. It means Love Flower."

"Flower of love," Asim counters. "Her eyes are much like Fareshta's. But Fareshta is more beautiful."

"Guys," I say, "please. We have to go back to that village."

another try

We decide to wait a bit, to avoid that police chief. This allows Asim and Ismail time for their afternoon prayers, while Roy, as if home on a lunch break rather than on a distant continent, performs the stretches a physical therapist has prescribed for his plantar fasciitis. But I can see in his eyes that he hasn't stopped worrying about Kyra.

Asim and Ismail kneel toward Mecca and recite the appeals they know by heart. I feel ill mannered with no god to pray to. No tradition to follow, just selfish pleas.

By the time we arrive back at the village, daylight has stretched lower, thinner. Even the animals and children appear quiet and still. The ancient toothless men are clearly concerned to see us back so soon. But Asim has come up with an excuse: that we need water for some part of the car that is overheating. The men offer us tea all over again, and we're led out to the well. Again we pass the neglected graveyard, the child-size lumps of earth.

They flew away.

That's when I glimpse Meena Gul. Not far from one of the clay huts, milking an indifferent cow, squirting thin streams of milk into a silver pail. I have Ismail come with me.

When she sees us, Meena Gul gives a start. Eye twitching, she greets me, shifting her gaze away from Ismail. She stands, wiping her hands on her skirt, and covers the pail with a lid.

"I think my friend Kyra is with Jorgen," I tell her, Ismail translating. "I love her and I'm very worried. I think someone told you not to tell us where she and Jorgen have gone."

Meena Gul looks down. She looks furious.

"We won't tell on you. Think of someone you love, think what you would do if that person were missing."

Meena Gul speaks in a rush, so fast Ismail can barely keep up. Something about a man here, Umar, and plans for Jorgen and another aid worker to visit some village. That Umar asked Meena Gul's older brother to watch over his goats and still hasn't been back.

"Which village? Did they tell you where they were going?" I'm wondering if it was that police chief's village. I'm already certain the other aid worker was Kyra.

Meena Gul's words are quick, distraught. It was a place she didn't know, and now she can't remember the name.

I ask where we might find a map. If it lists all the villages in the region, maybe Meena Gul will recognize a name. But Ismail doubts there are any maps out here; the villagers don't know how to read.

Then a voice pipes up. Not far from the well, Farid, the dull-eyed, lopsided boy, is speaking, squatting on his haunches, his baseball cap turned backward on his head. And though I'm worried we've been overheard, Meena Gul is saying something Ismail translates as agreement: Yes, that's the name, what Farid said, that's the place. Farid is her little brother. People think he doesn't know things, but he hears as well as anyone.

Meena Gul's eye is no longer twitching. And whatever she is saying now is delivered in a flat, matter-of-fact voice. "Umar is a good man," Ismail translates. "She doesn't think he would hurt anyone.

But some years ago he lost an infant son in a NATO raid. So he despises foreign troops. It's a sentiment he applies to all foreigners."

I want to believe her. But as we head back to join the others, my head is spinning. He's a good man, I repeat to myself, and think of his infant son. I think of what I would do if anything happened to Sean.

It was just curiosity at first, that day in the county courthouse. "Who's that little kid?" I asked my sister-in-law. "No one seems to be watching him."

"He's still here? Shit." She poked her head out in the hallway. "Sean, where'd your grandma go?"

"She's in the bathroom. She takes a long time."

"All right." She closed the door. "I don't know how much longer that poor woman can keep it up. She's been dying for three years now. Diabetes and hep C. We thought we had a new placement for him, but it fell through."

That was all she said about the boy. But when I left her office and he was no longer in the hallway, I felt a pang. I found myself thinking about him the whole way home.

Nolan and I had considered for some time that we might adopt. Treatment for childhood leukemia had left him sterile, so we knew that if we wanted children, it would take some doing. Not that I wanted very much to be a mother. But Nolan liked kids, and I wanted to make him as happy as he had made me. Because he was the reason I could have the life I had. I didn't need friendships, didn't need parties or a social life, never needed to reach out to anyone, because I had Nolan.

I called my sister-in-law, asked about becoming foster parents. Only after she had explained the process did I mention the boy. "He's the one I was hoping we could take in."

It wasn't quite so simple, she told me. For one thing, his mother was still around, in and out of jail, in and out of rehab. Addicted to methamphetamine—which, by the way, had probably affected her son in the womb. His grandmother tried her best but was often ill, so that Sean had already had a couple of stints with foster families. "Which didn't exactly go well."

I thought about this. "Well, I have to talk to Nolan about it anyway."

But I felt as certain as I had in the other deciding moments in my life. Just as I had felt about Kyra—loving her even before I knew why. And if this hard-headedness was misguided, then oh well. Yes, it was like falling in love: knowing that any exasperation or heartache this boy might cause would never be enough to stop me from loving him.

We leave quickly to reach Jalalabad before dark, making good time on the road. I'm still trying to understand what might have happened between Jorgen, Kyra, and Umar. Ismail is piecing together a timeline.

As the sky stretches into glowing strands of sunset, the men discuss a new plan. I realize I've made a wrong assumption. I didn't think we would be the ones going to this next village. I assumed some official would take it from here. "Enemy Central," I say, as a reminder.

"No, no," Ismail says, "that was just some of those cellphone records. The village Farid named is here in Nangarhar. Northeast of Jalalabad, but south of Kunar. So, yes, we're getting into the tribal zones, but I'm well acquainted with the area. Remember, only certain districts are problematic."

But my courage is waning. I ask if it might be better to hire some of Roy's "guys" to make the trip. "We need to be careful. They hide out there. Insurgents. Taliban."

"It's winter," Ismail says. "Taliban go to cities in winter. They take temporary jobs, wait the season out."

Winter is ending. Faint green bursts are visible on the hills under the setting sun. But Ismail and Roy are already well into their plan. Roy says his guys could fly a helicopter in, if necessary.

Asim, I note, sits quietly, saying nothing. Maybe he'll talk them out of it. But no, he needs the money. The bride-price. He wouldn't have us paying someone else.

What he says, when at last he speaks, is "My family is from there."

I frown at him from my seat in the back. "You said your family was from the south. Your father was a raisin washer."

"My mother, her family, they are from Kunar."

"We aren't going to Kunar," Ismail says. "The village is in Nangarhar."

But Asim continues. "When I was small we went to live with them because in our village was too much fighting. But then their village was bombed and we left."

I ask if he's been back.

"No way, man."

"See," I say. "Even Asim won't go there."

Roy growls, "We're not *going* to *Kunar*."

"Oh but yes, sister, I will go!" A small, pleased smile in the rearview mirror. "We will find this village of yours. We will go find your friends."

He says this so matter-of-factly, with such an easy nod of the head, all I can think is that he must really love that Fareshta. And that Roy must be paying him an awful lot of money.

We're back in Jalalabad by evening. Faint streetlights emerge in the gloaming. Roy and I settle back at the guesthouse, and Ismail and Asim—who are to meet us here at dawn—head off to evening prayers.

Auntie greets us like long-lost family, kissing my cheeks, plying me with her many polite questions. She urges us into the dining room, a handsome room covered in maroon carpets and draped with matching window curtains. There are tables laid with doilies, and a larger table laid for dinner. We're given tin bowls of water to wash our hands, and now here's the husband, pouring the scalding tea while chatting at top speed, he and his wife laughing at jokes we pretend to understand.

For the meal there's lamb stew, rice pilaf, steamed dumplings stuffed with minced meat, hot chewy flatbread, and a big fish with the head still on. But my body is still confused as to the time of day, or I am simply too exhausted to eat. Maybe it's nerves. All I can do is pick at the flatbread and dumplings and some sort of yogurt, forcing myself to eat so as not to insult my hosts. I keep thinking about tomorrow, remind myself that both Ismail and Asim know the region, that Roy's "guys" are here for us, that newspaper stories distort reality, focusing on kidnappings and violence and bad news rather than the everyday motions of daily life.

Roy appears confident as ever. He eats everything—stew, fish, naan—and nods at the proprietors' chitchat, checking his cell phone each time a new message pops up. In small movements of his face I glimpse the bright young man who stood on Grace's front stoop with his bottle of wine and the little cake in its shiny cellophane. Still see the careful way he kissed the top of Kyra's head. Feel the residue of that visit, of realizing who he and Kyra were to each other, long before I knew them.

His arm around her on the porch, pointing out the stars. Whispering to her as she lay on my mattress. A whole past between them, each the other's witness.

And there it is again, that sense of something Roy knew, that Kyra never told me. Some darkness she never felt she could share with me.

But how well can he really know her when, even now, he dismisses her feelings? A *phase* . . . As if she didn't know her own self.

Some experimental, temporary *phase* . . .

"Christ, Mim." Roy puts down his tea. "Now what is it?"

Kyra flitting morosely from one man to the next. So angry that time in the car, shouting at the squeegee man, *When a woman says no, she means no!*

Roy says, "At least stop squinting at me."

I say aloud the thought that must have been forming for some time—that now, because of Roy, has completed itself. "I think someone hurt her." Even as I say it I'm still deciding what I mean. "Maybe a long time ago. Maybe molested her when she was little, I don't know. Abused her in some way. Before I ever met her."

Roy watches me, unmoving, as if afraid to show anything on his face. When he speaks, it's in a humble tone I haven't heard him use before. "The thing is, Mim, I'm not supposed to say anything. She made me swear I wouldn't tell anyone. I couldn't make out whether or not she'd told you."

I can see by the way he rests his mouth against his knuckles that he doesn't like breaking his pact. And yet he seems relieved. "It was her second year of college. She never told me who it was. I think she knew that if she did, I would find him and do something."

"You mean she was raped."

He nods, and I feel myself tearing up.

Roy says, "She couldn't even say the word. She came home for Christmas and was even skinnier than usual. We'd finally gotten together the summer before. I'd assumed she would have her college escapades and after that we would be together. I think she thought so too. But that Christmas she was so strange. I kept asking her what was wrong. At first all she said was that she had gone on a date and it had ended badly. I guessed what that meant. But she blamed herself. Not for what had happened, but that it had taken her so long to admit it to herself. She hadn't reported it, hadn't even told any friends. She thought the way to move on was never to speak of it."

Roy takes a gulp of tea. "Honestly, I think by never talking about it, it just accumulated power. Became this big secret. I've never forgotten something she said when she first told me. She said she'd always thought she knew who she could trust, but now she knew that wasn't true."

From the look on his face, I have no doubt that if he knew who it was, he would strangle him. And I realize something else—that I was wrong to judge him so harshly. That when he made that comment about a "phase," he was probably thinking of this, that it had set Kyra off men, something like that.

"Jesus, Roy, I feel awful."

"Look, it's not your fault."

She was carrying that secret with her all that time.

"Ah, Mim, don't." Roy pulls his chair closer. "It's not like there's anything you could have done." He brushes my wet cheek with his fingers. With his thumb he strokes the tears away.

That's when his phone buzzes. Roy pulls his hand back and we both watch the cell phone vibrating on the table. For a split second it seems it must be Kyra, that she's heard us discussing her secret and is calling to say how angry she is.

Roy shifts away from me to read the number. His cheeks are flushed and he keeps his eyes from me, but already I see from his expression that this call is nothing to do with Kyra. "And here we go again." He sighs, leans back in his chair, answers the phone. "Hello, Sandrine."

I wipe the remaining tears from my cheeks. But I feel ridiculous, sitting here doing nothing. My phone is silent.

While Roy mutters in low tones to Sandrine, I look into my empty teacup, as if there might be some message there for me.

checkpoints

In the predawn morning, voices call out from the corners of the sky.

The electricity is out again, so I dress in the dark: thermal leggings, a long-sleeved undershirt, travel pants, and a baggy hemp tunic-dress. I grab my fleece jacket, harness my backpack, and head to the courtyard to wait for Roy.

It's been raining, and the wet air shimmers. Pleasant to sit under the canopy drinking my tea, reading my guidebook. When Auntie brings the breakfast, I make myself eat despite my nerves, and read more about Nangarhar Province, about the Kunar River, which begins in Pakistan and flows through Afghanistan roughly parallel to the Pakistan border before emptying into the Kabul River here in Jalalabad. I remind myself that we're simply going to a village northeast of here. At most thirty miles away. Roy's "guys" have given the okay. And Kyra and Jorgen might be there right now.

Roy still hasn't emerged. I check my watch. And though I know how pointless it is, I check my phone again.

The thing is, Nolan has always been the silent type. Not that it ever bothered me. Rarely have I felt the need to complain. Not the prideful public grumblings of so many wives, flaunting petty gripes along with their wedding bands and anniversary jewels. That kind of self-satisfied spousal complaining has never appealed to me.

And why is that, our counselor would ask. The same counselor every couple in our county sees. An eminently reasonable woman. *Why, Mim, don't you feel entitled to complain?*

Because Nolan is the one who allowed me this life, our quiet contentment in the house on the hill. I guess I never quite realized how I used him to build another island. He made me a wife, not just some strange woman living alone in the woods, and then Sean turned me into a mother. And still there are moments when I feel I don't deserve it—this life, this family. That at some point it will all surely crumble.

Perhaps now it has.

A gauzy rising sun is visible through the mist. I check my watch again and head back inside to knock on Roy's door. It's a relief to hear him fumbling with the padlock.

But when the door opens, Roy is pale and sweaty, the room thick with a rancid smell. "I'm sick," he says. "The fish." He flops dramatically back down on his bed. "Vomiting all night."

My heart starts thrumming. I ask if I should find a doctor.

"No, I've got medicine. But I can't go today. I can barely sit up." Before I can respond, he adds, "I don't think you should wait. Don't worry about me."

"I thought we were doing this together." Even as I see clearly how ill he is, some part of me wishes I too had an excuse not to go. "How do I know you'll be all right here on your own?"

"Just have the innkeepers check in on me. I'll text you." He waves me weakly away.

But I'm frightened and don't want to leave without him. It's one thing to have to rely on people one has just met; it is another to be the lone American.

All I can think to do is remind him to keep hydrated. I open one of his water bottles on the bedside table.

"Sorry to let you down, Mim."

"You're not letting me down. I'm just worried."

"Listen, my guys are working 24–7 behind the scenes. They have your back. I'll make sure they have your number and you have theirs."

"Okay." But I'm scared.

I shut the door, make my way down the dark hallway. This, I try to tell myself, is why I'm here. This is what I came to do.

Those letters in my backpack: Kyra sent them to *me*.

She called to me, and I came.

Ismail is waiting in the courtyard, the long wrinkles of his face looking somehow sadder. "Everything all right, Miriam dear? You look distraught."

I send him to check on Roy, as if he might somehow produce a better outcome. Then I tear open my bag and grab the packet of letters, scanning, searching, catching scraps of text that aren't the piece I'm looking for.

There's a newborn baby in the camp, they've named him Dakov. His mother is completely traumatized & her milk won't come in. Russian tanks shot at their Lada on the way here, she's still in a state of terror. So we're feeding the baby sugar water but he knows something is wrong. He just wails & wails.

Dad left most of his money to his wife Monica (a year younger than me!) but he gave me all his Exxon stock. I'll have to get rid of it when I'm home on break.

So my mom has Parkinson's disease. Remember how she was always eating ice cream? Turns out that craving is

212

one of the signs. Roy checks in on her for me. He lives in Providence, works for some company. You know, "Wealth Management." He & Sandrine have two little girls.

April always makes me remember. I'd never felt such happiness. Like flying.

"He'll live." Ismail is back, and I shove the wad of letters back into my pack. "Though he needs to stay put, that's for certain."

Asim has arrived and, informed of Roy's condition, heads inside to see for himself. Ismail doesn't appear to notice this small tussle for authority. "As for you, dear, I've brought you this." He takes up a bundle of fabric from one of the plastic chairs: a burqa, of thin nylon. "For the ride," Ismail says. "There could be multiple checkpoints. And as you know, it can be dangerous for Asim to be seen with us."

By "us" he means me. In his dirty wool pakol cap, with his sunbrowned skin, loose Afghan garments, and the patu blanket around his shoulders, Ismail could be a village warlord.

I ask him if we still need Asim to make the trip. After all, Ismail knows the land, and speaks both Dari and Pashto. "Does he really want to do this?" The money Roy is paying makes me feel complicit—that we're causing Asim to do things he wouldn't otherwise agree to.

"Could help us out to have a Pashtun with us," Ismail says. "And he has family nearby."

"Had."

And now here's Asim again, having confirmed for himself Roy's illness. Instead of his usual zippered gym jacket and denim jeans, he has transformed himself, with cargo pants, a pakol cap like Ismail's, a tunic with long, cuffed sleeves, a vest with many pockets, and the same fringed Afghan scarf round his neck. He still wears the fake rubber sneakers.

Ismail holds out the burqa to me, the shiny blue fabric limp in his hands. This is the first I've seen one up close, the embroidered cap at the top and the many pleats of fabric below. "Just for the road," Ismail says. "Can't have folks knowing you're *amrican*."

Asim nods. "Also, you walk wrong."

I stare at him.

"Like a dude. Too fast. You make long steps, and you stand too straight, your head is too high." He points at me. "See, no standing with legs apart like a dude. No standing with hands on hips."

I'm standing like this because I'm annoyed.

"Keep shoulders down. Keep head down."

Ismail agrees. "Best to play it safe."

"No loud talking," Asim says. "No moving hands around."

So, I'm to shuffle around in a burqa. I want to tell them both to screw off—but I take the thing from Ismail.

"No leaning forward when speaking. No looking up. No—"

"Is that what your girlfriend Fareshta is like?" I can't help asking. "Head down, soft voice?"

Asim laughs. "No way, man. She is a teacher—she is the boss!"

I pull the fabric over my head, tugging the embroidered cap onto my scalp, and attempt to arrange the crocheted section of little holes over my eyes and nose. It's a very small strip of holes. Not like the netting on some of those I saw in town. Yet to my surprise I'm not unable to see.

"Can you help me with this?" My voice seems closer, and my breath settles on my chin.

"What can I do for you, Miriam dear?"

"Help me put it on."

"It's on," Ismail says. "Good work."

But the fabric is man-made and doesn't breathe. The mesh creates lines and shadows, as if I'm peeking through a woven basket. "I don't think it's on right." The cap keeps riding up on my hair, and

I can't find any armholes or slits for my hands. With each breath, I suck fabric into my mouth.

Ismail gives the fabric a tug, and the garment is fully on. To my surprise, it reaches to my ankles; I've been given the least accommodating of styles—same length all around, and no flap to lift up from the face.

I shake my head, but the cap shifts on my hair and the mesh moves back and forth, obscuring my vision. "What about my backpack? How am I going to carry it?" I've conscientiously filled it with emergency supplies: painkillers, electrolytes, water-purification tablets.

Ismail says my pack is clearly American and will give us away. He has an old sheet and wraps it around the pack, so that it becomes a sort of cotton carpetbag.

"I will carry it," Asim says. With the cloth bundle, and the big scar across his face, and the pakol cap, he looks like a weary mujahideen.

"All right, then," Ismail says. "We're off."

I immediately stumble. Asim says, "No walking like a dude."

The trouble isn't the hem. It's the bars across my eyes and the fabric hanging before my face. Without peripheral vision, I have to bow my head to see where I am stepping, and with my hands restricted underneath the fabric, I'm oddly off-kilter.

I give up trying to walk with my usual stride. Grabbing the folds of fabric from inside, I shuffle along the wet ground, glad if my slowness means Ismail and Asim will have to wait.

This time we travel in Ismail's four-wheel-drive station wagon, which is in better shape than Asim's Toyota. I plug in my cell-phone charger, in case Nolan or Roy checks in.

It has begun to drizzle again, and traffic is already heavy on our way out. At first the road is smooth, but soon enough it seems to have deteriorated. We plunk along behind cars and motorcycles and colorful pin-striped trucks. The trucks are packed high and covered with tinkling bells. They jingle as they bump along, and spout black plumes into the air.

The diesel fumes leak into our car—but the fabric of the burqa acts as a shield. In fact, I find my anonymity a comfort. Yet I soon feel ill from the hairpin curves, nauseated each time we round a mountain bend. Through the crisscross of the tiny holes I search the brown landscape for something stabilizing, and fix my gaze on mountains in which are hidden, I suppose, bandits, al-Qaeda, Haqqani, who knows.

Soon the rain has stopped, and the sun sends bright streaks through the clouds. Already the air is warmer, though the road feels wet and gritty. And then we see, a good distance ahead of us, paused at the side of the road, a military convoy—a group of servicemen standing around. Not Afghans. Even from here it's clear from their size and posture that they are American. Bigger bones, broader chests in their pebbled camouflage, with matching brimmed hats.

This isn't a checkpoint; the soldiers must be en route and have stopped for some other reason. Already Asim has stopped the car, though we are nowhere near the vehicles. Ismail says, "Look, Miriam dear, your compatriots."

"Our foreign guests," says Asim, opening his window. Even at this distance I can see, atop one of the vehicles, a massive machine gun pointed at us.

I try to keep calm. Two of the soldiers, guns raised, are coming forward. Ismail has rolled down his window and holds up his hands, calling out, "Hallo there."

Asim too shows his empty hands. Under the burqa, mine have gone cold and clammy.

The soldiers are close enough now that I see they are mere boys. Late teens, early twenties at most. Sean's age, with short trim beards. One boy is freckled and the other looks maybe Latino. Tense, at the ready. Even through the crosshatch of the burqa I see how scared they are. Beads of sweat roll down the white boy's face. The tan one's jaw is clamped tight, his hands visibly trembling.

"Is it possible to pass?" Ismail asks. I'm hoping his British accent will help.

"Could you open the trunk for us, please?" the tan boy asks. Even his voice is shaking.

Ismail obliges, stepping out of the car and popping the hatchback, apparently revealing various tools and jugs of water and who knows what else. As he reassures the boys, I peer through my crosshatch at the other servicemen. And see that one of them is a woman.

Smaller, slighter, with a desert-camouflage headscarf instead of a hat. She wears sporty sunglasses and is holding a clipboard. I want badly, suddenly, to call out to her, to tell her I'm here too. But my job is to sit quietly and not make trouble.

When we're given the okay, the boy with the trembling hands nods and wishes us well. Asim restarts the engine, grins, and holds his fingers up in a *V*. The army boys laugh but still look nervous. I wonder how many of them will make it home. Which of them will laugh like they used to, and which will laugh the way Carl did, that low apologetic cough that wasn't really a laugh at all.

As we drive away I turn to look back and find the girl in her pebbled headscarf. I readjust the burqa's netting to watch as the girl and her comrades recede from view.

Those machine guns were pointed right at us. No matter how young or frightened the convoy was, I can't help thinking of that man Umar, his child killed in a NATO raid. I wonder how many times Asim has had a tank's machine gun pointed at him.

But when I ask him his thoughts about the soldiers, Asim says, "I like them."

"You don't have to say so for my sake."

Asim says, "I like their names. Mike! John! Rob! Very easy."

I laugh, my breath hot under the fabric.

Asim is nodding. "Americans," he says, "you are peacekeepers." Glancing at me in the rearview mirror. "Afghans, we are warriors."

The next roadblock is run by the Afghan military. They wear desert camouflage similar to the Americans but are smaller and leaner, with neat black moustaches. A long line of vehicles is waiting to cross. Some men are being made to step out of their cars so that they can be patted down.

Under the burqa I feel like an imposter. I'm scared and wish Roy were here to hold my hand. But by the time the mustached guard turns his attention to us, he's behind schedule and quickly waves us through.

We turn off the main road and watch the colorful trucks head away from us, toward Pakistan. As our car climbs higher, my ears begin to pop. The ground under our wheels feels muddy and slick, and through the shadowy bars of the burqa, I see a white fringe of snow at the side of the road. We pass another burned-up, blasted oil tanker. I ask who they think did that.

"Either some insurgent group," Ismail says, "or just locals who got fed up."

Just like with Kyra and Jorgen, whomever they've gone off with. Could be anybody.

"Maybe Taliban," Asim says.

"Or some offshoot," Ismail adds.

I think about this. "I thought the surge routed the Taliban. That they weren't much of a force anymore." My voice still sounds strange to me under the fabric.

"Depends on, like, the region."

"The province. The village." Ismail is nodding.

I know that, of course. What I'm really asking for is reassurance.

"Remember, Miriam dear, out in these villages it's the headmen, not the central government, who run the show. Local so-called commanders." Warlords, he means. "They raise their own taxes, have their own militias, their own pacts with each other. And when they're strong enough, the Taliban don't have the power to do much."

"Taliban, warlords," Asim says. "Two ears of the same donkey."

"But when villages are self-sufficient," Ismail says, "when they have water and food and schools and people to defend them, they don't need the Taliban or anyone else. They can band together and protect themselves."

"But they are always afraid," Asim says. "Always there is danger."

Ismail says, "Well, yes—"

"They are yellow with worry."

"Well now that's a bit dramatic."

"They tremble in their sandals."

I can never quite tell if he's teasing or serious. To make him stop, I say, "All I meant was that in the newspapers it seems things have quieted down. That there aren't so many Taliban now."

"Yes," Asim says, "but they are only waiting."

I ask what he means. When he doesn't answer, I lean forward, the burqa pulling against my forehead. "Asim, what are they waiting for?"

He takes his time before answering. "For our American guests to go home."

We pass two more Afghan checkpoints. The first is a plywood shack with a thatched roof, the next a hut propped up by sandbags in the middle of the road. Both are manned by stoned-looking boys barely past their teens. But they give us no trouble, and we seem to be making good time, though there's more snow now, thick banks of it, and the road feels icy in patches. Ahead of us, a car slips and spins off the road. We do not stop to help.

"We do not know who they are," Asim explains.

I look back to see a man stepping out, examining the damage. I feel bad leaving him there. If I were stuck, I would want someone to help me.

We turn up a steep incline and nose our way into the mountains, over ruts and frost heaves, past a line of men shoveling snow. Quite soon ours is the only automobile in sight. Even from under the burqa I sense how high we're climbing.

I tell myself I'm not really, truly afraid of heights. That I haven't, in coming here, made a colossal mistake.

"Please lean to right side," Asim says as we near a short stretch where a cliff-side portion of the road appears to be, quite simply, missing.

"Asim, no, please—"

"Now!"

We lean all our weight to the right, Asim speeding ahead with, it seems, just two of the car's wheels on the ground, the other two suspended, momentarily, in the air. With a heavy clunk, we land back on four wheels.

When my voice has climbed back up from the lower depths of my stomach, I manage to speak. "Never. Do. That. Again."

Asim affects not to have heard me. After a few minutes he begins asking questions.

"What does it mean 'revved up like a deuce'?"

"What is a 'freeze out'?"

"What is 'looking for some tush'?"

When the road has wizened down to something more like a trail, he says we are nearly there. I suspect what he really means is what Ismail points out: "Car probably can't go much farther. Higher up the roads just sort of disappear."

And sure enough, within minutes the road has petered out. We find ourselves at a small valley, more like a rut with a high wall blocking any view of the village behind it. Puffs of dark smoke float up from the hidden houses. Kyra and Jorgen, too, might be hidden there.

I remove the burqa, replacing it with my wool pashmina, glad for the warmth now that the temperature has dropped. Ismail pulls a woolen vest over his sweater and tunic. Asim manages to look perfectly comfortable as we all step out of the car and begin walking.

Gone are the balmy breezes of Jalalabad. The air nips at us. The ground is hard where patches of ice haven't yet melted.

At the high wall we wait before a big metal gate. It opens to display five men in long padded coats. They look to be Ismail's age, perhaps older. Behind them stands a phalanx of teenage girls, each girl holding a rifle.

The girls wear payraan tumbaan and rubber clogs, their headscarves draped loosely round their hair. I can't help staring at their rifles, while the men whittle their way through the introductions. They seem to know already who Ismail is, which I find reassuring. Then there's some sort of negotiation with the village mullah, a scraggly man in a knit skullcap. Each time the wind blows, his robes flap round his body like a flag on a pole. All the while, the girls with guns stand guard.

A dozen or so little children have flocked over, with probing eyes and nut-brown hair. Quite a difference from the unsmiling girls with their guns. No adolescent boys, just these girls—or young women, I suppose—keeping guard instead.

The men and boys must have gone off to make a living. Or to fight.

The girls are thin, with ink-black eyes. I can see them surreptitiously inspecting me, their gaze barely moving, taking in my clothing, my shoes, my face. When I catch one girl's eye and smile at her, dimples emerge on her cheeks; just as quickly the dimples disappear.

Since it is time for noon prayers, half of the regiment escorts Asim and Ismail with the men to the brush-and-mud shack that is the village mosque, while the children flutter around me, discovering that I really, truly have no gifts for them. I feel useless and stupid, and angry at Roy for falling ill, though of course it isn't his fault. I'd still be abandoned even if he were here. He would be with the men, and I would be alone with these gun-toting girls.

With their guns slung low in their hands, they usher me into a smoky hut where ten or so women stop their work to observe me. Half of the room is lit by a tunnel of light from the window, the rest in shadow. With no chimney for the clay stove, smoke swims above our heads. I hear the word "amrican" while my eyes adjust, and I take a seat on a cushion. Though the floor is covered in felt, with carpets splayed on top, I still feel how cold the ground is underneath, as the logs crackle and hiss, and the women return to their cooking, and I sip my tea and eat the raisins, dried figs, and almonds they offer me.

When we rejoin the men outside, the temperature has warmed, and the ground is dotted with flat, muddy puddles where the patches of ice have melted. The men's faces shine under the noonday sun. "It appears," Ismail tells me, "that Jorgen and Kyra have indeed been here. Twice. The first time seems to have been around that same day Kyra left her headquarters. They arrived with four men, one of whom is from the next village over."

"'Arrived with' as in of their own free will?"

Ismail is stoic. "No one has said otherwise." I can't tell from his face if he believes that. "The important information is that the group wished to stay here for a few days—but the mullah didn't want trouble and made them leave."

"Two foreigners is much trouble," Asim says, the irony of which is not lost on me.

Ismail says, "Doesn't take long for others to find out if Westerners are around. So the mullah sent them packing. The strange thing is that they came back."

"Six days ago," Asim says.

That recently! "But why would they come back, if they weren't welcome?"

Ismail says, "Apparently they had run out of supplies. Stopped by to 'refuel,' as it were, before heading off again."

"Into the mountains," Asim says. "Upon horseback."

"There's a village higher up," Ismail explains. "Not far from here, but horses have an easier time than we do on some of those trails. As for the men they're with, the mullah says the one from nearby isn't a bad person but that he's sometimes involved with some shady characters. Petty criminals. Not cruel, just out to make a quick buck, so to speak."

"So then it's possible he was"—what, exactly? "Paid to bring in some Westerners with credit cards?"

"Could be. The young men here have so few options. Most have gone off and joined the regional police or—other forces. But these gentlemen here tell me the fellow they know wouldn't hurt a fly. Couldn't, actually. Seems he has a birth defect. 'Flipper arms' they're calling it. Something like that. Only the other men were able-bodied."

But they must have used some kind of threat or force. If Kyra went with them of her own free will, surely she would have apprised her coworkers, rather than setting off this manhunt.

Ismail says the fact that they came back round and then set off in a new direction makes him suspect they have no concrete plan. "Or had to change plans. If they're criminals, they seem to be amateurs. My worry is that they might try to connect with some other group."

"Haqqani dudes," Asim suggests. "Or Talib dudes. Or HIG dudes."

"Either way," Ismail says, "we can get to them first. The mullah has arranged for one of his people to take us up. Rafiq here." He nods toward a stalk of a man with a rifle slung casually over his

223

shoulder. High cheekbones, a haughty nose, a neat short beard with sideburns, and one eye scarred shut. The other eye is a bright green.

The man could be thirty or he could be fifty. Hard to tell with the sideburns and beard. Despite the lines on his face, his hair is still dark. He wears the loose-fitting tunic and pants with a thick fleece vest, beige socks, and rubber moccasins. And a belt with bullets.

Asim says, "Rafiq he knows all the headmen."

Under his breath, Ismail says, "He's fought on multiple sides, if you see what I mean."

I look at Rafiq, and at the rifle, while Rafiq asks Asim something that produces a long answer.

Is this it, then, where I make some fatal decision—or where I give up and leave these men? As if that's even an option. Clearly I wouldn't be allowed to stay in this village. I suppose the fatal choice was one I made a long time ago.

The men converse, Asim at ease in his own tongue. I tell myself this man, Rafiq, will protect us. To Ismail I whisper, "You're saying he was Taliban?"

"People do what is politically necessary. And then the regime changes, and the people change too. Basic self-preservation. It's not always a matter of principle."

"And the gun is just for show, right?" I try to laugh. But now the man is looking at me as if I've done something wrong. He speaks gravely, and another conversation ensues. Whatever it is, the men quickly come to some kind of agreement.

Asim grins at me and says, "You will go as a dude."

"You'll blend in better that way," Ismail explains. "It will simplify things."

Asim nods. "Since you already walk like one."

big guns

Ismail wraps my turban for me. The cloth is very wide and long; he folds it multiple times to make it narrow enough. I pull on a small white snug-fitting cap, and then the fabric is wound crosswise around the cap and my head.

Over my thermal leggings, the baggy pants are loose at my hips, cinched at the waist with a cord I tie in a tight knot. Unlike the women's pantaloons, these taper toward my ankles. The fabric, crisp from being air-dried, has a wonderful wood-smoke smell, the long brown tunic hanging over my silk undershirt and past my knees. To complete the picture, Asim has me practice crouching down on the backs of my heels "like an Afghan"—a deep squat, my buttocks hovering above the ground. He seems to find my efforts amusing, though I suspect his laughter is also a cover for nerves.

"You mustn't speak if we meet anyone," Ismail tells me. "Our story is that you're a deaf-mute."

Oh, come on. "Ismail, this isn't some children's game. I can't play dress-up and pretend I'm deaf, *and* an Afghan, *and* a man, and everyone will just go along and believe us."

"Miriam dear, if we had a mirror, I would show you how convincing you look. Like a young man from the village." He must have tossed the "young" in to flatter me. Though I suppose it makes sense, in this land where even the young look weary. Rafiq, too, has deep creases at the tops of his cheeks, and lines fanning from his good eye.

All right, then. I'm about to say it aloud but nod, silent, practicing my new role.

Rather than horses, we're each given a donkey. Thick folded cloth tied on as saddles, and the reins are grubby pieces of string. The men's donkeys are brown, while mine is tan and looks incredibly bored, even as I haul myself awkwardly on top.

Rafiq has lit a smelly cigarette and looks as jaded as his donkey. Now that we're all settled, he holds out the cigarette pack to the rest of us—even me, as if I really am a man like him. I can't tell if he's offended that none of us takes one.

We amble toward the path. When I ask in a whisper where exactly we're headed, Ismail points east.

"Then why are we going in the opposite direction?"

"Just to exit the village. Rafiq says we had better avoid that first hill."

I refrain from asking who or what might be behind that first hill. I'd rather not know.

And so we ride into the crumpled brown mountains. Rafiq leads the file, with his smelly cigarette, then Ismail, his legs too long for his donkey, feet dragging on the ground. Then me, with Asim protectively behind me.

I pretend to myself that I've come here on a quick day hike. Try to think of it as a mere nature walk. But as the trail narrows and the slopes become steeper, my pulse starts to rush. Hard not to acknowledge the heights to which our donkeys might climb. Ahead, the trail spirals up into the cliffside. I keep my gaze cast down at the ground, where the donkey's hooves nick the earth, kicking up dirt and pine needles, rustling up a piney scent. That's how I come to see, among the hoof-blows, footprints.

Boot treads. Ones with good soles. Not the plastic sandals or rubber flip-flops everyone wears. I want to say something but am afraid to speak. I wait until we've paused at a fast-moving brook, the donkeys lapping up the cold, chuckling water. "Did you see the footprints?"

"I did," Ismail says. "Could be theirs, if they were taking turns on their horses. Of course other people use these trails too. But those treads looked like good boots."

Yet we encounter no one for an hour or so, until, as if out of nowhere, a pubescent boy emerges on the trail, stopping to exchange the requisite salaams before passing us. He is fair, with pale skin, blue eyes, and light-brown hair. I worry he might notice I'm not what I seem, but he doesn't seem to find us out of the ordinary, and heads on.

Our silent march sets my mind in a loop. I find myself thinking about what Roy told me last night. About what happened to Kyra. No wonder he could so easily discount her feelings for me. To him that time in her life was just a phase. A temporary aversion to men.

Maybe it was. What kind of love is that?

I must have sensed that truth even then. What to me was a grand love affair was nothing Kyra could sustain. That must be why I left.

But then why did she write those letters? Whom did she think she was writing to?

Not me, but the memory of me.

You're doing it again, the couples' counselor would say. *Making up stories about people.* That's what she called it, when Nolan and I were seeing her and I would claim to know what he must be thinking. She considered it a bad habit. *Writing your own version of reality.* But I don't know that my version is necessarily wrong.

The problem, she would say, *is that you believe it either way.*

I try to move past the thoughts, but they swirl back like snow. And though we haven't ridden long, I've developed a bad headache. "Probably the altitude," Ismail says. "You're not acclimated."

I ask for the backpack, to find the aspirin, when we stop to rest the donkeys. Rafiq lights another foul-smelling cigarette. I swallow two tablets of aspirin, my head throbbing, and feel, quite suddenly, despondent.

"There's a hill up over there," Ismail says. "I'm going to run up to see if I can catch a cell-phone signal."

"All the way out here?"

"The higher the mountain, the better"—though soon, he adds, we may be too far out to find any service anywhere. "Better try now, in case Roy has more information."

"If Roy's even still alive," I say, feeling hopeless.

Asim, always agreeable, says, "Yes, he was looking rather ill."

Ismail heads up the hill, becoming a small impression in the distance. It occurs to me that he could be calling anyone, really.

Rafiq smokes his cigarette, slowly, regally. Asim gulps water. "Good for me to take exercise. Fareshta will like me to be strong." He jokingly flexes his bicep, perhaps in an effort to cheer me, but my head hurts too much to laugh. Still, some distant part of me remembers what that kind of joy feels like. Being young and in love.

The way I felt with Nolan, finally doing this thing so many people manage to do.

Kyra, on the bench facing the ocean, telling me I was as brave as she was.

But I wasn't brave at all.

Ismail's back. He says Roy is recovering. There's been no new information on his end, but Ismail has updated him on ours.

Asim gives the thumbs-up signal, and I try to feel hopeful. Tell myself we aren't far behind Kyra and Jorgen. We remount our bored donkeys, and Ismail turns to me, twisting an imaginary lock and key over his lips.

Quite soon we spot a village slatted into the mountainside. Flat adobe dwellings, one atop the other, like lime scales clinging to rock.

They seem to defy gravity. And as we draw closer I see, clearly, wandering in and out of the houses, chickens and bedraggled goats. Even a big black hairy yak. It's like watching a strange and beautiful dream.

On a shelf of land higher up, a few sheep are being herded into caves. For a moment I'm so taken with the sight, I forget to wonder if Kyra and Jorgen are there. I forget to worry. But the shepherd must wonder who we are.

"Rafiq he knows the headman," Asim reassures me. I want to ask how exactly that works, how many villagers know people in other villages, especially in these remote places. I wonder if it has to do with what my guidebook says, that most villages are extended families of clans that go back generations.

The afternoon sun is strong, and when we at last dismount, our donkeys' bodies shimmer with sweat. For a moment it feels strange to walk again.

The village headman is a sharp-featured man in billowy pants and a tunic down to his knees. He carries a big gun. Though I keep waiting for him to notice my woman's hands and beardless chin, he doesn't appear to find me strange. In fact, he barely looks at me. Rafiq must have told him there's something wrong with me. Or maybe I really do look like a boy.

Other men have joined him now, some quite old, some younger. Lean faces. I search their eyes for some clue, some expression that will tell me we are in the right place. They wear muted colors, topped with patu blankets and pakol caps. A number of them carry massive guns, either strapped across their chests or at the ready in their hands.

Where I live, out in the country, there are plenty of guns, to scare coyotes away from chickens and dogs, to kill deer and pheasants, to protect the homestead. But this is the first I'm seeing a machine gun close up. I can't stop looking, even as we head into a mud-clay guesthouse and are served tea so hot the oldest men pour it from their cups into their saucers and slurp it from there.

Only after we have been fed a stringy meat stew and follow the men back out into the daylight do I understand that they have seen our friends. The headman points straight up, to high slopes etched with yak trails.

It's clear to me what this will mean: turning off the main trail onto a narrower path, needling our way through the mountain gorges, switchbacking up and up. I look at Asim and his rubber sneakers and tell myself he won't want to do it.

But he doesn't appear concerned. Nor does Ismail, though he must sense my unease.

I don't dare tell him that it's vertigo, as much as anything else, that concerns me.

Walking me well out of earshot, Ismail tries to reassure me. "There's a place they went to camp out, just a little farther up the mountain. Rafiq knows the mountain well. He knows where to go. We still have some hours of daylight. I have my compass. And you're strong."

But suddenly the entire enterprise seems preposterous. Like a schoolboy fantasy—me in my lame disguise, and Asim in his sneaker-galoshes, and Rafiq with his missing eye. He and Asim have lit their cigarettes, calmly smoking as if this trip is a mere pleasure jaunt, some weekend excursion. While I hardly know where I am.

Canteens are filled and strapped to our backs, patu blankets laid over our shoulders. Into our pack we load naan and little sacks of grains and dried fruit and nuts. One bag of provisions for all of us, as if this walk really will be simple. But I can't stop looking at Rafiq and his gun.

Just one more fact of life in a strafed country. Always on guard, never knowing whom to trust. Isn't that why towns huddle behind high walls, why a man's standing as friend or enemy depends on the type of hat he wears? Declaring oneself by tribe, by clan. Not so different from the U.S., I suppose, with our flags and bumper stickers and T-shirts.

It must bring an inner clarity, always knowing exactly who you are.

foothills of the hindu kush

It's decided we'll leave the donkeys here—can't risk a noisy animal announcing our arrival. So we leave on foot, a steady climb up paths I'm not even sure are trails.

The earth no longer feels packed down by travel; few people must use this route. Yet this is the way Rafiq has chosen for us, cutting across a shape-shifting terrain of boulders and gullies and copses smelling of spruce. My skin is really dry now, cracks of blood at my knuckles, dust trapped in the cracks and under my nails. The altitude makes every step a labor. I try to inhale slowly, as if that might help me take in more oxygen. Sometimes, catching my breath, I hear a sobbing sound.

Other times the mountain flattens out and my lungs rest from their exertion. We pass rushing brooks, and caves along the cliffs. A landscape of fairy tales—of magic forests, billy goats, ogres. Bin Laden might have hidden in these caves, or somewhere just like this, before he shuffled across the border to his fate.

I try to keep my gaze trained on the uneven ground, each step careful, exact. My nerves are beginning to get the better of me. I try to pretend this is nothing, there is no five-thousand-foot drop below. Retreat into my mind, round and round, endless verses of some interminable hymn. I'm not sure how much time has passed when I hear, beyond my circling thoughts, a humming sound.

The plane carves slow circles in the air. Fifteen, twenty thousand feet up in the sky. Ismail stops to view it through his field glasses. He passes them to Asim, who has a look and hands them to me.

The plane is unmanned, with struts and flaps sticking out like limbs. It looks like some mechanical space insect and seems to be hovering in a holding pattern, emitting a flat buzzing sound.

"Kyra saw these." I hold the field glasses out to Rafiq, but he shakes his head.

Ismail says, "Lots of drones out this way. U.S. keeping an eye on the Arab Afghans. And all the Taliban recruits coming in from Pakistan."

"Then they can see us too." Could be watching us right this minute. The plane surely has thermal cameras.

Asim says, "I never can understand. They see every small thing, how can they not find the Taliban?"

Ismail sighs.

"U.S.A. has satellites, they have night goggles, they have helmets. They have boots! Talib dudes they are wearing sandals. U.S.A. dudes are in helicopters, they are in tanks. Talib dudes their truck is always breaking. Their guns are older than me. U.S.A. dudes they have new guns. They have wires coming from their pockets."

They have nightmares and cold sweats. Mysterious syndromes and permanent brain injuries. No flak jackets or headlamps or night-vision goggles prevent any of that. Of course back when Carl was still alive we didn't know about those things. All we knew was that he didn't like to be in crowds, that in his sleep he saw dead Iraqis, that he woke grappling with the sheets, searching for his rifle. That his ears heard a constant ringing no doctors' tests could confirm.

And still Kyra and I thought *we* were the reason he did what he did. Put an end to it all with a gun. As if we mattered, more than the cold sweats and night terrors and hands that wouldn't stop shaking. We were so stupid. So self-centered, to think we had that kind of power.

Asim has stopped on the trail. "And why do they walk like that?" He hunches his shoulders, shifts his jaw out, lifts his arms out just slightly to the side, legs apart, as if puffed with invisible muscles. With each slow step, his shoulders seem to roll forward, arms never touching his sides. "Are they hurt? What is hurting them?"

He isn't joking. He looks truly perplexed. But how can I give a speech on American masculinity when I'm not to speak, when I have barely enough oxygen to breath. And what do I know, really. The only soldier I ever knew was Carl.

In just a short time my fatigue and nausea have worsened. Asim too seems short of breath. Yet the moment I stop moving, I feel almost normal.

We rest at a clearing before a glimmering lake. According to Rafiq we're nearly there. The slanting sun is strong here above the tree line. The lake quivers in the mountain air. Though my skin is cool to the touch, my brow is moist, and sweat has pooled in the shallow cleft at the center of my bra. Even my hands are sweaty, knuckles stinging where the skin has cracked. My lips too feel parched. When I lick them I taste salt.

Ismail removes the pack for a break, and Asim and Rafiq light cigarettes. Rafiq stretches his arms, wipes his forehead with the end of his turban. Veins pulse across the muscles of his hands. His beard glistens from sweat. In the sunshine his good eye is brighter, a sparkling green.

Ismail tells me what they're discussing. "Rafiq's daughter is addicted to opium. She's been stealing from her husband, selling off his belongings, so her husband sent her back home."

I tell Rafiq I'm sorry about his daughter. "Addiction's a problem in my village, too. Crystal meth. My son's mother died from it." I don't mention the selfish relief I felt knowing she was gone for good.

Ismail translates this for Rafiq, who says that methamphetamine is a problem here too. Leaning closer, forearms on thighs, he tells me about his family: three sons and two daughters. I keep expecting Ismail to join in, but he just translates for the two of us, never speaking of his own life.

I ask if Rafiq was born in the village where we met him, and if his parents are still alive. But Rafiq is not sure where he was born or exactly how old he is.

When they've finished their cigarettes, the men go down to the water to wash for afternoon prayers. I follow them there, to where the water's edge is lacy with ice. The lake looks like something in a movie, its shimmying surface a dark quivering mirror. That's how I glimpse myself—this odd new version of myself—in turban and tunic and loose pants. The baggy clothes make me look skinny, curveless, and for a moment I'm reminded of our neighbor Jorie back home, her slender, androgynous look. With the water blurring my wrinkles, I see in my reflection a lanky boy of twenty. Just like Ismail said.

The men complete their ritual and tug their shoes back on, and we head back onto the trail. But the moment we resume our march, I feel sick again. Soon my headache has returned, and even my eyes ache. My entire body feels strange. I have to breathe very deeply to catch enough air.

Ismail signals to us. Footsteps, coming toward us.

Where the trail curves into a shadow of the mountain, a form becomes visible. A large, humped, slow-moving creature. Some kind of hunchback, advancing with plodding steps. And then the creature emerges from the shade and in the light of day becomes a man, carrying something on his back.

A woman. Face yellow, eyes pinched shut, a wince each time the man takes a heavy step.

In the curve of the trail, the man does not salaam us. Deep concentration on his face. Rafiq says a few words, and the man continues on—toward Rafiq's village, Ismail explains when we're well past the couple. "There's a doctor there."

Hopefully it won't be too late. At the same time, I worry the man might mention us. "What if he tells someone we're on the trail?"

"He has bigger worries than us. But you're right, we should keep up our pace. We're getting close now."

"Yes," Asim says solemnly, "we don't want to bump onto the wrong dudes."

And so we continue, toward wherever it is that Rafiq is leading us.

caves

We must be nearing our destination. Rafiq keeps borrowing the field glasses, searching for something.

The late-day sun drags immense shadows across the cliffs. With each new layer of shadow, everything becomes more dubious—that Rafiq knows where we're going, that Kyra and Jorgen are alive. My every thought becomes dark. I keep thinking of what happened to Kyra before I knew her.

She trusted Roy with her secret but not me. Because we never had what she had with Roy. An adult love, and marriage, even if it didn't work out. A mature love, like I have with Nolan. Not carefree puppy love. We were so young! All these years she's been looking back on a fantasy. She said so herself.

I just finished The Soothsayer's Handbook. So, so
good, Mim! Of course I wanted a happier ending, but
that wouldn't have felt true. I keep thinking of the line
Lev says: *Having a relationship only in your mind is like
having a relationship with a ghost.* I guess I've done that
with you. . . .

Even after divorcing Roy she didn't seek me out. She chose to go farther away. What has she been seeking for so long, at such a distance? What has she found here, or in any of those places, that she couldn't find at home?

> We supply basic things like sugar, salt, vitamin-enriched
> flour & bottled water. Everyone ties up their rations to hang
> them from the ceiling so the rats can't get at them. But
> the child next to me is weeping because rats ate his teddy
> bear. . . .

> On the flight from Khartoum we changed planes at JFK, &
> in the restroom I couldn't stop staring at the tile floor. After
> a year of bucket showers & squatting over holes in the dirt it
> was like I'd never seen anything so clean & sparkling. . . .

> At each post I try to make my way down a checklist of basic
> goals—potable water, hygienic hospital, humane prison—
> but for every goal there's something in the way, a security
> authorization that never comes, or some intractable law from
> a hundred years ago, or crucial missing paperwork, or some
> bullying underling. . . .

She could have done humanitarian work without ever getting on a plane; plenty of help needed at home. The homeless congregation outside our apartment, the squeegee men trying to make a buck. Instead she ran away. The closest acknowledgment of this that I've found in her letters sounds almost flippant: *The joke in relief work is that we all think we can save people, when really we're as messed up as anyone.*

So she heads off to tattered lands far from her own. Up steep mountains, deep into the woods.

Mammoth shadows grow larger, reaching up the cliffsides. As we round another curve, I see, not far away, smoke.

It rises in puffs. Could be anyone, of course—but I see from Rafiq's face that he thinks we've found them.

Ismail takes up his field glasses. Shakes his head, indicating that he can see little other than smoke. Silently he motions for us to continue.

We walk on, the smoke becoming small billows. My heart beats fast. And then I hear voices. So small, so high-pitched, that for a moment they seem comic. Some sort of joke.

Children.

The loud high cartoon voices of the very young. I'd know that sound anywhere.

The voices ring out in the thin air. Rafiq looks confused. But he continues ahead, and we follow. When we've rounded the next bend, Ismail again lifts the binoculars. Under his breath he says, "Well I'll be damned."

Even on my tiptoes I see nothing.

"It's a family."

He hands me the binoculars. Adjusting them with clammy, fumbling hands, I find two women squatting on their heels at a campfire. One wears a long scarf over her hair. The other has secured hers round her shoulders like a cloak. They're stirring something in a large tin pot, while three little children play nearby.

I pass the binoculars to Asim and Rafiq to have a look, and see from their faces that this isn't right, this isn't who's supposed to be here. With the binoculars, Rafiq scans the mountainside.

He frowns, murmurs back and forth with Asim and Ismail. Probably those villagers gave us wrong information. At once I feel colder, weaker. Hungry. Exhausted.

Quietly the men weigh the possibilities: change our route, set up camp for the night, or continue toward this family. "They might be able to provide information," Ismail whispers. "Rafiq thinks it worth seeing if they might help us. But not a word out of you, Miriam dear."

And so we switchback up toward the campfire, until the mothers have heard our approach. Alarm shows on their faces; here come four strange men. I would be terrified too.

The children stop their game to stare at us. Toddlers, with weather-reddened cheeks and dusty brown hair. Three little boys, or perhaps they simply wear boys' clothing. Bright-colored pants and sweaters, and plastic sandals on bare feet. The skin of their feet and hands is black with dirt.

The men salaam the women, eyes averted. I raise my hand in greeting, shifting my gaze away. Rafiq says something clearly attempting to convey that we mean no harm. With surprise I realize that my overriding fear—that someone will hurt us—has been obliterated by the fear I see in these women.

Now that we're close, I see something else. Three cave openings. At the mouth of each cave, a frame of wood beams caulked around the entrance, held in place by mud bricks and mortar. On the ground in front of each doorway lies a dust-caked carpet.

These women live here. These caves are their homes.

Ismail has loosened the pack to remove some naan, holds it out to the children. They grab it with hands black as a miner's and tear into it. Up close, I see how cracked their skin is, much worse than mine. Their cheeks are raw and red.

The women are speaking now, slowly and then in a rush. I look at the toddlers' hands and feet, pitch black, and their red, chafed cheeks, their dust-matted hair. How can they survive here? It must be well below freezing at night. Already my sweat has turned cold.

But the children seem not to feel the chill that has slid into the dusky air. They squat on their heels and use stones to etch lines in the dirt. Even while drawing, they watch us with wide brown eyes. I suppose we're the most interesting things to happen by in some time.

Ismail holds up his water canister and asks a question. The mothers direct him, and he and I take all four canteens down toward the water. We soon hear the noisy crashing of a waterfall. Makes me thirsty just to hear it. And then we're beneath the falls, where the crashing sound is deafening and swirls of spring water become thick rushing tresses. I dip my bottle and drink in long loud gulps. My upper lip has split from dryness.

The noise of the falls obscures everything else. Leaning close, Ismail speaks into my ear. "They're sisters. Used to live in one of the villages below. Their husbands worked as goat herders. But there was some dispute with a neighboring family and their husbands were killed. Which of course led to retribution killings, more fighting, back and forth. The women fled. They live here now. Waiting for the fighting to stop."

"They couldn't go live with relatives?"

"Too much fighting. They feel safer up here."

Here in the granite cliffs. In the cold gray clouds.

"No indication yet if they've seen Kyra and Jorgen. We need to be careful about how we ask."

Right. I bend down to catch water in one of the canteens. "How do they survive up here? And with little kids."

"They say they make money by chopping wood farther down. One of them goes into town every few weeks to sell it. Quite a trek, but that's where they buy provisions. They hope eventually the fighting will wind down and they can return home."

Amazing. Dipping my bottle into the whirling stream again, I try to make sense of it—these superwomen trekking up and down the mountainside, their incredible fortitude. My fingers are already numb from the quick braiding water. Ismail closes up the bottles and turns to head back to the camp. I try to keep up with him but am overcome by another swell of nausea from the altitude.

By the time I reach the cave homes, Asim, Rafiq, and Ismail are conversing with the sisters. I try to gauge from their faces if they have any information for us, but their expressions are remote. Rafiq reaches into our pack and hands a small sack to the sister with the scarf-cape. She pours the contents of the sack into a pot, adds water from a canteen, and sets the pot over the fire, while Rafiq reties the sheet around our backpack and carries it to one of the caves. Only when the other sister fetches, from another cave, a thickly folded blanket, does it become clear that there has been some sort of nego-tiation, and that we are to stay the night.

Ismail gestures for me to follow him, and we enter "our" cave. He flicks on his torch, sending a bluish LED glow up the high dark walls. To my surprise, the cave is large, with dusty carpets splayed atop woven mats on the ground. Donkeys must have lugged them up here—the very effort seems to me fantastic. "Sun's about to set," Ismail whispers. "And we're all getting tired. These women have of-fered us shelter."

"Aren't they afraid of us?"

"They've asked us to guard them, actually. Seems they recently had a whole bag of provisions stolen at gunpoint."

"Who—do you think it was Kyra's group?"

"Young guys, doesn't sound like Kyra and Jorgen were with them. Of course we're still trying to find out if they might know something—but we need to be delicate about it. In case they talk to others who pass this way."

"As you know," I say, "my lips are sealed."

Sunset prayers are tendered, and tin cups filled with tea. Our din-ner consists of rice with lentils, scooped up with our hands, and what is left of the naan, eaten very quickly—even the children, no dawdling, just shoving hot food into hungry mouths with cold, burning fingertips. The meal is the most satisfying I've ever had. That's how hungry I am.

The light is gone, the fire dying down. We take turns relieving ourselves in the designated area, and the women and children head into their caves for the night. I can't help wondering that they don't see I'm one too—a mother, a wife, just like them. Deception makes my loneliness all the worse. Abysmal, actually, in my disguise, my silence, here in the "men's" cave, on a rug atop a mat on the ground, my turban folded into a pillow. The others attend to their prayers, while I tug the patu around my body, trying to retain the heat inside me, wondering what Nolan and Sean are doing now, if Sean would be in class, or the cafeteria, or his dormitory.

When we brought Sean to campus on move-in day, he immediately had a request for the dorm's RA: could he install the chin-up bar he brought from home? Of course he could, in that anything-goes place. Nolan helped him, and then we watched as he and his roommate performed dueling pull-ups.

There's Sean heaving himself upward, muscles shaking as he brings his chin over the bar again and again. Here on the cold cave floor, I see him, see Nolan, our home, our softly rising forest.

I barely sleep. In my fitful dreams I navigate a maze of villages, each leading to another, deeper and deeper.

a mistake

I wake to find the women pouring tea by the fire, the men at some distance from them, Rafiq and Asim smoking their cigarettes. That means they've already said their dawn prayers. I hurry down to the outhouse area, then to the falls to refill my water bottle, not to waste precious time.

But when I return, the men are still smoking, leisurely, chatting softly. The breeze blows ash from the fire, and the children chase each other, yelping with laughter. Even as my head throbs and I swallow more aspirin, I know I'm witnessing something remarkable. That these women have created something extraordinary here in the clouds.

I head back into the cave and attempt to wrap my turban. Ismail has followed me. "Here," he whispers, "let me do that."

"Why are we taking so long?"

"We were able to get more information. Those boys who stole the rice. Seems there was something wrong with one of them. They say he had very short arms. Not the usual amputee stubs. Short arms with fused hands at the end."

Flipper arms. "You mean the guy the headman told us about."

"Apparently they came via another route. From the north."

I consider what this means. "Then they've been on a completely different trail this whole time."

Ismail purses his lips. "Rafiq thinks he has a good idea of where they would have been coming from."

"In other words, we've been going in the wrong direction."

"It's just a bit of a detour." But Ismail looks very tired.

"How do we know these women are telling the truth? Maybe those boys with the guns threatened them. Maybe they said they'd come back if they set anyone on their tail." It suddenly seems absurd that among these peaks and valleys, this vast, rippled mountain, we could ever find anyone at all.

"I don't know if they're telling the truth," Ismail says. "I suppose there's no way to be certain."

I can't help but give a great, weary sigh. If that man was here, we haven't been entirely wrong—but why weren't Kyra and Jorgen with them? I ask Ismail if he thinks they are still alive. "That guy Umar hates foreigners."

"A dead foreigner isn't worth much. A live one can be ransomed, or sold off to some other group. It's possible Umar's crew revised their plan. Or those two men split off from the others."

But why would they do that?

Ismail must sense my doubts. "Kidnappers move around a lot. They're often figuring out on the fly what exactly to do with their captives. How to make the best . . . profit."

With that one word, *kidnappers*, Ismail has given up any pretense of Kyra and Jorgen having gone willingly with those men. And yet this acknowledgment, that they've been abducted, somehow comes as no surprise. Perhaps I've known it, too, all along.

"So, we should change course, then?" All that walking, and they are still so far away.

"If these women are telling the truth, then yes."

I consider the sisters. The look in their eyes when they spotted us. I trust my instinct, even if it means a longer trek. And anyway, if I were to balk, then what? Could I stay with these women while the men went ahead?

Not that it would make any difference. Only now is it truly sinking in, that I passed the point of no return a long time ago.

And so we follow a new trail, past gaunt trees and high chilly cliff walls, frost crunching under our boots. Rafiq is at the lead. His legs bow slightly, his weight on the outer edges of his heels.

Below us, wide banks of fog like ethereal carpets, and valleys of dead stumps where trees have been cut down. It is like inhabiting an ancient myth. I'm very cold, skin bumpy like a lemon rind. But soon enough the slopes have me sweating. I ask Ismail what elevation this might be.

"Maybe 2,500 meters. In feet that would be . . . eight thousand or so." It doesn't sound very high up. "We could cross at a lower elevation," he explains, "but if we take the main passages we risk running into people. Anyway, you don't seem in such bad shape now."

"No, no, don't worry." I'm determined not to hold anyone back. The labor of breathing becomes my focus, the scent of the pines cool and fresh. The glinting peaks of mountains flit in and out of view, and it even seems possible, despite what Ismail said, that Kyra really is all right.

Just think how strong she is.

And I was so weak. That must be why she didn't protest when I left her. She saw how weak I was.

Stop it! I try to imagine the thoughts evaporating, the words disappearing.

And yet it's true I was afraid. I was afraid of the truth—of who I was, of what it would mean for me to stay with her, with Kyra of all people, whom my world hadn't prepared me for.

What would it have meant, to try to step away from those fears?

The image that flickers before me is of Carl. Waiting for Kyra after the dance performance, carrying that bouquet tied with twine, as if bearing it for all of us.

Blink it away. Keep moving. Left foot, right foot. Here on the cliff edge of the world.

I keep my eyes down, continue at a careful pace. Until I spot a flash of something on the ground. Plastic. Purple.

DATA = POWER. But the plastic has torn at the W.

Broken bangles are placed on a woman's grave as a symbol of grief.

Rafiq is too far ahead to hear me cry out, but Asim hurries over. I hold out the broken bracelet. For all I know some sort of struggle tore it. "Remember these?"

Ismail has joined us, and Asim explains about the bracelets. Ismail nods. "Good work, dear." But I see the worry on his face.

"You think we might be too late. Is that it?"

"No, I'm concerned we might be seen, if indeed we're close on their heels."

"Yes," Asim says, "let us go."

I place the bracelet in my pocket. Rafiq is far ahead now, and we hurry to catch up, but I'm slower than the others, gulping air.

If only that bracelet weren't torn. Maybe then I wouldn't worry so badly.

And yet, improbable as it may be, it seems I was right to trust those women. That indeed we're on the right trail.

on the edge

Afternoon now, sun high and fierce. Rafiq has us taking a "short cut" that at times seems not to be a path at all. The track has narrowed, a mere slit in the side of the mountain. It seems to be gradually nudging us toward the ice-crusted edge. Like walking a tightrope, I try to joke to myself as I follow behind Rafiq and Asim. My pulse has begun to race.

Ismail, behind me now, must see what's happening: my knees knocking, the fabric of my pants trembling. More sternly than I've yet heard him, he says, "You're doing fine."

Asim gamely traipses ahead in his fake sneakers. Tears have begun to stream down my face.

Don't look down.

It's no use. We've arrived at a shelf of mountain that hardly seems wide enough for my body. I ask if there isn't some other, better route.

"If we're to catch up with them, we need to stay away from the main path," Ismail says bluntly. "Can't afford to be seen. And Rafiq says we'll get there quicker this way."

To one side of the tiny path is the cold stone wall of mountain, its jagged skin the only thing to try to cling to. To the other side, air.

A mere step off the ridge into the sky.

"It's only a few steps, really," Ismail assures me. "See, look over there. The trail is even wider than what we've gotten used to."

All I see is a never-ending path. Rafiq and Asim have paused ahead, waiting.

A stone—no, a heavy brick of ice—has settled into my chest. Lodged so tightly I can barely breathe. And then I'm down on my hands and knees, nose to the ground, weeping.

"What you doing?" Asim asks, alarmed.

"I'm dying."

Ismail is clearly annoyed. "Miriam dear, there is simply not room enough for you to crawl. Chin up and pull yourself together."

Slowly, I push myself to my heels. Very carefully, I stand, chest tight, my limbs so hollow a gust of wind might send me into the sky. I attempt to take a step and see that even my ankles are shaking.

Never have I felt like such a fool. I can't help but think of Nolan— that I've put him through something awful, all for this.

Rafiq has come over, very close, watching me steadily with his one, green, eye. The cigarette smell rises from his breath. Slowly he reaches out, and for a moment I think he's about to touch my face. But of course he would never do that. Instead, with great serious- ness, he begins to unwind my turban.

When he has freed a sufficient stretch of fabric, he drapes the cloth over my head in the opposite direction, so that it hangs like a curtain at the side of my face nearest the precipice. He arranges it so that it becomes a sort of blinder against the view.

When I understand what he has done, I tuck the end of the "cur- tain" beneath the collar of my tunic, into my undershirt so that it will remain in place. For now it seems secure enough, though my legs are still shaking and the cold block of ice remains heavy in my chest.

I peer ahead at the little ridge of mountain we're to skirt along. Think of those cave women lugging firewood down the mountain.

Meena Gul stomping off to the water well. The teenage girl gang with their guns. Those Jalalabad schoolgirls in their black veils.

It's time for me too, now, to become one of Jorgen's ninja warriors.

With the fabric of the turban obscuring my side vision, I no longer glimpse the plunging cliffside. I keep my eyes trained on the ground, one mincing step after another. With each step I think up a new way to trip, stumble, and drop into thin air.

One small patch of ice. One loose stone underfoot. One wrong step.

Come on, now, be a mountain goat, a quick-footed ibex. A ninja.

"There you go, dear. Don't forget to breathe." Ismail is right behind me, his careful words prodding me along. I want to say something but my tongue is thick. My heart thumps between my ears.

One foot forward. Now the other.

Kyra. I say her name to myself with each step. Left foot, right foot. Just one more. And another. And another—until at last we've shimmied our way around the precipice.

There, as if wrenched away from some bad dream, the path widens, soon returning to a decent distance from the cliff ledge. Only then do I allow myself to look up, at the mountains stretching ahead.

may you not be tired

Late afternoon and still we haven't reached our destination.

A line from Emerson plays in my mind. *From the mountain you see the mountain.*

The altitude has me moving at half my normal pace. But the men don't complain, despite the chill air and emerging dusk. They too seem to be moving more slowly.

Familiar thoughts braid through each other. That I was wrong to leave Kyra. That I wasn't wrong to leave her. That I did so for the wrong reason. That I was running away.

It's getting to the hour where we should be settling in for the night. But when we stop to drink from our water bottles, Ismail says, "I think we should keep going. Can you do that, Miriam dear? I know you must want a rest."

I picture Kyra scaling these trails, how cold she must be. Kyra in her many layered sweaters . . .

"I feel so crappy, it probably doesn't matter either way." I try to laugh. Really I feel dreadful. I've begun to shiver from the cold.

"Then let's keep moving," Ismail says, as the last patch of sunlight slides behind the mountain.

We walk all night, through groves of spindly pines and snow-tinged poplars, over earth patchy with ice, along the rearing walls of the mountain.

Under the crisp wedge of moon, ice patches glisten. Even our breath glows white. Yet we still slip, and grab at snow-crusted branches, and pick our way over stones and knots and every size of boulder. Night magnifies everything, even how filthy I am, the pungent-sweet stench of my dirty clothes and stale sweat. I can feel the dust caught in every crevice. Much of my energy is spent simply breathing.

Where the gorge opens up, the sky is immense, heavy with big plump stars. I've never, ever seen so many stars. They twitch in the sky like a strange language. Yet they're stars, just like those I see from my quiet hill in Massachusetts. For some reason this seems incredible, that a sky can stretch so far.

The teeming sky makes me dizzy. For some time now I've been in bad shape. Each time I haul myself over a boulder, or take a high step, my vision narrows and I find myself gasping.

"Slow slowly," Asim instructs when my breathing becomes even more strained. "Make short steps."

Frustrating to walk like that, such short paces, but to my surprise the mini-steps work. They stop my head from spinning. Soon I'm no longer gasping for breath. But they make my progress terribly slow.

"Sorry," I whisper, white puffs in the dark.

The others continue doggedly ahead. They have to keep waiting for me to catch up. Over and over we repeat this dance, throughout the night.

The moon is fading now, the stars snatched back, no light to help our feet find the ground. But even a match could give us away, so we wade through darkness, stumbling over stones, twigs catching at sleeves and pant legs. Without the moon, it seems even the mountains have disappeared. Yet I feel their presence all around me.

Asim keeps begging for a nap. I feel awful to have dragged him here. Each time he wants to stop, Ismail asks if he can continue for another twenty minutes, so that we make better progress. Apparently Rafiq thinks we're getting close.

Never have I walked nonstop like this, with little sleep and barely any food. My feet have passed from tired and blistered to battered and numb. My back wants nothing more than to be horizontal. Yet the aching of my body seems somehow separate from me.

It's much colder now. Rafiq has wrapped the long end of his turban around his neck as a scarf. When at last we pause for a rest, in the deep gray time before dawn, frozen condensation of his breath clings to his beard. I touch my face and even with numb fingers feel how puffy it is. I whisper, "Why am I the only one reacting to the altitude?"

"I've been out working in villages at four thousand meters for years," Ismail whispers. "You just arrived." But I can tell it worries him. "It's not good to take long breaks in these conditions," he says after a few minutes' rest. "Hypothermia. Frostbite and all that."

And so, under the faint haze of approaching dawn, we continue our march. Left foot, right foot, following the yak track toward the mountain pass, following night into day.

morning prayers

Gray almost-dawn. A quick break for water, the men performing hasty ablutions—running their wet hands through their beards and sort of patting themselves down. Speedy prayers, no time to lose. We keep moving, and the outline of mountains begins to take shape in the silvery morning.

Rafiq is at the lead. At a wide stretch of path pocked with caves, he stops. Raises a hand, signaling us to wait.

And then I hear what he must already have heard: the distinct ping of human voices. Relayed off rock walls, through the thin air. Hard to tell where the voices are coming from, or how far away. Just ahead of me, Ismail scans the area with his field glasses, trains his gaze some meters below us. He moves closer, behind a huddle of boulders, to watch.

Silently I join him, crouching low. To my great shock, there's no need for binoculars at all. They seem a mere twenty yards away—if many tiers down, along a granite plateau at a separate, lower, grade. I easily hear the echo of their voices, see their dark hair and the zippered vests over their tunics. Each carries a water bottle.

Five thin young men.

A bonfire has been lit, the first small puffs of smoke rising. A few yards away, a tarp stretches across wooden poles—a makeshift outdoor roof. The fire pit is wide and seems to have been there for some time, blackened logs and ashes piled up.

Ismail passes the binoculars to me, and with a jolt I confront the faces right in front of me. Boys—teenagers, early twenties at most. Sean's age, and skinny, with short wispy beards and thin moustaches. They've removed their shoes. No hats or turbans. Some have pistols tucked into belts.

With water from their canisters, they are performing their morning ablutions. Methodical, precise, each boy pushing up his sleeves to wash hands and feet, then face, ears, nose, mouth, arms, elbows. The choreographed sequence is much more measured than anything I've seen from Ismail, Asim, or Rafiq.

Another man has emerged from one of the caves. Not young, not dark, not wearing a vest. His hair is a rusty gray, his beard short, his complexion ruddy. He moves with awkward steps, seeming almost to sway from side to side. This is due, I see, to the chain round his ankles.

I look to Ismail, see his blanching face, and understand we have found Jorgen.

Considering that he's shackled, Jorgen doesn't look terribly put out. He yawns and stretches his arms, head tilted toward the sky. His wrists are free, and he's holding his own canister of water, which he opens to perform his ablutions. No one seems to be monitoring him, no one following him with a gun, no one paying much attention at all.

Now the boys and Jorgen kneel in configuration, one boy in front of the rest. No prayer mats, just their knees on the cold mountain floor. They look intent as they follow the lead boy's words and gestures. It feels wrong for me to be watching. I hand the binoculars to Ismail, and see that his hands are trembling.

Something about Jorgen's morning stretch, his unforced movements, allows me to believe that Kyra must be there, too. Or at least, I tell myself, that she hasn't been harmed.

Ismail motions for us to retreat and points to one of the nearby caves. It is very narrow, a cold, dark refuge.

"I don't think they're Taliban" is the first thing he says when we've huddled inside.

Asim isn't sure. Not all Taliban dress traditionally, he points out. These days some even shave their beards so as not to be easily recognized.

But they would have made a claim by now, or asked for ransom. "Whoever they are," Ismail says, "they're still figuring out what they want. Looks like they've been camped here for a while."

"But where's Kyra?" I can barely keep my voice down.

"They don't seem to have hurt Jorgen," Ismail says, as if that will comfort me. Or perhaps he's trying to comfort himself.

Asim says, "There are more of them than of us."

That's how I know he's afraid. That he thinks we might actually try to do something. "Only one more," I say, as if I think we could take them on. Well, were it not for their weapons, we could. They're young skinny boys. Mostly they look hungry.

Rafiq says something, and the men confer.

"Apparently there's a way to bypass them," Ismail explains. "We could cut east and call for reinforcement."

Reinforcement from whom? Where? It took us so long just to get here.

Asim says, "My family's village is not far from here."

"You said they moved away!"

"Many cousins still here. They will help us." He looks remarkably calm. But I don't want to leave without knowing if Kyra's here. I look to Ismail and can't even speak.

Ismail is watching me, those long wrinkle-streaks beneath his eyes. "Let's take one more quick look, see if we can figure out who we're dealing with." I sense that, like me, he needs to see his friend.

I follow him back to the stretch of boulders where we can watch the others without being seen. Having finished their prayers, the boys are passing around pats of naan. They tear into it, chewing, sipping tea that has been heated over the bonfire. Not sufficient for young men, surely. They must be hungry. They quickly chew and swallow.

Then they take out little pocket mirrors and scissors and, in the crisp dawn light, on this cold slope of mountain, set to trimming their beards.

There was a nightmare I used to have back when my mother was ill. I dreamed I couldn't find her, and in a panic would search and search. I always found her, but when I tried to call to her, my voice failed. There she was, so close, oblivious of my presence. And no matter how I tried, she never could hear me.

But this is no dream. From the craggy brown cave below, Kyra steps out.

Yes, it's Kyra, with a long rumpled tunic hanging loosely over baggy pants that are somehow too short. A scarf wraps her hair and upper body. She walks very slowly, because of the small chained weight around one ankle.

In my chest a fish leaps and plunges. Leaping, plunging. Never in my life have I wanted so badly to cry out.

A young man walks behind her. Short and stocky. Though he holds a rifle, he seems merely to be keeping an eye on her, his posture relaxed. At a remove from him, Kyra squats beside the fire pit and eats the naan they've left for her.

I grab the field glasses from Ismail and suddenly the campsite is too close, randomly showcasing some boys who, to my great surprise, are watching videos on their cell phones. Others, I see as I swing the binoculars wildly, are still squatting with their mirrors and scissors, pruning their beards and mustaches—yet they glance surreptitiously at the foreign being eating the leftover naan. I follow their gaze and find Kyra, her bony elbows and shoulders. Red marks on her ankle where the shackle has bruised it.

I train the trembling viewfinder on her face and for a moment lose my breath. It's the same face but thinner, with parched skin and tiny lines framing her eyes and mouth. This is Kyra. She is alive. Her lips are very chapped. Magnified by my lenses, she could be mere feet away from me. I could reach out and touch her.

Then she shifts her head, and her dark, impassive eyes look straight at me.

Of course she can't see me. Some part of me knows that. The binoculars wobble in my hands, and I have to stop myself from calling her name.

It still seems she's looking right at me. But even if she were, what would she see: some person hidden under a turban. She wouldn't know who I was.

She squints, as if trying to spot something, then gives up, takes a last bite of the naan. Then she stands and manages to walk, laboriously, away from the camp, away from the boys. Probably toward the outhouse area. The boy with the rifle follows her. She stops to adjust the shackle on her ankle.

That's when the boy nudges her with his rifle. Kyra turns and snaps at him. The sound of her voice, instantly familiar, shocks me. But the boy nudges her again. Kyra slaps him away.

The boy shoves her, hard. Kyra falls to her knees. He kicks her, so that she folds up into herself. The binoculars jerk and shake in my hands. Over by the campfire, the other boys don't notice what's happening. Meanwhile their comrade jerks Kyra's arms back and ties

258

her wrists with a strip of something, so that her hands are caught behind her.

Already Kyra has given in. No struggle. She lies limp, forehead on the ground, her arms torqued behind her.

I'm struggling not to drop the binoculars. The boy lightly nudges Kyra with the rifle point. Kyra manages, after a few tries, to stand. Then she continues, awkwardly, ahead, with the boy behind her.

Ismail tugs me away, to the cave where Asim and Rafiq wait.

"Isn't there some way for us to get help from here?" I ask. "Those boys were using cell phones. How do they even have cell phones out here? They were watching videos. Does yours work? Why doesn't mine?"

"Those videos were already downloaded." Ismail holds out his phone. No signal.

Rafiq says something, then Asim, and a whispered conversation ensues.

Ismail looks very pale. "Asim says if his people come on horseback they can be here soon. We just need to get to where we can reach them. According to Rafiq, we're not far from the Pakistan border, so we won't have to go too long to be near a cell tower."

"Then please go! But I'll stay here."

Ismail shakes his head. "We're safest together."

"But shouldn't some of us keep an eye on them?"

"They aren't going anywhere. They're still figuring out what to do. Meanwhile they've set up quite a camp." It's the first time I've heard him sound angry.

"I don't want to leave her."

Asim says, "Will be okay, sister. My people will be here fast." But I see the worry between his eyebrows.

We exit the cave, Rafiq leading us silently eastward. As badly as I want to take one more look, I'm terrified the boys might hear us, and follow behind the others.

a conversation

It is colder up here on the higher path. We pass saplings wet with ice melt, and shady patches thick with snow. We've walked maybe thirty minutes when Rafiq raises his gun, toward the lower hills.

At first I see nothing. Then I hear it. Somewhere below us, someone approaching.

All four of us pause. The air is so quiet, I'm sure we must have imagined it—but no, there it is again, soft but distinct, a rustle of motion from the trail below. And then I see them: a half-dozen men, all wearing camouflage jackets. They are big and burly, not skinny like the boys at the camp. They walk single file, their movements brisk and nearly silent. A donkey loaded with provisions sways heavily behind them.

Four of the men carry rifles. One carries a big jug of water on his back. Another is in charge of the donkey. No one says a word.

And then the man at the head, the brawniest of all, lifts a hand. Everyone stops moving. The man cocks his head, listening.

They sense our presence just as we sense theirs. All of them look up, guns at the ready. Time has never seemed so slow. And then I realize that all this while, Asim, Rafiq, and Ismail have been silently backing away, as far from the trail as possible.

I manage to pin myself back with the others. We no longer see the men. No way of knowing if they're still there, listening.

Then a voice floats up. Low but distinct. Another voice responds. They must have decided they're alone after all. The conversation lasts a good minute before we hear them continuing on.

When we're sure they've gone, we step back out and look down at the other trail. No one there.

Asim says, "Those men they were speaking Urdu."

Ismail nods. "Arab Afghans. Or maybe Pakistani."

"Maybe al-Qaeda," Asim suggests.

Rafiq says something no one bothers translating for me.

I must look scared. Ismail says, "Don't worry, dear, we're getting help." But as we head out again I see him glance back at the path those men were on. And from his face I can tell he's having the same thought I am, of where they might be heading.

It isn't much longer until we manage to make our call—first to Asim's "cousins," who agree to bring reinforcements, and then to Roy, who agrees to pay them one thousand dollars.

They'll be on horseback. Ten men, Asim says, and "many many" rounds of ammunition.

This cannot be real. All the way back along the same snow-lined path, I no longer feel tired. Each step seems to happen without my willing it, as if I've crossed over into a dream.

I keep looking for something I recognize, for signs that we're almost there. At last Rafiq gives the sign to be quiet and to stay as close to the cliff wall as possible.

We're nearly there. Help will be here soon. This thought keeps me going, until we reach the overhang from where we can see down to the camp. Rafiq's shoulders slump, and I see what he sees. The camp has been vacated.

The boys are gone, along with their canteens and guns and provisions. Gone too, the tarp that was stretched as a roof, and the posts that suspended it. The bonfire is out. Kyra and Jorgen are nowhere to be seen.

"Those men," I say, not bothering to keep my voice down. They must have done something to the boys. Taken them. Or scared them away. Or they all went off together.

Asim hangs his head. Ismail is visibly upset. I am furious.

Exhaling briskly as if to shake himself out of despair, Ismail says, "Well, if this has anything to do with those men, we've a good guess as to where they've gone."

Back toward Pakistan. As if Pakistan were yet one more village, not a country whose border stretches well over sixteen hundred miles.

"But we didn't pass them," I point out. The men converse in murmurs, and Ismail tells me Rafiq thinks he knows the route they would take. I ask about Asim's crew, if they can head straight to where those men might have gone. But it's all supposition.

"We need to contact them and regroup," Ismail says. "No point waiting around here."

I'm too furious to say anything more. While the men hold a rushed, anxious confab, I sit on the ground hugging myself, trying to calm down. That I ever thought this "plan" could work seems completely, utterly foolish.

And yet I hear myself say, "We need to follow them. We can't lose them. I won't let that happen."

"As soon as we reach Asim's people," Ismail says, "we'll do that." But I hear in his voice that he thinks it's hopeless.

blood for blood

We follow the same narrow snow-lined trail. Caves all around us, their dark open mouths. No speaking. No sighing. No crying. But I quail inside.

If I just keep on, we can reach her. We've made it so close.

There's more snow here in the shaded gorge. The path is lined with caves and large boulders. We are creeping along when there's a pop-pop sound, and voices shouting from afar. I feel something whip by my head.

Asim and Rafiq duck behind a massive boulder. More popping sounds, like fingers snapping. Ismail grabs my hand and dives at one of the caves—but my hand wrenches away and I feel my body twist, whipping around without my telling it to. I fall hard onto the cold ground.

This cannot be happening.

Bullets whoosh overhead. They seem to be higher up. I hear them bounce off the rock walls, feel shards of rock and blasted tree wood hitting me. Yet nothing in my body tells me to move. And though I see the cave, see Ismail lying there unmoving, I feel oddly separate from all of this.

Then my mind snaps back to itself, and I know what I need to do.

But when I try to crawl to Ismail, my arm gives out. And then I'm being lifted, pulled from under my arms, dragged backward off the trail.

In a niche behind a cluster of large boulders, Asim sets me down. His entire body—even his round young scarred face—is trembling.

Rafiq, alert, livid, is crouched low, rifle cocked, looking out with his one good eye. He doesn't shoot, just watches silently.

Lying here on the shale, my body has gone numb. Asim's face glistens with sweat. Even his lips are quivering. I try to thank him but all that comes out is a grunt. Then I see the blood. A small puddle beside me.

I look down at my chest—more blood. Only slowly do I understand that it's not my heart that's bleeding; it's my right triceps. In my confusion, I can't tell if the bullet has only scraped me or if it's lodged inside. Or maybe it's torn right through—maybe that's why my shirt is so bloody. I roll to my side and stare at the puddle as if it only remotely has to do with me. And then a clear thought floats up: I'm going to die here.

Sean will be pissed off. Nolan will never forgive me.

But I made that phone call he chose not to return. To Sean I wrote my letter. And though I know well the anguish of losing a mother—and that Sean has lost one mother already—I also know what people manage to do. They keep going.

Odd, the calm that I feel. The calm, I suppose, of understanding: that they will be all right without me.

How strangely freeing, to know that.

I must have blacked out. Asim is tipping water from his canteen into my mouth. I drink automatically, reflexively, muscles gulping. More gunshots, high overhead. I feel very cold. I can no longer see Ismail's cave from here. Perhaps he is dead.

Only as the bullets continue flying far above us, and gunfire answers from the other side of the gorge, does it dawn on me that whoever is shooting is not shooting at us.

As if to confirm this, Rafiq sets down his rifle. Yes, this is someone else's gunfight. We must have simply been caught in the crossfire.

I wonder if it's Kyra, her group, being shot at. I wonder if she's still alive.

Now Rafiq has seen the blood. His expression barely changes. In his calm way, he reaches for a pristine layer of snow. And as if I really am, now, a comrade, and not some untouchable woman, he begins to pack my wound.

The icy snow stings, then numbs, and turns pink from the blood. But it does seem to stanch the bleeding. Rafiq adds dense pats of earth. Then he removes his turban and with the fabric folded tightly wraps my arm.

"It is just a small hole," Asim whispers, as if to convince himself.

The shooting has slowed now. We wait for it to stop. My ears ring from the gunfire. Even when the fighting has ended, and the others seem to have left, we wait. A long time, listening to the silence, too frightened to move.

None of us says a word. We need to be sure everyone has gone. Still no sign of Ismail. Asim and Rafiq say nothing, just pull off their rubber shoes and turn them upside down, to shake out shards of rock and wood and grit. Rafiq's molded moccasins, and Asim's "sneakers" with the fake laces.

They took the laces out of his shoes.

Dizzy, I watch Asim slip the fake sneakers back on.

When a long time has passed, and the fabric around my arm is wet, Ismail emerges from his cave.

His face is dusty, his clothes filthy. He has removed his woolen cap, and there's a great bloody patch on his head.

Rafiq motions to him with his strong hands, and Ismail joins us, exhaling a long loud sigh. I realize he must have thought I was dead. Softly he says, "They nicked you, did they?"

Asim says again, "It is just a small hole."

"Your head is bloody," I manage to croak.

"When I dove into that cave I hit my head. Knocked myself out." His hooded eyes look very sad, with those wrinkles stretching down. All three men, I realize, are looking at me with gentleness. Ismail frowns at my wrapped arm. And then he says what I know is coming. What I know is the only thing he can say, what I absolutely do not want to hear.

"All right, Miriam dear. It's time we turned round and got you back home."

walking out

We "short-cut" southwest to Rafiq's village. We walk all day, and through the night, below millions of tiny stars.

A strip of the sheet from the backpack has been turned into a sling. At first I feel nothing—not my mud-packed wound, not my straining lungs or aching muscles or torn and bloody blisters. Not even terror at scaling the vertiginous stretches or scooching my way round tightrope ridges. My body runs on adrenaline, as if belonging to someone else. Then the pain comes. It keeps me moving.

The silence of the mountains is deep and still. Each slope becomes blackness blocking moonlight. I've never known such darkness, not even on my land back home. A few times, far below, the glow of firelight reaches through the dark. Other than that, no sign of anyone.

She never even knew we were here. I gave her no signal, no comfort.

She looked right at me. I saw her eyes.

What does it matter, now that we're heading away from her?

I see now that what I wanted was a fantasy, as impossible as this landscape, this besieged country. I've been no less deluded than Roy, thinking I could somehow touch the past.

Every so often I glance at my useless arm, to stop my mind from straying. But in the darkness, I see things. Visions. Not just Kyra in the loose pants and wrinkled tunic. The hilltop house I bought as if knowing already that Nolan and Sean would come to fill it. The three of us lying on the rug before the fireplace on a winter night. Sean, still small, in the too-big lawn chair, holding an ice pack on his arm where the wasp stung him twice. And with friends in his room, the sound of his young voice through the door:

Yeah, but I don't call her Mom, I call her Mim.

The sun rises again, washes us with pale light. At last Ismail's cell phone indicates we're in range. While he scurries up higher to call Roy, we rest.

Rafiq and Asim pull beat-up cigarettes from their pockets and light them with unsteady hands. I see them glancing at my arm. Nervous. We're too exhausted to speak.

Asim looks particularly weary. That he has joined this folly, risked his life for a bit of money, crushes me. One of his rubber sneakers is starting to tear at the back. I can tell from the way he moves that his feet hurt. If we make it home, I want to tell him, he can have my walking shoes. They're too big for me anyway, two layers of socks to help them fit. For some reason, this, of all things, is what I want to say. But when I try to speak, what comes out, in a parched voice I hardly recognize, is "You're not really that guy Ahmed's cousin, are you."

"Sister, in Afghanistan we are all relations." He even manages to smile.

"But you didn't have to do this. The money can't be worth it."

"It is worth it," he says plainly.

"You mean the bride-price—"

"With this money I will have *three* brides." He grins at his joke, but there's something else in his eyes. Fear, I think.

Feeling morbid, I tell him, "I wish I'd met her. Fareshta." In my weakened voice even her name sounds dubious. Probably she's not even real. Probably the bride-price is just an excuse.

Her name perks Asim up. "Let me show you." He takes his cell phone from his pocket as if not tired at all. I am female, after all—allowed to see her photo. When the screen has lit up, he holds it toward me. "This one is last month."

"Oh, Asim."

They stand side by side, Fareshta the same height as Asim, with an oval face and wide eyes that are a stunning greenish brown. She's wearing a yellow coat with a sash tied at the waist. The photo seems to have captured an unguarded moment, both Fareshta and Asim laughing at something off-screen. Even their eyes are laughing. And though they're not holding hands, not touching at all, the angle of their bodies reminds me of the way magnets rotate instinctively to-ward each other.

Because of whatever they're looking at off-screen, the angle shows only the unmarred side of Asim's face. No scar, just creases of laughter. His hair is thick and windblown, like some movie star. He wears dark pants, his zippered gym jacket, and an Afghan scarf around his neck. And of course the rubber sneakers.

I almost ruined this.

"Asim, I owe you my life. You could have been shot coming back for me." When he says nothing, I explain, "In the military, you'd get a medal."

He takes a drag from his cigarette.

"Asim, you saved me."

He just exhales a stream of smoke and says, "It is my job."

When Ismail returns, his face is pale. "Well, the good news is that Roy has fully recovered. He's sending help to come fetch us. And he's alerting his contacts with what we know about Jorgen and Kyra."

I try to read Ismail's face. "And the bad news?"

He squints, as if deciding whether or not to say it. "It seems your compatriots burned some Korans."

Apparently some Bagram inmates were writing messages to each other. "Using pages in books," Ismail explains. "So the U.S. soldiers burned the books . . . some of which were Korans." While we've been trekking in the mountains, the news has spread, along with riots and even revenge killings.

"A bloody mess. The U.S. consulate has declared a state of emergency. So we won't be going back into the city. The helicopter will take you straight to the airbase. And Roy has booked your flights back home."

Asim looks alarmed as he translates to Rafiq. I am filled with shame. I cannot believe that we have done this. That my country has done this. Not just the debacle with the Korans—I mean the entire bloody mess. The whole long winding path of handshakes and airstrikes and treaties and night raids. Of civilians blown to bits, and of caskets flown home.

Ismail is saying we need to be especially careful. "Not a peep out of you, Miriam dear."

All I can do is nod.

We enter Rafiq's village toward midday. I'm weak and afraid news from the city will have reached here, afraid of how the girls with guns will greet us this time. But they just whisk us to a hidden room where we are given food and tea and patched up by the doctor. He is a tall man with a neon-green windbreaker over his tunic. I want to ask after the man we saw, the one carrying the sick woman on his back, to find out if they made it here in time—but it would be too much to hear more bad news.

The doctor applies a numbing gel and some sort of antibiotic to my wound before stitching it up, unflinching, as if not hearing my cries. Over in the corner, Asim is making little hissing noises, applying an ointment and bandages to his blisters. Then the doctor tends to Ismail's forehead—quick work, since we must leave now, while the village has gathered for prayers.

Three sturdy donkeys stand by to transport us, with three old men to lead the way. As we say our farewells, Rafiq manages to look as if he hasn't just risked his life to help us. But he must be glad to see us go. It's too risky for him, for the village, to have us here.

When I thank him, he just gives a small nod. The unruffled posture, the fierce green eye. His graciousness moves me. In it I think I see what drew Kyra from her spartan room out to these steep winding trails. The formidable grace she knew was here, beyond the high walls and razor wire, beyond the boundaries of a world without forgiveness.

I see it too, now.

All this time I assumed it was pity, or maybe penance, that was driving her—to any of the stops along her peregrinations. When really it must be this.

Sorry my letters always sound kind of down. I should write you on good days too. I see amazing things, Mim. Incredible people. Incredible beauty. But I guess I mostly write when I'm feeling blue.

With help from Ismail, I manage to pull myself up onto one of the donkeys. Then he and Asim mount theirs, and the three old men lead us forward on foot. An easy amble, the village slipping behind us, as tears streak down my cheeks of their own accord.

Asim says, "Don't worry, sister, Rafiq he will pray for your friends."

On an open stretch of hard earth, Rafiq stands with his arms open before him, palms face up, as if holding a wide tray. The simple

271

beauty of his gesture, showing his palms to the sky. And the sun already arcing west, taking with it this long, long day.

I watch him as our lumbering donkeys shoulder us away. Angling my head, I keep him in sight as he becomes nothing more than a silhouette. A man standing with upturned palms, asking some question with no good answer.

Part III

THE WORLD

proof of life

Whenever I'm upset, or anxious, or blocked at some point in my work, I go for a walk.

Silent conversations flow easily, my thoughts loosened by the fresh air. Usually I follow the path my neighbor Jorie's horse favors, across the field, down to the creek, then circle back through the woods on my property. Always such bustle in those woods, such industry—the woodpecker knocking at some poor tree, and fat-cheeked chipmunks scrambling over rocks, and snakes or frogs or clever salamanders blending in with mud and moss and ferns. I love all the scurrying, the snapping twigs, the occasional rough crack of a dead branch breaking and plummeting to earth. These signs of hidden life always help to clear my head.

The air this morning holds that first nip of autumn before the birds gather to fly south. I might still spot the bright flash of a gold-finch, or a grosbeak with its bib of red. Even the garden still holds some color.

There was snow on the ground when I returned from my journey—well over two years ago now. I remember thinking that my few acres of woods and scrappy hilltop were nothing compared to where we had been, that I would never view them the same way again. And I was right. Now whenever I look across the valley, I see as through a scrim those other valleys and gorges, those smoky sheets of fog and clouds. And sometimes, when I look to the mountains, I glimpse shadows much taller and darker, as if cast from other, higher, peaks.

We hadn't yet left Jalalabad when we first heard from those men—the ones we'd seen on the mountain, in the camouflage jackets. AidNow had already been called, the FBI alerted. By the time we touched ground at Logan, a voicemail message was waiting for Roy.

I could hear the voice chirping from his cell phone. A man explaining, in superb English, that he was calling on behalf of the group holding Kyra, and that he would be calling again that evening.

"This evening?" Roy cried. "It's already evening." We were waiting in a long line at customs. Roy immediately called the consultants he had hired.

"I don't *know* when they're going to call," he grumbled into his phone as we inched forward in the queue. "He said sometime tonight." Roy looked so tired. I don't think he ever could have expected the spectacular disaster his "plan" had become. He had thought he would be taking Kyra home with him.

I must have looked just as exhausted—not to mention demoralized, with my lame arm in its sling. Ashamed too. Of everything I'd ignored about that country and about my own. And because I'd left my family to go do this thing that I had failed at.

Roy listened to the instructions from his consultants but had to break off to go through customs. I watched him pass through and then wait for me on the other side while I showed the customs agent my passport and smiled wearily at a joke about my bandaged arm. I remember looking across to where Roy stood, as if border lines really could contain a country. At that distance, weary and pounds thinner, Roy was no longer the specimen of privilege he once seemed. I felt a small pang to see he had become as rumpled and dejected as me.

"We're supposed to think of questions," he told me when I joined him. "Things only Kyra would know. To prove those men really do have her." And that she was still alive.

I told myself those men wouldn't harm her, that she was too valuable to them. I wanted badly to believe it. "Why can't they just put her on the line so that we could hear for ourselves?"

But who knew where they were calling from—most likely a different town, a different region altogether from where Kyra was being held. They couldn't risk her giving that information away. For all we knew, she was still huddled in a cave somewhere.

"Personal questions," Roy said. "Things no one else could know. Nothing that would be in public records."

We put our packs down and conferred. I asked if he and Kyra had had any nicknames for each other when they were growing up, or names other children in the neighborhood had called her. Roy tried to remember, while I considered other possibilities. A special day, or some private joke from when she and Roy were young.

And then Roy's cell phone buzzed. He pulled it from his pocket casually, glanced at the screen. "A blocked number. Can't be them. Can it?"

But I knew as soon as he answered who it was. Every little muscle around his mouth seemed to twitch. "Yes," he said politely. "Yes." He took a heavy breath and stood taller. "Before we move forward," he said, "I have some questions that Kyra will have to answer." He looked at me frantically, as if it were my fault we weren't prepared for this. "The first question is . . ."

"When her mother died?"

"They can look that up," he whispered, and then blurted out, "Ask what was her dog's name. When she was a little girl. What was the name of her pet dog."

I hadn't known Kyra had ever had a dog.

"The second question . . ." Roy looked to me.

"What street she grew up on?" I knew it wasn't very good. Roy grimaced but repeated the question into the cell phone. I pictured the big circular driveway, the gray stone house with the broad, curving porch. I still remembered that visit so clearly. Leaving the city, no idea yet that Roy was waiting there. Just me and Kyra in her borrowed car.

Which is how the idea came to me. I spoke slowly, the thought still formulating. "Have them ask her what she told the squeegee man."

Roy just looked at me.

"What she said to the squeegee man when she was driving with Mim." I was nodding, to convince myself my message would get through to her, that it would be understood. That recalling the words she had said would remind her that she was strong and could resist.

"They won't know the word 'squeegee,'" Roy hissed—then raised his eyebrows. "Yes, that's right." He looked surprised. His interlocutor, we would learn later, was an American, born and raised in Minnesota. But we didn't know that yet. "Yes, when she was driving with Mim."

She would understand that I was here, I remember thinking. She would know that I'd come back.

Roy listened to the man on the telephone. "I understand." The muscles of his face continued to twitch. "Yes, please call this number." And then the conversation was over, and Roy was staring at his phone as if it might again begin to speak. He shoved it into his pocket and gripped his hair by the roots.

They wanted, he told me, one million dollars.

Money, I remember thinking, hooray—Roy has money!

I was thinking of the money belt thick with cash. I also imagined there must be considerable funds from Grace's will; surely she had left her money to her daughter. I didn't know yet that Kyra had given nearly all of it away.

So, yes, one million was a tremendous sum, but surely Roy could scrounge it up. I was full of stupid hope as we made our way through the airport out into the cold New England evening. The crush of taxis and shuttle buses, the whiff of exhaust shocked us back to our old life. We agreed to speak the next day, then embraced lightly, awkwardly. But as we parted—Roy toward his driver and I toward a car service—Roy called to me.

He came to stand before me, his breath visible in the frigid air. "Listen, Mim. Please accept my apology. I had no idea it would come to—" He gestured at my arm in its sling.

"You were sick, Roy, you couldn't help it."

"I dragged you there. I put you in danger. I never meant to do that. I'm the one who got you into that situation, and then I wasn't there for you."

"It's not your fault." But I found it hard to look him in the eye.

"I'm sorry, Mim."

"No need to be sorry." But I could see this wasn't sufficient, that something kept him lingering on the grim sidewalk in the cold.

"I had all kinds of thoughts," he said, "when I was lying sick on that cot. A lot of things became clear. I know why Kyra sent those letters to me instead of you. She wanted me to know I was the messenger."

I didn't understand. "You're not just some messenger, Roy."

"She knew what she was doing. That if I hadn't had to face you, I could keep up what I've told myself all along. Those things I said to you, about Kyra and me, or about her with you. I was ignoring everything I didn't want to be true."

He shifted his feet on the cold sidewalk. "I was the messenger. But the message all that time—in those letters—was for you."

Before I could reply, he lugged his bag back up, gave a crisp salute, and walked briskly away, as if to prevent me from witnessing his emotions. I was still standing at the walkway, travelers wheeling their luggage to and fro. I searched for a bench, hurried over, tearing at my backpack, feeling inside for the packet of letters. I tugged the pages up and didn't stop searching until I found the one I remembered. The one I knew was there and had to see again.

August 23, 2011

Mim, I just finished <u>Foils & Follies</u>. So heartbreaking! You can tell he really loves her but is tricking himself into thinking he doesn't.

Eternal love is romantic & pure but such a trap. How can we understand our feelings if we don't even acknowledge them? I guess that's what you've been working through in your novels. I have to admit I see myself in them. And you're there, too. Different names, but each time I know it's you, loving me (or the me you've turned into some much more interesting person!). It keeps me going.

Funny, I just realized: We've both been writing to each other this whole time!

Me with these lame letters & you in your beautiful books. Messages. We've been calling out to each other all along.

I've read every one of yours. Maybe someday you'll hear mine.

Love,
Kyra

I had messaged Nolan before leaving Jalalabad to let him know I was coming home. In his reply he said he would go stay at his sister's, to "figure things out."

Just like two years earlier, when my not wanting to join him on vacation (I had a deadline for a book) was interpreted as evidence that I was not a full partner in the marriage, that I might go off and leave, something drastic like that. Sparked a whole big drama. Nolan said he felt me retreating, had felt it for some time. Only our counselor's diagnosis—the drifting apart that can happen to couples at this stage—helped us make sense of things.

Now, though, I realized as I let myself back into the cold empty house, I *had* gone off. I *had* done something drastic.

I had gone away, and failed, and had my arm in a sling to prove it.

It didn't matter whether Nolan wanted me back or not. It didn't matter if he decided to forgive me. Because without even meaning to, I'd already given him my answer.

In our muddle of fatigue, I hadn't thought to give Roy the answer to my proof-of-life question, and he hadn't thought to ask for it. But in the wee hours, my phone pinged with a text from him:

when a woman says no she means no

For the first time since my return I cried, big hot wet stinging tears. For Kyra and the big tangle she had become part of, and for everything I had done and hadn't done. For the deep sad yearning inside me, and for being alone again in my house on the hill. For Nolan on his path away from what we'd been together. And because all I could do was to type back to Roy, *That's right.*

one hundred and sixty-five million

That's how much the U.S. Treasury estimates was paid in ransom to al-Qaeda and its sidekicks from 2008 through 2013. France, Qatar, and Oman paid the most, then Switzerland and Spain. I couldn't have guessed, in those early months of 2012, that I would become an expert on such matters.

For a week or so we had no news. I checked my messages constantly, called Roy to ask about negotiations, but his interlocutors had gone silent. I was so anxious, it took me a few days to understand that the stomach ailment keeping me up at night was no mere symptom of worry about Kyra or Sean or Nolan, but a diagnosable illness from something I'd ingested on our trek.

"Unhygienic food supply is the most common cause," the doctor explained after learning where I had traveled. For some reason he thought it helpful to add some comment about the drinking water being tainted with feces.

I lost weight and barely slept. Not the best circumstances for my lame arm trying to heal. And then came a letter. Not to me, but to Roy. The Pakistani government also received one.

Roy called to tell me. I was still using my left arm for everything, and it felt strange to listen with my other ear. I was sitting at my desk in my study, as if it were a normal day, listening to the sounds of spring outside, the trickle of after-rain through the gutter, the birds in a delighted frenzy.

The letter made no mention of the million dollars. Instead, the authors requested the release of eight hundred imprisoned Balochistan nationalists. The signature on the letter read *Balochistan Liberation United Front.*

"Who the hell is that?"

"Apparently they want Balochistan to become its own independent nation. Look, don't ask me."

With a thick black marker, I printed BALOCHISTAN as Roy spelled the name. Another crack in the globe, glimpse of a grievance I hadn't known was there. I asked him why in the world they would have Kyra.

"It's not clear that they do have her. Balochistan is in the south, nowhere near where we saw her. It's possible they simply heard about Kyra and are pretending."

That seemed crazy too, though.

"That said," Roy explained, "apparently they often have ties to Taliban and al-Qaeda. So it's not out of the question, given the group we saw."

I thought about this. "Eight *hundred* prisoners?"

Roy started laughing then. At first I didn't know why. "Oh, you know," he said, "just eight hundred." He laughed harder, and I realized that since all of this started, I hadn't heard him laugh. "A mere eight hundred," he managed to say, and the sound of his laughter caught me too. Soon both of us were howling, until I realized I was crying.

It didn't matter. Roy's "people" were unable to confirm anything— not even that Kyra was alive, let alone in the hands of the separatist group. And then came the long hard stretch of months when we didn't hear anything at all.

Roy and I were speaking by phone once a week at that time. In early June, on my way to pick up Sean from college (he was coming home for the summer, to apprentice with a carpenter we know), I decided to take a detour to Newport to see Roy.

We met for lunch at a loud, airy place near the water. I spotted him seated at a table by the window and for a moment was stunned. He seemed almost to glow, a halo of sunlight on his hair. Up close, worry still creased his brow, but he appeared energized, bright with confidence. Though we spoke briefly of Kyra, I was glad to move on to other things. I told him how much I was looking forward to having Sean back for the summer, that I hadn't realized how lonely I'd been.

Roy was nodding. "I've been spending more time with the kids and Sandrine. I have to admit it's done me a world of good."

So, that was it. The reason for his health and good cheer.

"It's amazing," he continued. "Sandrine finally understands. Ever since I came home, she doesn't resent the time I spend on Kyra. Not the way she used to."

"She knows she's no longer in competition with her." I said it before I could stop myself.

"Hmm, maybe you're right." He didn't seem to wonder terribly much either way. But I think I was correct, that by giving up the fantasy of winning Kyra back, Roy had finally freed himself. Or rather, I suppose, Kyra had freed him.

For a brief moment it even seemed to me that she had brought us together for that very purpose. That she knew that to be released, he and I would each have to learn from the other—learn who the other was to Kyra.

But as soon as I thought it, the notion seemed embarrassingly wishful, and I dismissed it.

It's quiet down here near the creek. Sometimes I see my neighbor Jorie riding her old tired gray horse, but today there's just the little trickling current of water, and some jays in the treetops chastising each other, and my footsteps crunching the dirt road. Left foot, right foot. Not a car in sight. Early yet. Sean has already left for work. He didn't return to school last year. Instead he's been working for the carpenter he apprenticed with.

Next week he flies to Virginia for boot camp.

A recruiter in the Price Chopper is to blame. That's what a mother gets for insisting her son help run errands. Apparently the recruitment table had been set up right across from the checkout aisles. Sean came home with a bunch of brochures.

He stood there in the kitchen looking proud, like he'd found the solution to a problem. Big brown eyes shining the way they do when he gets excited. I asked if his roommate Ben had put him up to it. Last year, instead of returning to school after spring break, Ben joined the marines. "Just because Ben joined doesn't mean you have to."

To myself I was thinking, Nolan will blame me for this. If we hadn't separated, maybe Sean would be content to stay here at home. Maybe he'd even still be back at school. But no, that wacky college never had enough structure for him. It was too free-for-all, too loosey-goosey. I know this, just as I suspect that I've failed him.

"I could do really well there!" he said, holding up the brochures as proof. "I have all the right qualities."

The recruiter must have said that.

And yet it's true. Sean's a fast thinker, emotionally tough, never afraid to make quick decisions. Plus he's physically strong. Started lifting weights when he was fifteen, running miles and miles each day. He likes to push himself to extremes. And I have to admit he does well in structured environments. Why, I've known this since he was five years old. And yet it never occurred to me that he would go and do this.

"Of course you could do well there," I told him. "You can do well at anything you set your mind to." I've tried so hard to make him aware of this. Of choices, opportunities. Tried to undo everything those very first years of life taught him.

And this is what he has chosen.

He said, "I want to serve my country. I mean it! I love the United States of America. I want to stand up for freedom. I—"

"There are other ways to serve. You don't have to go into combat."

"Who even knows if I'll go into combat! Look, I'm doing this, okay?" He opened his eyes wide. Not defiantly but—to my surprise—pleading.

That he was asking my permission melted my heart. So I said the true, fair thing. "I love you." And then, "Okay."

publicity

There was no more news of Kyra until this winter.

Nearly two full years since she went missing. Sean had a girlfriend he stayed with in town, and I'd grown used to my solitude, alone in the house on the hill. By then everyone knew that Nolan and I had split up. Running errands in town, I found myself wanting to explain. But when one nosy woman went so far as to ask what happened, all I could say, mumbling, was, "I went away."

Roy meanwhile was back with Sandrine, living in his old house with her and the twins, deciding whether or not to have another child. We still spoke weekly but rarely saw each other in person. Even so, I could sense the peace he seemed to have achieved.

I was finally finishing up the novel I'd begun before my journey, but my heart wasn't in it. I had other projects now. From my desk I would look out the window and see mountains.

I imagine Kyra must have felt it too, each time she had to leave any of the places where she lived. In fact, I suspect it's the freedom of leaving that makes us feel it. The duty that comes with bearing witness. That to witness is to be implicated.

It had taken some thought to figure out how I might best act on that. The rest of my free time I mostly spent cooking and listening to the radio. I remember I was pouring boiling water into the coffee press that cold morning when the top-of-the-hour news came on. "A group calling itself Soldiers of the Caliphate says it will free an American aid worker abducted in Afghanistan in exchange for the release of six Guantánamo Bay detainees."

I managed to stop the kettle from spilling.

"A videotape shows the relief worker alive and apparently un-harmed. Her companion, a Danish citizen, was released from cap-tivity yesterday through negotiations with the Danish government. The two had been missing since February 2012. The American's exact whereabouts are unknown."

Then the announcer traipsed ahead to some new headline, some other spot on the globe. More brisk dispatching of the day's disas-ters. I immediately called Roy.

"I was going to tell you," he said, "but I didn't even have confirma-tion about Jorgen until this morning. We were told to keep it under wraps. They say we risk encouraging the kidnappers if we publicize their demands."

"Then why is it on the fucking news?"

"The kidnappers sent them the video, obviously." Roy sounded weary.

"Who are these people?" Already I felt that prickle along my scalp, my hairline sprouting sweat.

"Some new group, apparently they're Kazakhs. Used to work with the Taliban and al-Qaeda but now it seems they've got some global affiliation. The men they want released are Pakistani. In the video they say they're making their demands 'in the name of the Islamic Caliphate.'"

I said, "The U.S. is never going to release those prisoners."

Roy ignored this. "We just have to keep them engaged."

I asked why they wouldn't accept ransom money. They had for Jorgen, clearly. "Wasn't that what they wanted in the first place? I mean, I know the U.S. doesn't encourage it—"

"Believe me, Mim, I've tried. I offered them everything I have."

What had seemed to me a solution was no longer even possible. "What about a rescue operation?" There would surely be new information from Jorgen, and possibly from that videotape the newscaster had mentioned. "Your guys are looking for her, right?"

Roy had a slew of people working for him by then—not just his private investigators and the FBI but also a professional negotiator and an Afghan liaison who specialized in kidnappings.

"They're working on it, but it's hard to keep track of these people. They're in the tribal areas and keep moving her around. Look, the most important thing is that we prevent any sort of public deadline. If they set a deadline, and the deadline becomes public, they'll have to follow through if they want to be taken at their word."

I refrained from asking what, precisely, he meant by "follow through." I could guess, of course. Who knew what they were doing to Kyra, already, what they might have been doing. Had they beaten her, tortured her? Raped her? The thought had come to me many times, ever since I first saw her on the mountain. Usually I managed to force the thoughts away.

I said, "They don't execute women, at least." At least we knew that.

"Apparently this new group executes anyone."

Standing there gripping the telephone, I saw in my mind, as I often did, Kyra on the mountain floor, her hands pinioned behind her. How she lay there, no struggle. That was what had stayed with me: the fact that she did not yell or cry or say anything at all. So different from the Kyra I'd known, the one I first encountered at the train station, straight-backed, proud, in her imperial-looking coat. The Kyra who marched after the squeegee man, telling him to come back and finish what he started.

That night, late, the sound of coyotes woke me. The whooping and skirling of some pagan celebration. Usually it lasts just a minute or two. I love the wildness, the sudden burst from within the darkness. I went to slide the porch door open and stood at the screen, cold air rushing in. Soon enough the coyotes stopped howling.

In the sky of bright stars, I searched for familiar configurations. I wondered if Kyra, wherever she was, looked out at the stars. If she might have found some peace in tracing their constellations, in telling herself their names.

And all at once it seemed utterly strange that we give names to the stars, to galaxies, the Milky Way and its planets. As if by naming them we might claim them, these things so far beyond us.

an international industry

I learned something new today. About the word "martyr." It originates from the Greek word *martus*, meaning "witness."

The word was a secular term, not a religious one. A "martus" was anyone who testified. To any fact or knowledge that had been gained from personal observation.

And bearing witness did not necessarily result in death.

For a week, there was no more news of Kyra. Just reports from the papers about Jorgen's ordeal. How he and Kyra had been intercepted en route to a village they had previously visited, how each place their abductors tried to hide out wanted nothing to do with them, how they had been traded to another group, and then another. . . . I could hardly bear to read it. And then one afternoon toward the end of February, as I set to chopping vegetables on the big heavy wooden board, a newscaster said that the kidnappers of humanitarian aid worker Kyra Thornton-Greer had announced they would execute her if their demands were not met within three days.

I tried to listen to what little more I could glean, but there was an awful pounding in my ears. I hurried to my study to telephone Roy and realized I was still holding the knife.

I grabbed the phone but saw on my computer that Roy had sent a message. An email blast. Asking every human he could reach to sign the attached petition. "Friends of Kyra" read the subject heading, and then a long plea for signatures, to urge the U.S. government to make the trade.

Recipients had been using "Reply all," vowing to call their congressmen, to pray for her, little notes of support. A Facebook page had been created and the petition posted there, already shared hundreds of times.

I added my signature to the list. And then noticed, in my email queue, a message forwarded from my publisher. The subject heading read: Urgent?

Dear Mim—

I am here at my desk perusing the news online and have just read of the American woman held by terrorists. The photograph in the article looked like your Kyra. I am concerned and wonder if this is true.

Please let me know. And I hope you are very well.

With my best wishes,

Jacques Catalano, PhD

Award-winning author of *Parallel Voices: Colonial Dominion and Sexual Domination in the Literature of the Maghreb*. Read more at www.drjacquescatalano.com & follow me on Twitter: @drjacquesnumero1

I hadn't heard from him in years. Later I would see from his website that he was a fellow at an institute in Florence, editing an anthology of poetry from the Maghreb. According to his biographical summary, he lived "in Rome and New York."

But first I wrote back: yes, it is Kyra—and included the link to the petition Roy had sent. Please sign this, I typed, though I knew such efforts were futile. After all, who was Kyra to the U.S. government? To the universe? A citizen who tramped from one wracked country to another, trying to do some good.

No doubt in my mind what Kyra would think about that petition. All this hubbub for a single American. Meanwhile entire nations struggle, entire populations flee. To buses that never leave. To boats that never touch land.

Imagine what Roy's belt of money could do for *them*. I have a feeling that's what Kyra would say.

I dreamed of her that night. I found her in a cave like the ones where those dusty children lived, with the improbable carpets out front and the caulked wood-and-clay doorframes.

Instead of the dust-caked children, though, Kyra looked up at me. She looked confused. She didn't understand that I was there to save her. I was shouting, *We need to go!* But she didn't understand.

I kept shouting, until I shouted myself awake. Then I lay in bed for a long time, listening to the soft "tsk, tsk, tsk" of the clock.

no negotiation with terrorists

By the morning of the second day, a rally was taking place. If I still owned a television, I could have watched it—the crowd gathering outside the White House, with their lollipop signs and the photo of Kyra, the one with her face partially in the shade. But Nolan took the TV with him when he moved out, and I hadn't felt the need to replace it.

The reporters on the radio didn't mention Roy's petition, but they spoke of the growing crowd, and of a prayer circle that had formed nearby. Not so different from Roy's efforts, I remember thinking. Prayers, after all, are petitions to the gods.

There came a voice I recognized. "We're here because we feel strongly that it's time to negotiate. This is an American citizen who risked her life in the name of peace, and now it's time for us to give Kyra her due."

"That was actress Adrienne Brightly," the newscaster explained. "She's one of a small but growing group of supporters urging the U.S. government to release six Guantánamo detainees in exchange for humanitarian aid worker Kyra Thornton-Greer."

Adrienne's voice said, "Just as our government supports its men and women in uniform, it should come to the aid of its civilians who have put their lives at risk in the name of international peace."

I always find it embarrassing when actors discuss foreign policy. Still, what a score for Roy, I remember thinking. Adrienne Brightly has been a household name ever since she landed the role of the president's chief of staff on one of those HBO dramas. I hoped her fictional association might lend her some authority in real life.

"We can't just look the other way," she told the reporter. "We can't keep pretending it doesn't have to do with us. The U.S government needs to do the right thing."

Adrienne didn't mention her personal connection to the hostage in question. But because of her involvement, the news correspondent explained, a large contingent of Hollywood heavyweights were now supporting the prisoner-hostage trade-off.

When next I checked, the number of signatures on the petition had quadrupled.

In less than forty-eight hours, I remember thinking, the entire episode would be over. A morsel of history, the newscasters already on to some new atrocity.

I tried to busy myself with one of the projects I'd been working on since my return: a pen pal program between Afghan students and their American counterparts. With the help of Fareshta—she and Asim are now married—I had paired an English class from her school in Jalalabad with students from one in the town next to mine. The idea had taken off, and we were rapidly connecting more age groups, in other schools and classrooms.

My other main project is a writing workshop for veterans. I lead weekly writing sessions in three different locations, with a psychologist who is himself a veteran. We hope to add two more counties next year. With the program expanding so quickly, we'll need to hire an assistant soon. There's so much work to do.

I don't know what my next book will be. Taped to my computer is a stanza by Horace:

> Many heroes lived before Agamemnon
> But they are all unweepable
> Overwhelmed by the long night of oblivion
> Because they lacked a bard

emancipation

I understand, of course, the government's policy of not complying with terrorist demands. I understand not wanting to set such a precedent. I do not disagree with this philosophy.

Sean, I want you to know this. I want you to know everything—who I was when I was your age, and what I did, all that happened. The people I have loved. That sometimes, in spite of love, we spin off from each other like stars.

I never felt any panic when you left for college. No mother-hen worrying that you still needed me around. That school seemed to me a haven, a place for precious young eggs to incubate. Now, though. The army will be the opposite—you are beyond my protection. Fine, I accept that. I'll even admit how proud I am of you, of this instinct to launch yourself away from our small town, out into the world.

Left foot, right foot. Moss and old fallen leaves glisten, crushed beneath my footsteps. I'm following the trail back through the woods, to the stacked gray rocks that mark where our land ends and the rest of the world begins.

This is the route I took that final afternoon, when the deadline for Kyra's release was to expire. I had to do something; I could not sit still. I kept hearing the seconds ticking off, the clock stuttering forward. Like that New Year's Eve party so long ago, standing with Kyra in the smoke-filled room, counting down to midnight. To everything to come, all that had yet to happen.

Just hours earlier, via Roy's liaison, new proof-of-life questions had been conveyed to the men holding Kyra. The hope was that they were bluffing. But the questions, Roy informed me, had been answered correctly.

So it was true. Kyra was there, with those men. They meant what they said.

I felt ill and could barely think straight. With just an hour or so until the deadline, I pulled on my parka, boots, gloves, and blaze orange hat, and headed out.

Left foot, right foot. The sun was sliding west, drawing flat sullen winter shadows across the hills. Disconsolate crows called to one another. Soon enough the clock would strike the hour, and all across the planet—not just in Kyra's cave, or wherever she was—staggering atrocities would take place.

My plan was to stay out until I was certain the deadline had passed. Maybe by the time I returned home they would have come up with some alternative. Negotiated some other, better solution. Some kind of truce. Though I knew better, I wanted very badly to believe it.

I tucked my hands into my coat pockets. The broken rubber bracelet was still there. Proof that I'd made it so very close.

Yet still I hadn't reached her.

If only I could have reached her.

I touched the bracelet every so often as afternoon bent toward evening. I thought it might comfort me. But the image that kept coming to mind was those clay lumps in the ground, untended mounds of dirt. Asim saying, *Their spirits aren't here. They flew away.*

I told myself that, too, would be a kind of liberation. Her spirit set free. But it was poor solace. Soon the sun was no longer visible, just its refractions off the mountains. Where the ground was covered in shadows, the snow had hardened again and crunched under my boots. And then the last of those refractions, too, slipped away. In the dimming light, the snow glowed electric-blue.

Stunning, the blueness. Pale and neon at the same time. Even the birch trees had turned from white to periwinkle. It seemed to me they had never looked that way before. Through webbed branches, the sky, too, glowed a gauzy luminous blue.

I knew the deadline had passed. I turned back toward the house, to return before dark. But everything looked suddenly unfamiliar. The black eyes of birches staring. The capsized tree trunks lying sideways, their roots extended like long, fossilized tresses. Broken stumps like giant jagged teeth. Everything was strange, even the crackling of dead leaves underfoot. Squirrels, I told myself, or deer. But the sounds unnerved me. I looked into the blueness, and stopped.

I could feel her there, among the trees and sky. And then it was as if I could see her. The vision took shape, strong limbs, thin knobby branches, the reaching boughs. Kyra, in the loose pants too short for her and the wrinkled tunic that surely could not be warm enough. She stood before me, her face very thin, worry lines across her forehead. Sleepy almond eyes, but with creases at the corners. Her jaw was trembling. Her entire body was trembling. She gave that little closed-mouth smile, perhaps to try to stop the trembling.

I tried to say her name but I was frightened and my chest filled with spasms. My limbs felt weighted down. A voice was saying, *Sorry, sorry.* It was her voice from when we were young. The figure before me shook her head as if about to laugh at something hopeless, something inevitable, Well, what can you do?

My entire body shook, I could not stop it. I felt her touch my coat, the lightest breeze. Then she took hold of the lapels and gently tugged me toward her.

I stopped trembling. Kyra leaned into me, and I nearly felt her head against mine. She was still holding the edges of my coat, pulling it close, her hands lifting it up toward her ears. She must have been very cold. She burrowed into my coat, like the girl who once slipped into my bed, under the covers, beside me.

I could feel the last of her breath on my collarbone. Could feel her trying to pull the coat around both of us, as if to hide inside, the two of us together. As if that might be all it took to make things right.

So I stepped in close and wrapped my coat around her.

Author's Note

For firsthand insights into Afghanistan, the eastern border regions, and humanitarian aid work, my gratitude to Zohal Atif, Xavier Collard, John Crowley, Stephen Landrigan, Qais Akbar Omar, Elsa Vargas, and Dr. Dave Warner. I am also grateful to all those who have written about their experiences in the region. Any errors are my own.

For their expertise regarding Desert Storm, the U.S. military in eastern Afghanistan, PTSD, and veteran life, my deep gratitude to Tony Schwalm and Dr. Joseph Christenson. For answering my questions about the pieds-noir in Algeria, my thanks to Jarrod Hayes. And for pointing me to these experts, my thanks to Cat Parnell, Rob Friedman, and Nancy Miller.

For reading the many drafts of this manuscript, infinite thanks to Jessica Berger Gross, Morgan Frank, Leah Kalotay, Jill Kalotay, Judy Layzer, Chris McCarron, Tom McNeely, Kirsten Menger-Anderson, Ron Nemec, Emily Newburger, Rishi Reddi, Julie Rold, Mandy Smith, and Mako Yoshikawa. A huge thank-you also to Kathy Daneman and the NUP crew.

Blue Hours was created with support from the Corporation of Yaddo, the Bogliasco Foundation, Catwalk Institute, and the Virginia Center for the Creative Arts—for which I am ever grateful.